-Elk o

Book 1

Lee Nicol

-Chapters-

- The Road To Bramwich -
- Shambolic Hollow -
- Cold Blooded Barrage -
- Gila Vision -
- A Crick's Temperament -
- Press To Dirtbere -
- Tribe Amora -
- Mossguard -
- Anti C -
- A Rekindling Entrapment -

-About the author-

Dear Reader,

Thank you for showing interest in ***Elk of Eshia***.

My name is Lee Nicol. I'm 35 years old, I live in Scotland with Sara, our 2 children (one of each flavour) and our favourite pooch Holly.

When I'm not writing, I enjoy spending time with my PS4, and my family… wait I better rephrase that…
(I'm only joking), I enjoy spending time with my family more than I enjoy playing my PS4.

I hope you enjoy reading ***Elk of Eshia*** as much as I've enjoyed writing it. I've started writing the sequel to ***Elk of Eshia***, so watch out for it.

You can find details at the end if you would like to contact me.

Once again, thank you for your support.

Lee

-Summary-

Delph, Elk and Kadence find themselves thrust into the unknown on a journey of friendship, discovery and uncertainty with a dash of humour.

Faced with a fresh hell in the form of an ancient enemy that has surfaced after a long hiatus, bringing with them an unquenchable thirst to plunge Eshia into darkness.

Can the friends hold it together long enough to defeat the savages once and for all or will they surrender to the darkness?

And the most important question of all... will Elk ever eat enough to satisfy his insatiable appetite?

There's only one way to find out!

Grab a seat, hunker down and welcome to Eshia.

Chapter One

-The Road To Bramwich-

'Why won't they leave us alone? That's twice this week those creatures have attacked us. I've had enough,' moaned Elk.

'Elk, can't you sit at peace for longer than five seconds? I can feel a headache starting and your pacing back and forth isn't helping. Check yourself over for any wounds,' ordered Delph.

'Can you blame me though, Delph?' Elk asked. 'There's no way I'll be settling down any time soon. Didn't you see the size of that monster's teeth?' he shuddered.

'Come on guys, settle down. There's no point fighting with each other, we need to focus. Those beasts could come back at any moment and I'd rather be ready if they do.' Kadence said.

'To be honest, I'm surprised we came out of that last fight unscathed. It felt like we struggled, the fiend was relentless,' said Elk. He got himself comfortable on a moss-covered log and checked himself over for cuts.

'Where are we anyway?' asked Kadence; looking around for something she might recognise.

'I'm sure this is Blue-pine Forest,' Delph replied.

'What makes you say that Delph?' Kadence asked.

'Well, see all of those blue pine trees,' smirked Elk; pointing all around them.

'Always the joker eh Elk,' sighed Kadence, cringing at his smug expression.

'What are we doing here?' Elk asked.

'We didn't have the time to check where we were going and we had to get off that road at any cost. Don't worry though, the path we were on leads through this forest. All we have to do is find it and join it again,' Delph replied.

Lack of sleep had been playing a major part of the trios life recently.

The last time they had the luxury of a bed was a few nights ago when they arrived at the sleepy town of Ellendale. Furtive whispers of an ancient enemy were running rife throughout the small town which still gives them shivers up their spines when they think of them.

Elk was certain the monsters they faced earlier must have been the ones the townsfolk spoke of when they told the group the tale of the bearer of the pure soul and how it had been the scourge of the J'yoti for many years.

The only thing truly capable of quenching the J'yoti's insatiable thirst was capturing the one with the pure soul.

In years long forgotten the J'yoti had searched tirelessly for the pure soul, attacking any unwitting travellers they found. They were intent on finding the bearer and ridding whoever it may be from Eshia once and for all.

It is not known by any living man or woman if there ever has been anyone that lived with the burden of harbouring the pure soul, so it's unclear if it's a tale told around a campfire in the days of old.

However, it has been foretold that the bearer of the pure soul is the only one capable of stopping the master of the J'yoti.

It's thought that only the bearer of the pure soul is the one that can prevent Eshia from plunging into eternal darkness.

The J'yoti hadn't been seen by anyone for many years and it was thought by all to be extinct.

The friends had never experienced this type of cloaked enemy themselves and they weren't sure yet on the best way to deal with it.*

One by one dark shadows appeared around them, just like they had done previously. Delph, Elk and Kadence were surrounded.

'Oh, come on, not again!' Elk yelled.

Delph and Kadence both sighed in sync with each other.

Gruesome shadows pulsated and produced a low buzzing noise which gradually increased as they drifted closer together. As the shadowy forms drew closer, Elk now knew the plain, outright fear on the villagers' faces had been genuine.

* To be fair, they had no intention of establishing a rapport with the beasts, neither had they a flowchart that they could refer to that described the best way to handle oneself when faced with such foolery either.

The J'yoti had indeed returned, and the friends were about to witness first-hand the reason for that unforgettable look of desolation in the old man's eyes as he'd watched Kadence, Delph and Elk leave Ellendale.

Elk used his initiative and ran away from the commotion and only when he was at a distance comfortable to him he turned around to verify the whereabouts of his friends. Delph and Kadence hadn't been as quick off the mark. Seeing the ring of darkness consuming his friends horrified him, he knew he would have to make his way back and help his friends.

In the next instant, all sounds merged into one and the only noise they could focus on was the bellowing shriek coming from the shadows.

Everything started turning black as the darkness overcame and engulfed everything in the ancient forest, from its tallest trees right down to the friends. The colour drained from them all, just as it drained from everything around them. Delph rushed to shield Kadence as she panicked. It seemed like they had only just recovered from the last fight and now they had no choice, but to do it again.

The creatures they met earlier were practically mutes compared to these shrieking fiends.

They hoped they could escape these evil attacks and be free from the surrounding threat, however, their hopes were growing little to none after recent events.

At that precise moment, the beating darkness receded as an intense surge of light came rushing towards them, forcing them to shelter their eyes as they instinctively shrank from its glare. The light seemed to last forever when in fact it only lasted a few seconds; they were relieved when the brightness started dimming even if it did leave them with blurred vision. However, within mere seconds their relief quickly changed to horror.

In the returning darkness, two cloaked forms and two shadowy creatures appeared before the trio like an unwanted gift and they moved towards Delph and Kadence with an undeniable purpose.

Elk ran back to join his friends, and they faced the oncoming enemies together.

They struggled to make out the exact definition of the figures because they still had little specks of light swirling in their eyes to contend with as well.

As the creepy horrors surrounded them, they desperately scanned their surroundings for a way to escape, not finding any, they realised that the only way they had a chance of surviving was to fight these foul brutes.

The three friends stood there, shivering in the damp forest with their hearts pounding and their chests full of apprehension, besieged by these horrific dark creatures.

Delph the self-proclaimed leader of the trio knew he would have to make a move 'You take the cloaked one on the left. Elk and I will take the other three' he yelled to Kadence.

Kadence pulled a little jar from her satchel. She drank its contents in one big gulp and she vanished. She sneaked around behind one of the cloaked fiends whilst reaching for her flame-gold bow, the hungry savage turned around expecting to find its prey, only to find nothing at all.

Kadence stayed as still as she could, she wanted to be sure she was invisible to the swine. She slowly inhaled and held it in and only releasing it when she was certain the creature couldn't see her.

She reached for a five-pronged, jade-sharp arrow from her quiver and carefully taking aim she drew back the string and held it tight. She released her arrow with precision; it ended up lodged in the creature's neck.

The creature screeched as it dropped to the ground and writhed in pain. She flexed her fingers then pulled out her dagger all whilst dodging the creatures determined claws. It fell silent as she quickly finished it off with a swift stab to its temple.

Elk withdrew his angel-ray gun and aimed it at his target, he lined up his shot just in time to see his enemy hurling something at him; he wasn't quick enough to react and immediately felt a sting in his waist; looking down he saw a pincer needle sticking out of it.

A chilling sensation entered his body, originating at his waist and then flowing down into his legs.

He tried stepping forward, and it was at that point, he realised he couldn't move.

The needle had paralysed his legs. Frustration and dismay took hold. He knew he would need to take control of the situation before the creature could advance on him, so he did just that.

He channelled his fear and projected it to the back of his mind. He remained focused on the task at hand and shot a bullet towards his foe in retaliation. His shot was direct, the impact was deadly and his foe crashed down, lifeless on the cold mossy ground below.

'That's karma right there,' Elk mused.

Kadence reappeared in front of Elk; startling him.

'You'd think I'd be used to that by now Kadence,' Elk laughed nervously.

Kadence glanced at Elk and gave him a half-hearted smile. She was concentrating on saving him and hadn't heard what he had said. She quickly reached into her satchel and pulled out a small blue vial and handed it to him.

Elk pulled the cork out of the vial and poured the contents into his mouth, screwing up his face as soon as he tasted the foul concoction.

'I know it tastes disgusting Elk, it is powerful though,' said Kadence.

He felt a warm sensation running down the full-length of his legs. He was relieved and took it as assurance that his limbs were returning to normal.

'Thank you, may the debt toll* continue. I can feel my legs again' Elk cheered; stamping his feet on the ground to get his blood flowing.

'A little help over here would be good guys!' Delph yelled.

Kadence turned around and ran over towards Delph. Elk got up and followed her, he was still a little unsteady on his feet.

'Where are the other two, wasn't there four?' Elk asked Delph.

* The debt toll is something that is known as the "I owe you one" to the trio of friends.

'I have no idea where they are though. I thought you were taking care of them!' Delph said.

Neither of them could see the other two enemies anywhere.

'I'll climb up that rock over there and hopefully, it'll be high enough for me to get a decent look around,' said Kadence.

'Good idea. Just be on your guard up there and be careful, it looks jagged,' Delph warned her.

She ran over to the rock, checking for beasts as she went because the last thing she wanted was for one of those creatures to sneak up on her. She crouched down and had a quick look around and when she knew there were no enemies near her she began climbing, carefully choosing where she placed her feet because she didn't want to slip and fall.

As she reached the halfway point she quickly checked for the missing enemies again. She gasped when she pinpointed exactly where one of the missing fiends was.

Delph spotted the enemy at the same time as Kadence. 'Elk, drop to the ground now!' he yelled.

The beast leapt over Elk just as he ducked, narrowly missing his head with its grotesque feet. Elk was thankful that he heard Delph's warning.

Delph sprung into action. He ran over and sliced his green acid-sword right through its two front legs. The great hulking beast screeched as Delph's sword cut through its body and as soon as it dropped to the ground, he raised his sword up and drove it down into the beast's head, silencing its anguished screech immediately. It all happened so quickly.

Elk was still lying on the cold grass covered in the creatures still warm blood, staring up at the sky in disbelief; trying to take in how lucky he had just been.

He felt extremely grateful towards Delph, who was wiping the monster's blood on the grass.

'I believe that's one kill for each of us then. Where is the last one?' Delph asked, as he held out his hand and helped Elk up to his feet.

Elk used his sleeve to wipe the beast's blood off his face.

Kadence had only just climbed down from the rock when she was taken by surprise and thrown on her back. She shrieked as the air was driven from her lungs.

Her vision was blocked by the ferocious brute as it forcefully stopped her from getting back up. She instinctively forced her hands up and grabbed the beast by the sagging skin around its neck, locking her arms into place.

The beast's guttural snarling frightened her. She couldn't take her eyes off its serrated teeth as it snapped its jaws at her, she worried that it would rip her face off at any given moment. The smell of its putrid saliva made her gag as it hung down from its sagging jowls before dropping onto her face and rolling down her neck. She shook her head frantically to lessen the risk of any of it from getting into her mouth.

The great, heaving hound sank its razor-sharp claws into her shoulder, pinning her further to the ground and no matter how hard she tried; she couldn't move.

She was struggling to draw breath and her vision was becoming blurry, she feared that she would pass out at any moment.

A loud bang rang in her left ear and she felt the crushing weight lift from her body. Air rushed into her lungs quicker than her body could take, forcing a coughing fit. She saw the creature slump to the ground with a thud. It sounded similar to that of a small tree falling and landing just to her right. She felt no remorse when she saw the fiend laying lifeless on the grass.

Kadence looked over to her left. She could see Elk standing there grinning with his gun pointing in her direction. 'I believe that means my death toll has now been repaid,' he yelled.

Kadence remained on her back, confused and shocked and each strained breath burned in her tight chest.

Delph and Elk ran over to Kadence to help her up. She gasped and inhaled harshly as soon as she stood up. She felt a sharp pain in her shoulder from where the beast's claws had dug into her skin, she looked down and panicked when she saw blood oozing through her clothes.

'You're bleeding Kadence,' Elk gasped.

'We need to stem that flow,' Delph said.

'It feels like a knife has been dug in and is being twisted around. Let me stand still for a moment,' she groaned.

Delph and Elk stood by her to support her weight.

Once the pain subsided, Kadence could hobble slowly. They knew they would have to find shelter, so they kept going until they came to the perfect spot.

It had big rocks and trees with over-hanging branches, which was perfect to protect them from any rain and wind.

'This will do nicely, let's get our camp fixed,' Elk said; helping her get into a comfortable position between the rocks.

'I'll go out and gather wood for a fire, so we can get some heat and then I will make us some food when I get back,' said Elk.

A gust of wind tore through their camp, stirring up dead leaves on the ground. They all shuddered.

'Great idea. I'll stay here and make sure Kadence is comfortable and then I'll make a base for the fire.' replied Delph.

Kadence thanked them both.

Elk set out to patrol the surrounding area for wood and herbs. His grandfather taught him about herbalism when he was a kid, so he knew which herbs and plants could be used for cooking and which ones he must never touch.

Back at the camp, Delph reached into Kadence's satchel and pulled out some bandages, some water and a solution that would help heal her wounds fast. He passed her a clean jumper, He wiped away any blood he found whilst he cleaned her wound.

The beast's putrid saliva left her neck sticky to the touch. He shuddered at the thought of the huge terror on top of her and he didn't want to think about how close he came to losing her. Once he had finished cleaning her wounds, he applied the solution and wrapped the bandages around her shoulder and then cleaned the saliva from her neck.

'Your wound is deep, you've stopped bleeding though. How does it feel now?' Delph asked.

'Still sore,' she gasped: 'I can't help worrying that we'll be attacked again,' Kadence added.

'I'm not worrying, so you shouldn't either, try not to worry just now Kadence, if they come back we'll deal with it. Nothing will prevent us from getting to Bramwich village, just get some rest and we will make our way there in the morning.' Delph replied.

Delph gathered a few small rocks and when he had enough, he arranged them together in a circle to make the base of the fire.

Elk returned with his pockets full of herbs and his arms full of kindling. He threw the wood on the ground and crouched down to arrange it in the firebase.

He lit the kindling once he was ready, then fetched a pot, dried meat shavings and the last of their water containers from his backpack.

He watched the fire for a moment to make sure the fire took hold.

'Continue preparing for dinner and I will go out and hunt us some bokbit,'* Delph told Elk. Delph wandered off into the forest.

Keeping as low to the ground as he could, he weaved in and out of the trees, using the natural sounds of the forest to his benefit and only moved when there was another sound to mask his own.

He knew all too well that he would have to be quiet as the creature he was hunting was able to perceive sound exceptionally well.

A familiar feeling growled in the pit of his stomach, forcing him to stop dead in his tracks, it was at that moment he noticed how silent the forest birds had become.

An intense scent of a bokbit filled his flared nostrils. His eyes turned yellow, his eyesight and hearing both sharpened.

* The bokbit are a hybrid species of rabbit and deer. They're the size and shape of a small fawn with long ears that dangles down.

He knew he was shifting and there was nothing he could do to stop it, all he could do now was prepare for his transformation to run its course whilst he still had some control of his natural self, so he knelt down to lessen any sound that his body would make when it slumped to the grassy ground.

He groaned unwillingly as his skin tightened around his body. He growled wildly as his teeth protruded through his gums; he ran his tongue over his sharp teeth, and he glanced down at his hands and excitement rushed through his body when he saw that they were now big silver fur coloured paws with razor-sharp claws.

He knew that his form change was complete, and he was now a silver fox. A cooling breeze flowed through the air, muffling the crunching of the dry grass as he slithered through it. The breeze helped to keep the temperature of his fur covered body down as it flowed through his thick fur.

His heart fluttered with excitement when he heard a bokbit close by, he kept his pace steady until he was a foot away from it.

He stopped to watch his unsuspecting prey for a moment as it licked the dew from a moss-covered rock.

He couldn't contain his suspense any more, so he seized his chance and pounced on top of it, sinking his teeth right in. The startled bokbit wailed with pain and bucked him off its back.

Delph caught his balance and dashed at the bokbit. He yipped with joy as he tore its back leg open with his razor-sharp claws.

Primal frenzy rushed through his body as he watched the bleating creature limping away from him. He rested for a few moments to catch his breath; he knew the deal was done, and all he had to do was follow the trail of blood it left behind and then waiting for him at the end would be his kill.

He tracked the blood trail until he reached his prey; it was slumped in a heap underneath a bush it was trying its hardest to hide in.

Its staggered whimpering gave it away, Delph walked over to the cowering beast and stared in its petrified eyes and for a split second, he felt guilty.

He brushed his conscience aside and gripped the beast by its and with a powerful bite he snapped the creatures neck, silencing its whining.

He hauled his trophy back to Elk and Kadence by the scruff of its neck. It took twice as long to get back to camp because of the heavy load he was bringing back with him.

He arrived back at the camp and dropped the bokbit on the grass, startling Kadence. She had only just started regaining her strength again, when she tried to jump up, she misjudged her footing and slumped back down to the ground, so she reached for her bow instead. Delph saw this and dashed out of the camp and took cover in some bushes.

'That's Delph, don't shoot!' Elk screeched.

Kadence lowered her weapon and apologised to Delph.

The bushes that concealed Delph shook, after a few moments of shaking and grunting, Delph poked his head out, he had returned to his natural form.

Kadence looked at Elk for an explanation, then she turned to look at Delph and then back to Elk.

'Don't worry about it. That's not the first time I've scared someone whilst in another form' he laughed nervously. He threw Elk a sarcastic grin and Elk grinned back although he was less sarcastic. Elk had experienced this happening to Delph on numerous occasions and he always found it amusing. Delph, however, did not.

'Elk, pass me some clothes out of my bag please,' Delph said.

Elk picked up Delph's bag and walked over to Delph and the closer he got to Delph, the more Delph crouched down to protect his modesty, Elk threw the bag into the bushes and made his way over to the bokbit.

'Nice catch Delph' Elk said, crouching down beside it.

'S'alright isn't it,' Delph beamed.

Elk stood up and dragged the bokbit over to the fire before letting go of it and watching it flop to the ground.

With some difficulty, he was able to manoeuvre the bokbit onto its back; the creature dropped on to its side twice before he noticed one of its legs had folded under itself.

He pulled on it to free it; it took a few attempts before it even budged, he found a technique that seemed to work although it crunched with every movement and with one final twist; the leg popped out of its socket and Elk could move it with ease.

Elk looked over at Kadence, who was displaying a look of disgust.

He reached for a knife and with one quick stab he made an entry point between its hind legs. He dragged his knife along its stomach and couldn't help smiling when he saw the layer of fatty meat, envisioning the stew he would be making.

He finished gutting it out, separating the consumable from the waste and placing it in a pot. Kadence felt queasy and had attempted looking away several times, however, it fascinated her and continued watching.

It wasn't the fattest bokbit that had ever walked the land, it was, however, a good catch and would feed them well. Elk utilised what he had and used as much as he could; so it's death wasn't in vain.

He garnished the meat with the herbs he had gathered earlier, whilst Delph dragged the remains off to one side so any forest critters could feast as it broke down.

Whilst waiting for their dinner, they spoke about the old days, the new days, but mostly about what had happened that day. When dinner was ready, Elk scooped out a healthy helping of his bokbit stew for each of them, they discussed the enemy they fought earlier, as they ate their food.

'Those monsters that attacked us. What were they?' Kadence asked.

'I'm not sure.' replied Delph.

Kadence nodded.

'Remember when we passed through that weird village the other day, I'm sure someone mentioned a sighting from the J'yoti, they described it as an "old enemy" or something along those lines. Although the man who told me looked a little odd, all I could focus on was his left eye, it kept rolling around in a circle and do not even get me started on that little girl's teeth, or lack of them I should say.' Elk said, shuddering as he remembered.

'Elk, that's mean,' laughed Kadence.

'It's the truth and you know it,' laughed Elk.

'The J'yoti were around in my dad's day, surely those fiends are not the same ones. He told me they were gone.' Delph replied.

'What do you mean when you say gone?' Elk asked.

'Gone, as in dead-gone and no longer here, I'm sure those cloaked figures we battled earlier used to live in the wide valleys of Booroff and once roamed the great fields of Avaalon, or so I understand. They were a peaceful race and weren't vicious or dangerous like the ones that attacked us.' Delph explained.

'What do you think made them change?' Elk asked.

'As far as I know, it's Viacorp's wrongdoing. One night a few Viacorp lackeys broke into Queen Tybressa's home while she slept, they murdered her guards and took her captive.' Delph explained.

'You would have thought she would have had more than enough security around her to prevent such an attack,' said Elk.

'I don't suppose they would have had many enemies. They had preserved the peace for so long, so they would have no need for a stronghold,' Kadence replied.

'You would think that, wouldn't you?' Elk asked.

'Poor Queen Tybressa. Why did they do it?' Kadence asked.

'Viacorp strongly suspected that there was some sort of power force deep within a cave and they desperately wanted it for themselves, but because they were few and the J'yoti were many, they simply didn't have the power to reach it without conflict.' said Delph.

'Bloody J'yoti.' Elk cursed.

'So they used Queen Tybressa's capture to make sure that her people would aid them and once they had the Queen, they could control the masses by forcing the weaker ones into slavery and turning the stronger ones into warriors, in a bid to take over Eshia.' Delph said.

'How horrific. Queen Brana was a peace bringer, or so I've heard anyway,' said Elk.

'Elk, will you address her properly please,' Kadence scolded, raising her eyebrows.

'Does it really matter? She's no longer here is she?' snapped Elk.

'It makes no difference, she was a queen, you know fine well I'm a stickler for formalities Elk,' said Kadence.

'Okay, *Queen* Tybressa then. I'm sorry,' Elk apologised sarcastically.

'If there was so many J'yoti, why aren't they around now and what happened to them?' asked Kadence.

'I'm unsure about the race as a whole, but as the old tale goes, it was on a cold and stormy night, dingy rain lashed against the great dwarven warrior Gloram Brundhir's time-worn face as he lay alone near the peak of Jaadfaul Point armed with only his mighty primoth-cirox axe. He lay wounded and feared that his own demise was impending, having just defeated the last of the J'yoti. They've never been seen since.' Delph explained.

'Well, not until today anyway,' stressed Kadence.

They scraped any remaining food into the fire and washed their dinner plates down with the remaining water.

'That was lovely Elk, thank you,' Kadence said.

'Yeah, definitely one of your best meals,' said Delph.

Elk nodded, he was modest and didn't require compliments to boost his ego. He also enjoyed his meal, so much so, he added it to his ever-growing list of favourite foods.

Kadence yawned, which set Elk off then Delph off

'Since the sun is setting and we will have a long journey ahead of us tomorrow, I think we should try to get some sleep. Shall we take it in turn to guard the camp on a two-hour rotation?' Elk suggested.

'Good idea Elk. You can go first since you volunteered,' Delph replied with a cheeky grin.

Elk smiled at Delph sarcastically.

Kadence smiled.

'How are you feeling now Kadence?' Elk asked.

'Still a little sore although that solution Delph applied earlier has worked wonders, thankfully it's fast acting.' Kadence replied.

Elk nodded.

They each had their own sleeping bag and blanket, they took them out of their bags and unrolled them around the campfire.

They were thankful that it was a calm night and the wind had settled. Delph was first to fall asleep in the calming orange glow of the fire.

A silvery-pink tinge flared across the sky as the sun set. Elk sat close to the fire watching it flickering back and forth, relishing the heat on his face. It wasn't long until the light dwindled.

As the darkness enclosed around him, he couldn't help recalling the horrors of his day, he couldn't help replaying the events of the day over in his head, be grew ever more anxious every time the J'yoti appeared, so he stood up and put a few branches on the fire, revitalising it.

The forest had long gone to sleep and Elk's tiredness had come and gone. Every enhanced crackle from the fire echoed around the trees.

He watched the orange glow dwindle once more and couldn't help imagine one of the J'yoti lurking about in the darkness watching him from just outside the light of the fire.

He picked up the last of the branches and held the end of it in the fire creating a torch; he walked around the camp listening for any sinister signs of movement.

He settled his mind by doing this and chose just to let the others sleep on.

Elk amused himself throughout the night while keeping an eye on their makeshift camp, he patrolled close by for signs of any enemies and luckily for him there wasn't any trouble at all.

He gathered some fallen branches and carried them over to the camp, and after refuelling the fire he lay down and counted the stars, it was something he hadn't done for many years; he felt like he never got the chance to relax and just watch the world go by any more.

There wasn't a cloud in the sky and Eshia's three moons shone down illuminating the darkest parts of the forest.

He was happy that the night was mild, he watched the night sky and he listened attentively to the wildlife until the sun rose.

Kadence and Delph awoke with the first light of the sun as it broke through the trees. Delph sat up and asked Kadence how she was feeling.

'I'm a little groggy this morning, I stirred for most of the night, I feel better than I did last night,' Kadence replied.

'What about you Delph?' Kadence asked.

'Yeah, I'm okay' replied Delph, shrugging his shoulders.

'ARGH!' came a shriek from nowhere.

Kadence and Delph both jumped up from the ground and frantically searched for their weapons. Both turning around fast to face their attacker only to find Elk hunched over, holding his stomach and laughing.

'Elk, you git. What a fright you gave me' gasped Delph; laughing nervously.

'Elk, you're a moron, we could have killed you. You're lucky I didn't have my bow to hand or your day would have been over as quickly as it had begun!' Kadence yelled.

'Calm down Kadence, it was only a joke, you need to chill out. I've kept myself amused with that idea for the last two hours!' explained a slightly shocked Elk.

Delph shook his head at Elk's level of stupidity.

'Sorry Elk, I'm still a little jumpy after what happened yesterday,' shuddered Kadence.

'I thought you would have woken one of us up. Why did you stay on watch for the full night Elk?' Delph asked.

'I chose to let you sleep on. I didn't think Kadence would be up to it after what happened to her yesterday and I saw you yawning all day yesterday, so you must have needed a good sleep Delph,' Elk replied.

'Thanks for that, but in future please stick to any set routines. We all have to be fit and able, just in case we run into any trouble,' Delph said.

'I hear what you're saying, but I'll be okay. I'm a big boy Delph, it's not the first time I've stayed awake for a full night you know.' Elk replied sarcastically.

Delph frowned.

Elk refuelled the fire before poking it with a stick, he watched the embers swirl into the air.

'We don't have any water left, so we can't have any tea, but I saw a little river just on the other side of those trees over there, I can make us some tea if you're happy to drink the water from it?' Elk asked.

'Fine by me' replied Kadence.

'It won't be the first time we've drunk river water, Elk' said Delph.

'Yep you're right there Delph. I'll nip over and fill up one of these containers and I'll make tea, when I get back,' said Elk as he took off.

'Delph, I can't believe you can turn into animals. It's brilliant,' Kadence said.

'Uh yeah, it's amazing isn't it.' said Delph, his cheeks turned slightly pink as he laughed nervously.

'Delph, last night you spoke about Viacorp. Who are they?' Kadence asked.

'Viacorp is an organisation that built machinery they used to dig out the old caves of Booroff, in search of gold and useful minerals. My dad once told me of the fated day they found the power force they had been searching for.' Delph said.

'What was the power force?' Kadence asked.

'It was a mysterious element called unuprium and unknown to the slaves, a vicious spirit from an older generation was concealed inside. It festered in the cave and lay in wait for many years until it was powerful enough for its very own uprising.' Delph explained.

'What did it do for all of those years?' asked Elk, jabbing the fire again.

'During those years it had evolved into the resting creation which was disturbed one direful day when it was found by an unfortunate slave.' explained Delph.

'What do you think happened to the slaves?' Kadence asked.

'First of all, the unuprium consumed any slaves that were in the vicinity when it was found. Their stolen lives fuelled it with the power it required to secure its own uprising and when it had enough energy, it was strong enough to enslave the others and drive the unrequired slaves insane by mentally touching the men and women in the head.' Delph answered.

'That's horrific,' said Kadence..

'Yep, it drove them crazy until all that remained was maniacal servants of the ancient demigod Oona-Ciara. They craved the boost of unuprium that Oona-Ciara would serve to them if they were lucky enough,' Delph explained.

'I wonder why they didn't just flee from Oona-Ciara. If that were me, I would have made sure I was as far away as I could get,' Kadence said.

Elk nodded his head in agreement with Kadence. He screwed his face up; envisioning Oona-Ciara.

'I suppose they were hooked, and they needed their fix of unuprium. I'm sure I heard from my dad that some tried to escape, but their addiction overwhelmed them and they stayed where they were out of fear and the need to satisfy their addiction.' Delph explained.

'How unfortunate. Why did Oona-Ciara do that to all those poor men and women?' Kadence asked.

'In a bid to overthrow Eshia and control its people. It's evil you see,' Delph answered.

'Why do they wear the cloaks?' Kadence asked.

'You're full of questions this morning Kadence,' laughed Elk, returning with the water.

'I know, I'm just interested in our history and since we've now come up against the J'yoti on more than one occasion, I'd like to try to understand them a little more than I do at the moment,' Kadence replied.

'Apparently, they were scolded with molten whips if they didn't fulfil the tasks that Oona-Ciara dished out, usually resulting in their skin being scorched right down to the bone—' Delph was cut short by Elk.

'Toasty' Elk said out loud.

'I suppose they could use the cloaks to hide their deformities, although I'm not sure, maybe they clawed their own skin off, who knows.' answered Delph, grinning at Elks comment.

'Those poor men and women, how awful' Kadence said remorsefully, wiping a tear away, she shuddered at the thought of them being tortured.

'Should we have breakfast with our tea before we set off?' Elk asked.

'Is that you offering to make it Elk?' Delph asked.

'Yeah, I suppose it is. What do you two want? Just the usual?' Elk asked.

'Yeah' replied Delph and Kadence.

'We don't really have any other choice, do we Elky boy?' Delph laughed.

Once the trio had finished their breakfast, they cleaned up any mess and put out the campfire and made their way to the stone path.

Three weeks had passed since they had left the safety of their village and each of them was missing their home. It was a warm day, the sun shone fiercely, and some rays had pushed through the dense forest right down onto their faces.

A smooth cooling breeze flowed through the trees. They listened to crickets chirping, frogs croaking and birds singing a beautiful melody which helped to pass the mundane chore of getting to the path they had started their journey on the day before their battle had begun.

They reminisced about many things, including the life they had back in the village after they all met.

Delph is twenty-four years old. He grew up in the city of Elmoira. His black hair flows down past his ears. He has wild piercing icy-blue eyes and wears a lion heart earring in his left ear.

He also has the same emblem around his neck, he wears them proudly to represent and honour his father Kai, who was known as 'The Lionheart.' He lost his life in battle. Delph, like his father before him, is an excellent warrior.

His mother passed away when he was only four years old, this meant that he only had his mother's love for a small period of his life. He had to grow up fast and never had much of a childhood since his father was a general in the colossal war of Tastona.

Delph is a Therianthrope, so he can transform himself at will into various animals. He inherited the gift from his mother, who gained it from her mother. He met Kadence when she was twelve. She had no family around her, so he took her into his care, protecting her from any harm as best he could and making sure she kept out of trouble.

Kadence is twenty years old. She grew up in Bramwich. She has long braided silvery-blue hair that flows right down to her lower back, her calming eyes are ruby garnet red which offset her rosy cheeks perfectly. One day her younger sister Florence disappeared whilst she was out playing in the old woods.

One morning a few months after that horrible day Kadence woke up to find a golden-edged letter from her parents. They had mysteriously left her to survive on her own, she couldn't understand why they would just leave her.

Dear Kade,

It is with great sadness that we have to write this. We are so sorry, it's not something we've thought about at all trust me. We have to get away; you need to keep yourself busy and do not speak to anyone about this, if anyone asks about us, just make something up. I know you won't understand; I don't understand it myself, my sweet child. We are so sorry to leave you after our recent tragedy with Florence, I can't believe we are doing this, one day we'll meet again Kade and until that day, keep strong and stay safe. Oh lord of Eshia, keep our daughter safe. With all my love, mum, xxx (I'm so sorry.)

Kade,

We are so sorry my darling; I need you to do something for me, I need you to finish your training, it is important to our bloodline, and it is with utmost importance that you don't discuss your training with anyone other than someone trustworthy. Make your way to Elmoira, there are still a lot of good people there, I have faith, that we will meet again. You need to fulfil your prophesy training, that's all I can say, we must go.

All my love, my sweet daughter, Love dad xxx

Kadence was able to stay in Bramwich for a few months until she ran out of food, it was then she packed some items and left. She made her way to Elmoira like her dad had told her to. She slept rough in makeshift camps and stole food from market stalls for a few weeks until she met Delph, who invited her to stay with him.

Delph cared for her like an older brother. He wanted to make sure she achieved something in life, so he enrolled her in further education. She learned about potions and mastered the arts of potionology when she was only fifteen years old and has since mastered a vast knowledge of different types of potions. Her favourite is invisibility potions, she's found these useful in the past and used them any time she needed to escape from troublesome situations.

Elk is also twenty-four. He has short spiky green hair. His eyes are emerald green and he is a keen herbalist which means he can gather herbs and cut titbits from edible plants and shrubs ensuring he's never hungry when he's out in the wild, he also knows which ones to pick and use for medicinal purposes.

He learned the trait from his paternal grandfather when he was a little boy growing up in his hometown of Moorwarth.

Elk met Delph and Kadence when he was travelling to Elmoira on a supply run when he stopped to restock his herbs. It was then that he ran into some trouble from what seemed like a whole tribe of Wild-claw Crawboks.*

They were hostile to anyone that entered their territory, the Wild-claw Crawboks took nothing lightly.
They presumed that Elk was invading their area, therefore they surrounded him.

Delph and Kadence were close by and they heard the commotion, they came to his rescue and the trio has remained close friends ever since.

Soon after that Delph invited Elk to stay. Delph and Kadence helped Elk move all of his belongings into Delph's home.

* They were a tribe of men and women that chose to live in nature, much like naturalists... except, they were wilder and much more... crawbokier.

They had been on the road for what seemed like an eternity and Elk liked to remind them about it at every opportunity, so not only did they have to deal with sore feet from all the walking, they had to put up with Elk's constant griping as well. It had been a long day; they were just thankful that they didn't meet any other monsters.

It was early evening by the time they reached Bramwich village. Bramwich is a little village, there weren't many buildings. The buildings were a mix of houses, shops, a church and an inn.

Overall, it was a pretty worn down, dimly lit village. Elk watched as eerie, chilling smoke rolled past them and swirled up in random spots.

'Well, this place is weird' Elk whispered to the others.

Each house had grubby, straw-thatched roofs and a few of them had boarded-up windows and broken white picket fences surrounding them. A couple of houses had flowers laid across the doorstep. The ones with flowers had three red crosses painted on the doors.

Light from a poorly lit street light bounced off of an old red stained window, which drew their attention to movement over at the old church. They noticed a few people dressed in black cloaks entering the church, they dashed into a shadow to conceal themselves from the strangers.

They watched the cloaked figures for a few moments until goosebumps flashed up Elk's arms, shoulders and head making him shudder loudly, the sinister beings stopped suddenly and tilted their heads as if to smell the air. They were certain that they were on the verge of having another battle. They breathed a sigh of relief when they saw the cloaked strangers continue walking into the church.

Kadence stared over at a house and ran her eyes over the three crosses on the door, she closed her eyes and shed a few tears. It was the house that she grew up in, Elk noticed Kadence's tears, so he walked over to her and gave her a comforting hug.

'What's wrong Kadence?' Elk asked.

'Just memories, I'll explain later' replied Kadence, her voice was soft.

They looked up at the old worn down inn.

'Shall we stop here for the night?' Delph asked.

'I don't fancy our chances of travelling through the night.' said Elk.

'Let's go in,' said Kadence, wiping her eyes.

They pushed open the heavy red door and entered the inn.

There was no one there, so Elk walked up to the cluttered front desk and pressed the faded brass bell and when there was no jingle he pressed it a second time harder than before, this time it jingled.

He scrunched his face up in disgust when he felt a grimy residue on his fingers left over from touching the bell. The thought of smelling it crossed his mind although he went with his better judgement and he settled on wiping his hand on his trousers.

The innkeeper appeared from a beaded door frame that was behind the desk, he approached the desk scratching his wild, unkempt ginger beard.

He cleared away some dusty parchments that had built up over time by swiping them onto the floor behind the desk, leaving a trail of falling dusk specks in tow.

He leaned on the desk staring at them blankly, showing prominent signs that he never graduated from the school of people skills, he watched them suspiciously for a few moments without saying any words.

'Hello' Elk said; breaking the weird silence by waving his hand in front of the innkeeper.

'Sorry, I was miles away. Welcome to my inn. How may I help you?' the innkeeper grunted at them.

'We're looking for a room for the night preferably with three beds if you can manage our custom?' Delph asked.

'And how much will it cost for one night's stay Elk asked, looking down at the innkeeper's messy beard imagining all sorts of creatures nesting inside it.

'Aye, we have a couple of rooms left, we would happily welcome your custom, it'll be ten triarps* for each of you for one night, that includes dinner and breakfast,' he replied.

'Why is the town so eerie and what's happened to all of those houses?' Elk asked.

The innkeeper looked at Elk through tired and weary eyes.

'They showed up again a few nights ago,' grunted the innkeeper, rubbing his itchy eyes.

'Who did?' Delph asked.

'Can't talk now, I've got too much to do, I'll explain at dinner.' the innkeeper said.

'I bet you're hungry. I'll get someone to take care of the desk and I'll ask the chef to prepare your food, is there anything you don't like?' the innkeeper asked.

'No, we pretty much like everything.' Delph answered proudly.

* Triarps is the currency of Eshia.

Kadence took the money out of her pouch and placed it down on the untidy, grubby counter, it was only down for a split second before the innkeeper snatched it from the desk and placed it in his own money pouch.

'Okay great, let me speak to the chef and get someone through to watch the desk and then I'll show you up to your room,' confirmed the innkeeper, before disappearing through a door, leaving them to their own devices.

'What do you think he meant when he said they came again a few nights ago?' Delph asked.

'I'm not sure, but I don't fancy staying here more than one night in case it returns.' Elk replied.

'It will be the J'yoti. Remember what the man in Ellendale told us,' Kadence replied with a shudder.

The innkeeper returned with one of his staff; instructing him to watch the desk.

'If you'll come with me, please' he told the friends; pointing towards an open door to the left behind the desk.

They followed the innkeeper through a door which led them along a dimly lit corridor until they came to a crooked set of stairs. Kadence felt bad for cringing at the state of the décor.

'I will hate staying here tonight.' Elk whispered to Delph.

'Shh' Delph whispered back, grinning at Elk.

'Look, even the wallpaper hates it here, it's trying to escape.' Elk whispered to Delph, pointing his head to the walls.

Delph laughed louder than expected, He cleared his throat trying to disguise his laughter as a cough.

The green paper on the walls wasn't as vibrant as it once was, showing its age by hanging down at the corners. Dark damp patches lurked in the corners. Kadence had to step over a few tattered rips in the old brown carpet to save falling over.

'What's your name innkeeper?' Elk asked.

'My name is Rhoadan Brundhir,' replied the innkeeper.

'Brundhir... are you related to Gloram Brundhir?' Delph asked.

'Yes, he's my father. Have you heard of him?' Rhoadan proudly asked.

'Wow, yes we have,' Delph replied.

Rhoadan smiled.

'What are your names?' Rhoadan asked.

'I'm Delph Ferox. This is Elk Blake, and this is Kadence Erin,' said Delph; introducing the trio.

Rhoadan smiled again. 'Your room is just up these stairs and along the hall.' he said.

Rhoadan led the way up the crooked wooden stairs where each step groaned louder under his feet than the one before it. When they reached the top of the stairs, they followed him along a cold musky hall, passing many flimsy looking doors. This floor was in a similar condition to the one below except there were fewer damp spots strewn across the walls.

Rhoadan stopped. 'This is your room, I hope you find it adequate and cosy enough,' he said.

'Thanks, I'm sure it will be perfect,' replied Kadence.

'Kadence, before you go in, I have a question about your surname, it's a name I recognise. Do you have family in the village?' Rhoadan asked.

'Not now, but my family used to live here,' replied Kadence.

Rhoadan smiled and nodded.

'Dinner will be ready soon, so just make your way back down to the reception when you're ready and I will show you to your table,' explained Rhoadan.

They thanked him and pushed the door open. The room was surprisingly fresh smelling, which shocked them somewhat based on the state of disrepair in the décor.

There were three individual beds and one window which had a view of the forest they had just travelled through.

Over in the corner was a table with one lamp, it had no shade, just a bare bulb, there was a threadbare rug on the floor, the room was free of damp spots and the paper was intact.

'Let's dump our stuff and head down for dinner, then we can try to think about where we are heading next and what our plan of action is.' Delph said.

'Can we make sure we leave as soon as we're ready in the morning?' Kadence asked.

'I wanted to have a look around in the morning. Why do you want to leave as soon as we're ready Kadence?' Elk asked.

'I grew up here, I've got many happy memories, in fact too many to count, but I've also got a few not so happy memories. I used to live in the house across the path at number four with my mum, my dad and my little sister. We lived here for years and we were happy until that horrible day and it all went downhill from there.' Kadence replied.

'What happened?' Delph asked.

'When we were younger, my little sister Florence, and I were playing in the woods behind our house and when it was time for us to come in, I raced ahead and she never appeared. My parents and I went out to look for her, but we couldn't find her, she had just vanished. I haven't seen Florence for eight years and although it's wonderful to see my home village again, I only wish to make it a swift visit. The town is full of sad memories. My parents left me here alone, so I wasn't even able to complete my training.' she said.

'That's terrible,' said Delph, lowering his eyebrows.

'What training Kadence?' Elk asked.

'Prophesy training. It's something I'm supposed to do which will enable me to do something when I'm old enough, but I never completed it because my parents left me on my own and I never got to finish it or find out why I had to do it. I just know it's something I must complete, it's something important in my bloodline to enable safe handling of some sort of prophesy, apparently. I know that doesn't explain very much, but it's all I know.' explained Kadence, unenthusiastically.

'I'm sorry to hear about Florence,' Delph said.

Elk smiled empathetically.

She thanked them both.

'We'd better make our way down to dinner, we don't want to feel the dwarf's wrath. I'm already feeling the wrath of my stomach and that's harsh enough as it is,' said Elk, rubbing his belly.

'No we do not' Delph laughed.

'I wonder what's for dinner, I'm starving,' said Elk.

'You're always starving.' laughed Kadence.

They made their way down to the reception area where Rhoadan was waiting for them.

'Welcome back. Follow me and I'll show you to your table. Dinner's almost ready.' said Rhoadan.

They followed Rhoadan through the reception and into the well-lit dining room. There was four wide windows stationed evenly along the wall on their right. There were ten beautifully presented tables in front of them, with high back wooden chairs around them.

Rhoadan led them to their table and pulled out a seat for each of them to sit down. They all thanked him as they sat down, making Rhoadan smile.

'I'll go check on your dinner' he said as he headed for the kitchen door across the room.

Kadence and Delph watched Elk fidgeting in his seat.

'What are you doing Elk?' Delph asked.

'Getting comfy' he replied.

'You're making some amount of noise on that chair' Kadence groaned, cringing at every squeak of the seat.

Elk sighed childishly and shook his body to make a few more squeaks. A sarcastic grin appeared on his face quickly following the final squeak.

'Okay, here is what I suggest. We should finish our dinner and then head up to bed, in the morning we should have breakfast and then go. If you two are okay with that?' Delph asked.

'Yeah' replied Kadence.

'Fine by me, I need to get a decent sleep tonight.' Elk replied.

The kitchen door creaked as it swung open, drawing their attention to it. They readied themselves when they saw Rhoadan coming towards them with the dinner trolley. He presented them with bokbit stew and marl piper potatoes, mango bread and ginger ale tea.

'Mmmm I love this, it's my favourite' cheered Elk, grabbing his plate from Rhoadan's hands; making the chair squeak again.

Rhoadan muttered something about manners under his breath.

Delph and Kadence thanked Rhoadan as they took their plates from him. Rhoadan nodded and turned around to wheel the trolley away. Elk had almost finished his food before Rhoadan had the chance to reach the kitchen door, they made a quick job of clearing their plates before washing it down with the ginger ale tea.

They all shuddered at the same time with the final gulp, it was sweet tasting going down, but the residue at the bottom was bitter, leaving them with a warm glow inside.

'How was your meal?' Rhoadan asked as he joined them.

'It was perfect thanks.' replied Kadence.

'We have a few questions. Would you like to join us?' Delph asked.

'Okay sure. Would you like some rootberry wine?' Rhoadan asked. He then called for someone to fetch the wine and glasses and he pulled up a seat next to them.

'You mentioned that you would like to talk,' Rhoadan said.

'What's happened to the village? When I lived here, I remember it was so full of life, now it seems so lifeless.' Kadence asked.

'And what do the crosses on the doors mean?' Elk asked.

'The village was full of life. We used to have a busy market as you will remember Kadence. We had traders passing through every day. I had business all the time, and every room was constantly booked out, but now I'm lucky if I get people booking in every now and again. I even tried reducing the price of a nights stay, but it didn't do me any good.' Rhoadan said.

He sighed, feeling sorry for himself.

'I can't even cover the cost of running the place. I'm sure you've noticed it's not in the best condition. I'd do anything to get that kind of custom again. It would give my life meaning once more. It all went wrong when those attacks began.' explained Rhoadan.

'What attacks?' Kadence asked.

'About eight years ago some villagers noticed cloaked individuals watching them from the woods and it wasn't long until the sinister feeling swirling around the village had everyone on edge. One night two men had been drinking and had struck up enough courage to confront the watchers. The cloaked figures vanished without a trace when the men got close to them and everyone thought they had seen the last of them. That was until they were spotted lurking around the trees again, and within a few days little Florence disappeared and the men that went into the woods to confront the creeps were found dead in their houses,' explained Rhoadan.

Elk shuddered as he looked over at Kadence.

Kadence nodded her head as tears welled up at the mention of her sister's name. She felt her legs trembling, so she tried pressing her hands down on them to stop the jittering.

Elk and Delph turned to look at each other, goosebumps ran up their body and their face was as horrified as the one looking back at it.

'You asked me about the crosses,' said Rhoadan.

'Yes, what do they mean?' Elk replied.

'Those are the houses that my neighbours, unfortunately, died in. We painted crosses on them hoping their souls survived the journey to the sacred land. We won't ever know if their souls made it though, we just take some peace in thinking they made it.' Rhoadan added.

'It will be the J'yoti!' stated Delph.

'The attacks and those dark figures must have been connected,' said Rhoadan.

'It certainly sounds that way,' said Elk.

'They appeared again a few weeks ago and everyone is scared; so much so that I've seen people leave Bramwich every other day. I can't keep my business running any more, I want a fresh start in a busy lively and safe town.' said Rhoadan.

Kadence remained silent, she tried to hide her trembling chin, and she was quick to wipe away any tears that trickled down her cheeks.

'Florence was my sister.' she said.

'I wondered if she was your sister when you told me your surname earlier, but I didn't want to presume or mention it until you told me just now in case it upset you. I'm sorry for your loss.' said Rhoadan.

'We're heading out of Bramwich tomorrow, you should come with us Rhoadan,' Delph suggested.

'Is that okay with you?' he asked, biting the ragged corner of one of his nails.

'No problem at all.' replied Elk.

Kadence nodded.

'I'd love to. I would have to say a few goodbyes and tie up some loose ends here first, it shouldn't take long, I've been thinking about packing up for a few days, so I already have most of my belongings and supplies packed, plus I have a carriage and Brightbane to take us.' Rhoadan said.

'What's a Brightbane?' Elk asked.

'It's not a thing. Brightbane's my horse,' laughed Rhoadan.

'That will certainly make our journey a lot easier.' replied Delph.

'I also have something I would like to do before we leave.' added Kadence.

'That's settled then. Let's have a few more rootberry wines and discuss our plans before heading to bed to prepare for our journey tomorrow.' said Rhoadan.

They had a few more drinks and when they were slightly worse for wear, they all decided it was best to head to bed. In the morning Kadence would be glad she only had a few wines whereas Delph and Elk would regret it, Delph more than Elk.

The light of the sun had just begun peeking over the top of the hills and it shone straight into the room. Kadence smiled as she embraced the sun's warm glow on her face. She lay awake in silence staring at the ceiling, tracing the whirls and cracks in the plaster with her eyes.

'Snccchhhhhhaaaa' came from either Elk or Delph, she was unsure who it came from because they both lay there snoring their heads off, disturbing the serenity of the morning.

She sat up and threw a pillow at each of them for good measure and when neither of them budged, she got up and walked across the cold floor and stood on the rug to warm her feet before making her way over to Delph's bed first to give him a shake.

'Time to get up Delph, we need to get ready.' she said.

He rolled over and lazily opened one eye: 'Sore head,' he croaked, before rolling back over to face the wall, pulling the covers over his head.

'Well, you should learn to limit the rootberry wines,' Kadence said as she smiled.

Delph groaned.

She walked over to Elk and nudged him: 'Elk, it's time to get up,' she whispered in his ear.

He threw his covers back and sat straight up, startling her. Squinting at her through half open-eyes, he smiled and nodded his head: 'Morning,' he muttered hoarsely. He dragged himself out of bed and slowly made his way to the bathroom for a long overdue drink to satisfy his dry throat.

Kadence headed into the bathroom to get ready once Elk had finished in there and when she got out she noticed Elk had already left. She sighed at the sight of Delph lying half slumped over the bed as she made her way down to the dining room where breakfast was already laid out. Elk was already halfway through his breakfast.

There was a choice of toasted nut bread with jellied syrup or a mixed oats mash. Kadence chose the toasted nut bread and jellied orange syrup. Delph's groaning drew their attention as he shuffled over to the table.

'I feel like death' Delph groaned as he slumped down into a seat.

'You should learn to limit your wine then,' Kadence laughed unsympathetically.

'You're getting old. You can't handle it any more.' said Elk with a smile.

'I'm the same age as you,' grunted Delph.

'I know you are, but at least I know *when* to stop.' laughed Elk.

'Do you want me to fix you any food?' asked Kadence.

Delph shook his head, groaned and reached over to the coffee jug.

Rhoadan appeared and wished them a good morning: 'It shouldn't take me long, I've said my goodbyes to friends and now I must now speak to my staff, this is the part I'm not looking forward to.' he said, before disappearing into the kitchen.

'I wouldn't like to be him right now.' Elk laughed.

Rhoadan had previously asked his staff to meet him in the kitchen for a meeting.

He'd only been in there for a few minutes when the group heard a clutter of clanging and banging and once the storm had calmed, the staff stomped out of the kitchen, one by one shaking their heads.

A few moments passed before Rhoadan appeared from the kitchen covered in the aprons that his staff threw on him: 'Well that could have gone better,' he said with an awkward smile, before walking through the dining room door to the reception, peeling off the aprons as he went.

He peeked back in and said: 'I'll just finish packing, why don't you have a look for items around here that might be useful to you. You're welcome to anything' before he disappeared.

Elk got up from the table and went into the kitchen.

'I'll try not to be long. I'm going over to see my sister's grave. My parents made a grave for her in our old back garden. Even though she was never found, we still needed somewhere to mourn.' Kadence explained.

'Take as long as you need Kadence,' Delph said.

She pushed her seat out and grabbed the flowers from the vase in the centre of the table, she nodded at Delph and headed for the door and walked out of the inn.

Delph helped himself to more coffee. He felt ill, but the coffee seemed to help, he lifted his cup from the table and joined Elk in the kitchen. They both looked through cupboards and drawers for anything that would be of use to them on their journey. Elk found bandages and some sterilising liquid.

Delph opened the fridge and found some smoked hog flanks, he took them out and placed them on the worktop. He finished his coffee and lifted some nut bread and jellied syrups along with a few other items he thought would be useful and put them to one side.

'Let's take water because we ran out back in the forest and I'd rather not let that happen again.' suggested Delph.

'Good idea, look here's some bottles we can use' replied Elk, taking the first one to the tap to fill it.

'There's no point in taking this lot upstairs only to bring them back down again. Let's leave it all in the reception area and we can grab it all on the way out.' said Delph.

They lifted their supplies and carried it all through to the reception before dumping it on the ground, then went up to their room to get their bags.

Kadence threw the door open surprising them both. Her eyes were red and puffy, they could see she had been crying. She fixed her bag and once she had finished, she lifted it and muttered: 'Meet me out in the courtyard, around the back.'

Elk and Delph made their way downstairs once they had finished fixing their own bags. They put all the supplies from the kitchen into their bags and went outside. They walked around the back of the inn and into the dingy courtyard where they joined Kadence, Rhoadan and Brightbane.

Chapter Two

-Shambolic Hollow-

Rhoadan was already seated in the grand wooden carriage when Elk and Delph arrived.

'Set your bags in the back then jump up here with me and take a seat,' Rhoadan said.

They put their bags in the back and discovered that Kadence was settled in there with her back turned to them.

They walked around to the front of the carriage and stopped at Brightbane. She was a huge black steed, her mane and tail were golden, she looked down at Elk and snorted her nostrils.

'Would you mind if I clap her?' Elk asked.

'No, not at all, but be gentle, try not to make any sudden movements as she doesn't know you and isn't keen on being startled,' Rhoadan replied.

Elk nodded, he looked up at her and clapped her side.

'Look at her hair, it's so bright,' said Elk.

'It shimmers when she runs.' said Rhoadan.

'Right Elk let's get up onto this carriage,' said Delph, as he climbed up.

'Just coming, give me a hand up,' Elk said, holding his hand up to Delph.

'Climb up yourself, You're in better condition than me today and I managed it,' laughed Delph.

'I'll miss Bramwich, I've lived here for most of my life ever since I was a little nipper. It's making me nervous to think this could be the last time I see it,' said Rhoadan.

'I can relate to that,' said Delph.

'You could always come back for a visit,' said Elk.

'I know I can. Where is it we're going anyway?' Rhoadan asked.

'We're planning on heading to Dirtbere,' replied Elk.

'Dirtbere you say, I love Dirtbere. I used to go there with my family when I was younger,' replied Rhoadan.

'I haven't been,' said Elk.

'I have. Dirtbere is an amazing market town. It has its own harbour with magnificent boats, I heard once that there's even flying ships that have golden wings and sails, but I've never seen one,' said Delph.

'Yeah, I've heard that as well. The ships bring in goods to the market. I've heard Dirtbere's wares are famous throughout the land, if you ever need anything then Dirtbere's the place you'll get it and if you can't find it there, then it's not worth having in the first place. It's a beautiful town, and it never rains, the sun always seems to shine, there's something magical about it.' Rhoadan explained.

'Dirtbere sounds wonderful. Do you know how long it takes to get there?' Elk asked.

'I'm sure it takes a few days, so if we leave now though we should make good progress,' replied Delph.

Rhoadan had one last look around at the place he's called home for more years than he could remember. He cracked Brightbane's reins to let her know he was ready to move on.

'Let's go girl' he said softly.

The group hadn't stopped once since leaving Bramwich, the twinging in Elk's stomach told him it was nearing lunchtime.

'How about we stop for a while to let Brightbane rest her hooves?' Rhoadan suggested.

'Great idea, I could do with a stretch.' Delph replied.

Rhoadan clicked his tongue, the sound alerted Brightbane, and she slowed down faster than Rhoadan had intended. She halted abruptly, jerking them forward.

'I'll just let Kadence know what we're doing, then I'll gather firewood and make a fire so I can cook us some lunch,' said Elk, steadying himself in his seat.

He jumped down and stretched his arms and legs, the long journey had not only numbed his mind but his arms and legs as well. Once the natural feeling had returned to his limbs, he made his way to the back of the carriage.

'Kadence, we've just stopped to have lunch. Would you like to come and help me gather some wood for the fire?' Elk asked.

Kadence looked at him and smiled. She climbed down and stretched her legs. She had it easier than the others, she had the luxury of lying in the back of the carriage and could stretch out whenever she liked without the risk of toppling over the edge of the carriage. She followed Elk into the trees where they both looked for wood.

'How are you feeling Kadence?' Elk asked.

'I'm still heartbroken, I'll never get over her, I have learned to live without her around though. I still miss my little sister and visiting Bramwich was hard for me,' she replied in a soft tone.

'I'm not surprised you're upset. I've never lost a sibling so I can only imagine how you're feeling, if you ever need to talk about anything, I'm always here for you,' Elk said.

'I know you are, thanks, Elk' replied Kadence, shunning all eye contact.

They barely had enough time to scratch the surface of the forest when they heard Rhoadan yelling at Brightbane to calm down. Kadence and Elk both looked at each other with widened eyes.

'We better grab some wood and head back,' Elk said.

They hunted for wood, picked it up and ran back to the carriage. The first thing they saw was Rhoadan waving two white wooden staves in front of Brightbane and rather than causing further agitation, they kept clear of Brightbane and joined Delph.

'What's happening?' gasped asked.

'We were sorting lunch when I saw a black creature lurking over by the trees, that's when Brightbane freaked out, she must have seen it as well,' explained Delph.

'Oh, no are they back? Have they found us?' fretted Kadence.

'No it's not the J'yoti this time, at least I don't think it is, it looked different. It was much smaller than the ones we faced before,' Delph explained.

'What's Rhoadan doing?' asked Kadence, with her brow furrowed.

'Beats me' Delph replied, shrugging his shoulders.

'Brightbane, calm down girl,' Rhoadan stated; waving the sticks about.

'Do you need any help, Rhoadan?' asked Elk.

'Yes, I thought you'd never ask. Pass me a few sugar cubes from my orange satchel,' he answered.

Elk hurried over to the satchel, opened it hastily and rummaged through it, cursing every sharp object in it. He pulled two cubes out of a little side pocket and hurried over to Rhoadan.

'Slow down, bring them over to me slowly. Brightbane is spooked out enough as it is already.' Rhoadan warned Elk.

'I'm sorry I didn't think' replied Elk, as he slowed down. Elk handed the cubes to Rhoadan and backed away, joining Kadence and Delph.

'Don't worry about it, you weren't to know.' said Delph; patting Elk on his back.

'Now girl, take these nice and don't even think about biting my finger this time' Rhoadan warned Brightbane. He held the cubes out with an open palm and rubbed her neck until she settled down.

'She's settled down now thankfully,' sighed Rhoadan, joining the others.

'Why were you using those sticks Rhoadan?' Kadence asked.

'They aren't *just* sticks, they're staves. I purchased them from an old Orkapi trainer many moons ago when she was a foal. The old man told me to wave them in front of her face when she is hyper like you just saw, and it's supposed to calm her down, although I think she would prefer to kick me in the face when she lays her eyes on them.' Rhoadan explained.

'A what trainer?' Kadence asked.

'Orkapi. You know those giant blue birds, sharp teeth, one eye, two tails with a fiery temper,' said Rhoadan.

'I've never heard of them,' said Kadence.

'There's not many of them around these days, that'll be why I suppose,' said Rhoadan.

'Do the staves work?' asked Delph, running his eyes up to the crescent moon at the top.

'Yeah they do, but I actually think it's just the cubes that calm her down, she's a chancer,' laughed Rhoadan, he put the staves back in the carriage.

'I wonder if Brightbane saw the same thing I saw,' Delph said.

'I'm sure I saw a shadow lurking about by the trees. It looked like an animal, either a wolf or a dog, something like that, although it was too far away to see it properly. It scampered away when Brightbane started braying and kicking her legs in the air,' shuddered Rhoadan.

'I'm going to start making our lunch and then we can be on our way. I'll make something quick to eat in case it comes back, I really don't want to meet whatever it was,' shuddered Elk.

'What are we having?' Kadence asked; holding her growling stomach.

'I'm not too sure yet. I'll have to see what we have,' replied Elk.

Elk crouched down to look in the bags. He took out the nut bread and smoked hog flanks he got from Rhoadan's kitchen and lifted out a pan and slice to cook them with.

Delph lit the fire and Kadence took out some bowls and forks.

'Do you think Brightbane will eat some of this?' Elk asked.

'Nah, it'll be too rich. I'll just fix up something for her,' Rhoadan said; he lifted out Brightbane's food bag.

'What's she having for dinner?' Elk asked.

'Mixed oats and apple cores, it's her favourite,' Rhoadan said.

Elk threw the flanks into the pan and placed it on the fire, he sear fried them till they were brown; he broke it up and put the flanks on the bread and served it to the group.

'I'm worried that we'll get attacked again,' stressed Kadence.

'Try not to worry about it Kadence, if it happens, then it happens. We will take care of whatever comes our way,' replied Delph.

'Plus we now have Rhoadan on our team and he looks like he enjoys smashing skulls,' laughed Elk.

Rhoadan scowled at Elk and grunted something quietly to himself* then continued eating his meal.

'Let's finish our lunch and then we can leave before that thing comes back,' said Delph.

'Well I enjoyed that,' said Kadence.

'Yeah, it was nice. Cheers,' Delph said.

Rhoadan grunted again.

'No problem' replied Elk; he began clearing away the dishes.

'I'll put out the fire. Are you okay to get the bowls Kadence?' Delph asked.

Kadence nodded her head.

Rhoadan gathered all the bags and put them into the back of the carriage.

* **'It will be your skull that I'll be smashing if I get any more cheek from you laddie.'**

Kadence climbed in the back and Elk, Delph and Rhoadan climbed up front.

'Let's get going, I want to make good progress before nightfall, it's not long after lunchtime and we've already had a scare, I don't want too many surprises today,' said Rhoadan.

'Good idea. I'm happy with that,' replied Delph.

'Giddy up girl, let's be off now,' Rhoadan said.

Rhoadan cracked Brightbane's reins until she started walking and he kept it up until she was in mid canter. They travelled for a few hours with minimal conversation, still full from their big lunch.

Delph broke the silence and asked Rhoadan about his father.

'Rhoadan, you told us who your father was back at the inn. You don't see many dwarves any more, what happened to him and your race?' he asked.

'I think your the first dwarf I've ever seen' Elk replied with a big grin on his face; resisting the urge to lean over and pat him on the head.

'I can't answer much on the latter part of your question, however, I can tell you what I know of the former part. My father was a magnificent warrior in the colossal war of Tastona. He lost his life whilst fighting the J'yoti, not long after the war ended.' Rhoadan replied.

'My father lost his life in that war,' said Delph.

'I'm sorry to hear that Delph. What was his name?' Rhoadan asked.

'He was known as Kai the Lion heart, he was a great man. Perhaps you've heard of him?' Delph asked.

'I have. I've heard tales of his war stories, I've heard he was a magnificent general who was great and powerful. I'm certain he and my father would have been great friends.' Rhoadan said.

Delph smiled.

'As for the latter part of your question, what I understand from rumours is that the true dwarf race almost ended with that war. I lost my father when I was just a child and I was too young to know anything about the dwarves, really.' Rhoadan replied.

'I've heard different stories about the war from various people over the years, one thing that's always consistent though is a vast number of people lost their lives whilst fighting in it. What was the reason the war started and who were they fighting?' Elk asked.

'There were four holy beings known as The Guardian Four, although their names escape me, right now. I heard they could sense that there was some sort of interference happening throughout Eshia. They were connected to Eshia via Eshia's life source which was draining at the time. Therefore, they decided that they would monitor the interference, in doing so they discovered that Viacorp were at the source of it and that they were damaging Eshia.' Delph added.

'So they recruited all the able-bodied men and women they could find; that was still stable in the mind and untouched by unuprium. They formed a masterful army to save Eshia and stop it from being overrun by Viacorp. They lay in wait until the darkest day, in which the enemy made their move.' Rhoadan explained.

'They sound like a right nasty bunch,' Elk said.

Delph and Rhoadan both nodded their heads.

'I heard the war started when Viacorp had become so strong they were on the verge of taking over Eshia and in the process plunging it into eternal darkness. We launched our attack where Viacorp were based and we battled tooth and claw until we believed the J'yoti were gone.' Rhoadan said.

'Numerous lives were lost, but in all the sadness we had finally got rid of the J'yoti, once and for all, or so we thought, until that fateful day up on Jaadfaul Point, where my father defeated the last J'yoti,' Rhoadan explained.

'If your father defeated the last of the J'yoti, then why have we been fighting them recently?' Elk asked.

'That part is unclear, which is why I'm nervous. He passed away a short time after his battle, due to the injuries inflicted upon him by that wretched J'yoti. I fear that Viacorp may be up to their old tricks again.' Rhoadan answered.

'As far as I know, Oona-Ciara was defeated in the colossal war. If she was, how can they be on the rise again?' Delph asked.

'I have no idea. We will need to stay safe though because—' Kadence caught Rhoadan's attention.

'It's back, we're being followed.' Kadence interrupted Rhoadan.

'What's back? What do you mean? Where is it?' Delph yelled back.

'I'm not sure what it is, it was too far away to get a proper look. It's black, it must be the same thing that frightened Brightbane before,' replied Kadence.

'It better not be those J'yoti hounds again,' Elk shrieked.

'Okay stop the carriage, let's have a look,' Delph commanded.

Rhoadan whistled for Brightbane to stop. A suspicious-looking shadow lingering further up the road caught Elk's attention.

Elk and Delph jumped down from the carriage and walked around to see what Kadence was referring to, Rhoadan stayed in front of the carriage and kept an eye on the motionless shadow that lurked further up the road from where they stood.

'Can you show me what you saw Kadence?' Delph asked.

Kadence jumped down onto the dusty road below. She looked further along the road to where she had last seen the beast.

'Well that's strange, there's nothing there, there was something following us, I watched it for a little while and it was just following from a distance,' Kadence told Elk.

'It just disappeared,' Rhoadan shouted.

Elk, Delph and Kadence ran around to the opposite end of the carriage to where Rhoadan was standing.

'What's disappeared?' Kadence asked.

'That thing has, the thing that was sitting up there, whatever it was,' Rhoadan replied.

'These things are truly starting to annoy me,' he added; whilst pointing up to where it was sitting watching them from.

'We spotted another one sitting on the road up ahead when we were coming round to you, but it's also vanished,' Elk explained to Kadence.

'Now what are we going to do?' Kadence asked.

'We should just keep moving and hope we can find a safe place to park up and take shelter for the night,' said Rhoadan.

'Look, there's another one up there,' Elk said; pointing in the direction.

'Let's hope we make it to a place of safety before we run into any trouble,' stressed Kadence.

'Don't you think if those creatures were going to attack us they would have done it by now?' Elk asked.

'What's making you say that?' Delph asked.

'Well let's put it this way. How many times have we seen them now?' Elk asked Delph.

'That's been twice now,' Delph recalled.

'Well then, that's twice that we've not been attacked. Is it not?' Elk asked.

'You're right, but on those two occasions, they've just disappeared,' Delph replied.

'Yes I know that, but they still had the chance to launch an attack on us. What if they're not our enemy?' Elk asked.

'Well let's not hang around any longer to find out,' suggested Rhoadan.

'Kadence, would you rather sit up front with Delph and Rhoadan and I'll keep watching from the back?' Elk asked.

'Good idea, I was getting bored before,' admitted Kadence.

'We can't just sit here and wait for them to return, we need to get ourselves moving and get off the road and get some decent rest,' Elk added.

'We don't have long until it gets dark and I really don't fancy our chances of travelling through the night on this road. I think it would be best if we look for a place to stop for the night sooner rather than later,' suggested Delph.

Kadence, Delph and Rhoadan all climbed up to the front of the carriage while Elk made his way round to the back.

'It looks clear from this end, from what I can see' Elk yelled.

'It's all good over here,' Rhoadan yelled back.

'Let's move on then girl,' Rhoadan said to Brightbane as he cracked her reins gently on her back.

They made their way along the dusty road until they were faced with a massive rock that blocked their path, they couldn't continue any further, they surveyed their surroundings to reassure themselves that they weren't being followed.

'Right guys, we've come to the end of the road. We can't go any further,' said Rhoadan.

'What do we do now?' Kadence asked.

'I wonder if we can get around it,' said Rhoadan.

'Why have we stopped?' Elk yelled.

'There's not a hope of a chance, look at it, that rock is massive. Even if we could get around it, just look at the drop at the other side, there is no way around it,' said Delph, ignoring Elk's yell.

Delph jumped down from the carriage to have a look and check for alternative routes. Elk joined him.

'Look over there, is that another path?' Elk asked.

'I'm sure that is a path and if we go down that way we should be able to bypass that rock,' said Delph.

They searched further along the road until a cave came into view.

'We should make our way down there and check it out,' suggested Delph.

'Sounds good,' replied Elk.

'I don't like caves,' Kadence confessed.

'It's not as if we have any other choices. We can't go any further and if we were to stay on the road for the night we wouldn't make it,' Elk said.

'Shhh,' Delph whispered, holding his hand up to his ear.

'What is it?' Elk whispered back.

'I thought I heard someone calling my name. Let's carry on.' replied Delph.

Elk and Delph climbed back up onto the carriage.

They headed off the dusty road and make their way down the beaten mossy path towards the cave.

The carriage was too bulky to get down the path easily, so it made for a bumpy ride.

Little to their knowledge there was a set of watchful eyes staring at them intensely from afar, observing every move they made.

The light began to disappear as they made their way down to the cave, so they took it slow, they didn't want to risk taking a chance of rolling right over the cliff edge.

They reached the massive entrance to the cave without too much hassle.

'It's dark in there,' Kadence fretted.

'It should be. It's a cave. Do you know of many well-lit caves Kadence?' Elk joked.

Delph jabbed his elbow into Elk's ribs to stop him ridiculing Kadence, he also received a sarcastic stare from Kadence. He preferred Delph's elbow to Kadence's icy stare.

Elk thought it was best to refrain from further jest.

'Let's enter the cave,' Rhoadan proposed.

'I think we should find some wood for a fire before we go in,' said Delph.

'Don't worry about that, there's loads in the back of the carriage,' replied Rhoadan.

'Brilliant, let's get a few torches lit, so we can see where we're going when we get in,' said Delph.

'Rhoadan, you failed to mention that you already had wood before Kadence and I went into the trees to collect some before lunch,' said Elk.

'I forgot it was there. I've only just remembered. I'm getting old. My memory isn't what it used to be,' laughed Rhoadan. They all laughed.

Delph searched through his rucksack and found some fire rag, Elk handed him three pieces of wood he had just fetched from the carriage.

'Here you go, wrap some of that rag around the end and I will light them,' Elk said.

He pulled his lighter out from his pocket and set fire to the first one, the light from the rag shone brightly around them.

He passed the first torch to Kadence, he got his own one from Delph and lit it as well, Delph lit the last one and kept it for himself.

'I wouldn't recommend anyone sitting in the back of the carriage with one of these torches. So I'll walk alongside the carriage and we can find a safe spot to rest.' Elk said.

'Good idea' said Rhoadan.

Delph and Kadence jumped back up onto the carriage and sat on either side of Rhoadan, they held out their torch-bearing arms, to reduce the risk of setting something on fire accidentally.*

Rhoadan whipped Brightbane's reins gently to let her know he wished to continue into the cave.

'Can you see anything Elk?' Rhoadan asked.

* **Or more importantly, Rhoadan, as much as having a beard of fire would help with their lighting predicament, Rhoadan would rather not have one.**

'Not really. Just the ground, some stones, and a few rocks, it's all very exciting stuff down here.' Elk joked.

'What about you?' Elk asked.

'Nothing yet' replied Kadence.

'Let's keep moving, at least it's dry I suppose,' said Elk.

They continued until they found a hollow section of the cave.

'Let's stop here, it looks perfect,' suggested Elk.

'Great, we can finally get off this carriage and relax without the constant bumping and shaking,' said Delph, as he lunged down to the ground. At that point realising how unappreciative he sounded, he quickly added: 'I mean no offence Rhoadan, I'm grateful for your carriage, just not the persistent jiggling.'

'Don't you worry your head lad, I'm built from strong stuff, I have thick skin, no offence taken' Rhoadan replied with a grin, as he clambered down from the carriage and landed with a heavy thud on the stony ground below.

'I nearly fell there, did you see that?' Rhoadan laughed.

Kadence jumped down from the carriage, she, however, did not create a scene like Rhoadan had just done.

'Right Kadence, could you fix us a fire?' Delph asked.

'Once that fire is ready, I'll make us some dinner, I'll have a look and see what we have to offer,' Elk said.

'I'll get the unpacking done, and see what we'll need for the night, then see to Brightbane,' said Rhoadan.

'I'll have a scout about and check our surroundings,' said Delph.

'Before we do any of that, we should set up torches around the camp so we can at least see what we're doing,' Elk suggested.

Elk lifted some wood from the back of the carriage and threw it down on the ground while Kadence fetched some fire rag from the rucksacks. She put the rags down by the wood that Elk had just brought.

Rhoadan wrapped the rag around the wood and handed it to Delph, who lit them one by one, as each torch lit up, they were carefully arranged around their temporary camp.

The immediate area radiantly lit up like someone had just switched on a dozen lamps in a dark cellar.

'Good job everyone, let's get our camp set up.' said Delph; as he walked away to scout the area.

They had used all the wood that Elk brought them earlier on the torches, so they fetched more from the carriage. Rhoadan wandered over to Brightbane and Elk searched through the rucksacks for food.

Gghrgrhrhrhrhgrrhrhghgrh.

Kadence stopped what she was doing and turned around to investigate.

'Shhh, stop. What was that noise?' Kadence quietly asked.

'I didn't hear anything. What noise?' Elk asked.

They listened for a few moments, but the only sound they could hear was the distant crunching of gravel that Delph made as he patrolled the cave.

They could also hear Rhoadan making some noise as he tended to Brightbane, they couldn't hear anything else, so they both carried on with what they were doing.

Gghrgrhrhrhrhgrrhrhghgrh.

This time it was louder.

'There it is again, please tell me you heard it that time?' Kadence asked, fearing she was starting to hear noises that weren't really there.

'Yes, I heard it that time. What was that?' Elk replied.

He stopped searching through the rucksack and looked around quickly in all directions to try to catch a glimpse of the owner of the ghastly sound. Kadence reached for her bow as did Elk with his gun. They both listened intently for further sounds and had all sorts of horrible creatures going through their imaginations, they waited silently for another few moments, but there weren't any further sounds.

'Rhoadan' said Kadence softly.

Kadence waited patiently for a reply that never came.

'Rhoadan' said Elk a little louder than Kadence did.

They looked over at Rhoadan, awaiting his response, they could see him crouching down over by Brightbane.

'Do you think he's okay?' Kadence asked.

'I don't know. What is he doing?' Elk asked.

'I'm not sure, but I think we should go over and check.' suggested Kadence.

Kadence and Elk cautiously walked over to Rhoadan, trying not to draw any unwanted attention to themselves from the hidden horror that they couldn't lay eyes on. Elk tapped Rhoadan on the back when they reached him.

'Rhoadan, are you okay?' Elk asked.

Gghrgrhrhrhrhgrrhrhghgrh.

Kadence got a fright and she let out a sharp yelp which multiplied several times as it echoed around the cave.

The noise startled Rhoadan, he jumped up and almost knocked poor Elk flat on his back. Rhoadan turned around sharply to see Kadence and Elk stood with their weapons drawn, they were staring back at Rhoadan, as though he was a three-headed monster.

'Are you okay?' Elk asked again.

'Yeah. Why?' Rhoadan asked.

'Didn't you hear that noise?' Kadence asked.

'What noise?' Rhoadan asked.

Gghrgrhrhrhrhgrrhrhghgrh.

'That noise' Kadence replied.

'That's just my stomach, I'm starving, what's for eating?' Rhoadan laughed; slapping his belly.

When they learned that it was only Rhoadan's massive appetite that made the noise, they returned to what they were doing before. Both chuckling out of embarrassment as they went. Once they reached the carriage, Kadence lifted the wood that she had laid out on the ground earlier and carried it over to a spot she thought was perfect for making the fire.

Elk continued looking through the rucksacks for some food, he found some nut bread, some dry smoked bush boar legs and some root tuber potatoes, he took it all out and walked over to Kadence.

'I'll just put these down on this rock, then I'll go and fetch the rest,' Elk said as he placed the items down.

'Okay' replied Kadence.

He walked back over and picked up the rest of the supplies.

Elk still had the pots, bowls and cutlery to bring back, he picked them up and carried them over, one of the pots slipped from his grasp and made an almighty clatter as it hit the hard ground below, Kadence jumped up and let out another yelp.

'Sorry, sorry it's just me,' Elk quickly apologised.

Brightbane snorted her nostrils and whinnied, kicking her two front legs up into the air, knocking Rhoadan onto his back.

'What a commotion you're making tonight,' moaned Rhoadan, as he stood back up and settled Brightbane again: 'There, there girl, settle down it was only that daft lad.' he added.

Elk laughed nervously.

'I'll go back to fixing the fire, now my heart has stopped racing, what a fright you gave me there,' laughed Kadence.

Elk grinned awkwardly.

Rhoadan was able to settle Brightbane, so he joined the other two and he brought blankets with him.

'I don't fancy sleeping on the ground tonight it's mighty jagged.' said Rhoadan; stomping the ground.

'The last time we camped out, I stayed awake all night to let Delph and Kadence sleep on,' said Elk.

'Try to get some sleep this time though Elk,' said Delph.

'Yeah I will, how about we do a two-person patrol?' Elk asked.

'I'm tired, but I don't know if I'll be able to sleep tonight,' said Kadence.

'Hopefully, we all manage to get some sleep,' replied Elk.

Kadence finished setting up the fire. Elk handed her his lighter, she gripped it tightly and flicked it until a small orange flame danced out of it, she held it to the wood and it quickly caught fire.

They smiled gently as the fire warmed their faces.

As the fire grew from the base up, it lit up the parts of the cave the torches hadn't been able to reach, shadows danced on the walls and ceiling of the cave as if they were performing an ancient tribal dance.

Elk let the fire die down a bit before using a stick to push some of the embers from the bottom. He moved them to the area that he had designated for cooking. He clumped the embers together and placed his pots on them and put in the smoked boar and tuber potatoes.

'I'll make us some tea while we're waiting for the food' said Kadence. She gathered the items she needed from the carriage and returned to the preparation area.

'We're going to have some delicious night tea,' Kadence said.

'What's night tea?' Rhoadan asked.

'Well, it's like normal tea you see, except we have no cream.' she laughed, as did Elk and Rhoadan.

'That'll do me nicely and the food smells good Elk,' said Rhoadan.

'Yeah, it smells good, even if I do say so myself.' replied Elk.

'Do you think one of us should go and check on Delph?' Elk asked.

'He's been gone for a while now, our food will be ready soon,' he added.

'If he's not back soon, I'll go and have a look,' replied Rhoadan.

'Don't worry, I'll give him a shout,' said Kadence; she walked over until she was a foot or so from the edge of the firelight.

'Where are you, Delph? Are you there?' she waited patiently for a reply.

Kadence was sure she heard something moving in the shadows, but she wasn't able to see anything, it was too dark to see past the line of light she lingered in front of, and when she received no response she shuddered and returned to the others.

'Anything?' asked Elk.

'Nope, no response, although I think I heard something scuffling about in the darkness, I couldn't see anything. Do you think we should we go and check?' replied Kadence.

'Someone would be better staying here with Brightbane,' Rhoadan said.

'Well, that won't be me. I don't fancy staying here on my own,' said Kadence: 'I'll go with whoever goes.' she added.

Just then they heard movement behind them.

'I think our dilemma has been resolved. No one will need to go, he's back.' explained Rhoadan.

'Tea is ready. What took you so long Delph?' asked Kadence; she was relieved to see him.

'Did you find anything?' Elk asked.

'I'm not sure, there was nothing at first, but then I found some tracks—' Delph was cut short.

'What kind of tracks were they?' Rhoadan rudely interrupted Delph.

'I'm not sure, I wouldn't say they were the tracks of those hounds we saw earlier, these tracks were of something with large claw-like feet,' Delph said.

Kadence gasped.

'I followed the tracks until they disappeared and it was too dark to see anything and that's when I turned around and came back.' Delph explained.

'Did they look like fresh tracks?' Elk asked.

'No, there wasn't any scent in them, so I'm not sure how long they've been there,' Delph replied.

'I'm not sure if that's a good thing or a bad thing.' said Elk.

'Well, we can't tell at this precise moment, so I think we should eat some food in case it does turn into a bad thing,' suggested Rhoadan.

Elk had finished cooking the food. He dished it out and handed each of them a bowl, Kadence handed out tea, Rhoadan took his bowl, as did Elk and lastly, Delph reached out for his own.

'Ah night tea, my favourite. You haven't made this for ages.' said Delph, he smiled.

Elk and Rhoadan looked at each other. 'Well these days we always seem to have cream,' answered Kadence.

'Well except tonight that is,' laughed Elk.

'When we were younger, I used to make this all the time, we would have lots of sugar cubes in it, of course since we've got older we've cut back on the cubes.' said Delph.

They all began eating dinner, Rhoadan sighed with contentment as the food hit his stomach. He couldn't get enough and began gulping it down.

'This is lovely Elk,' said Kadence, finishing a huge mouthful.

'Mhph munmggblrr' grunted Rhoadan.

'I never caught that fully Rhoadan,' laughed Elk.

Rhoadan finished what he was chewing. 'Sorry, I was saying, I agree, it's delicious,' he laughed.

Delph remained silent.

'Delph, your eyes are really weird, they're yellow. In fact, if my eyes are not deceiving me, they're glowing,' Rhoadan gasped, he stood up and stumbled over some wood, almost landing in the fire in his haste to get away.

Delph crouched down, accidentally dropping his bowl and cup, they clattered to the ground, spilling the contents everywhere.

The noise startled everyone, including Brightbane. He had begun to shift into his wolf form, he shrunk to the height of the creature they saw outside. Silver fur covered his pale skin, his hands and fingers were replaced by paws and claws, he howled and darted off into the shadows.

'Erm guys, what the' Rhoadan yelled, he was shaken by Delph's sudden departure into the darkness.

'Rhoadan, there's something we probably should have told you by now. Delph's a Therianthrope.' said Kadence.

'Excuse me, a what-mi-thrope?' Rhoadan asked.

'Long story short, Delph can shift into any animal form he wishes to,' Elk explained.

'I would've appreciated some pre-warning, my bowels almost gave way there.' Rhoadan laughed nervously.

Elk laughed and Kadence cringed at what Rhoadan just said.

'This is all too much, I can't get my head around it. Is there anything else that you would like to share with me before it's sprung on me like just now?' Rhoadan asked anxiously.

'You'll get used to it, after a few times that is. There isn't anything else to share just now that I can think of, plus I've not long found out myself that he can do that, I'm just glad he hid the fact he can do it from me for so long.' replied Kadence.

'A few times? It'll take more than a few times for me to get used to that I think.' replied Rhoadan in disbelief.

'I've known for a while that he can do that and it still makes me nervous when he does it,' laughed Elk.

'I suggest we forget about the food for now,' said Kadence.

'I'm not hungry after seeing that,' replied Rhoadan. 'We should prepare ourselves!' warned Kadence.

'There's got to be a reason Delph darted away fast like that and I want to be ready for whatever comes our way,' said Elk.

Elk unattached his angel-ray gun from his belt, Kadence fetched her flame-gold bow and her quiver from its resting place and they aimed them out into the darkness, into the direction that Delph ran.

'I suggest you equip yourself with something Rhoadan.' Kadence said.

'We have no idea what's coming back with Delph when he returns, but I suggest that you're ready!' Elk warned.

Rhoadan ran over to the carriage, he reached into the back of it, shifting his bags about until he found his twin hatchets, each hatchet's shaft was brown and almost half the length of Rhoadan's arm, the blade was a silvery blue colour, they matched, so Rhoadan had always called them Brother and Sister.

He lifted them from the carriage and he ran back to the others and joined them as they awaited whatever cruel hand the near future was about to deal them.

Without any warning, the torches went out one by one until the only light that remained was the light that came from the fire and even that had slowly begun to abandon them as it itched away bit by bit.

Their hearts pounded as they waited in near darkness, standing with their backs to one another trying to make sure they had the best view from all possible angles.

Chapter Three

-Cold Blooded Barrage-

They concentrated as they struggled to see through the darkness. Brightbane's scared whinnying along with the cracking of the remaining fire embers broke the silence.

'Settle down girl,' Rhoadan said with a short and sharp grumble, trying to sound as reassuring as possible at the same time.

A loud howl echoed through the cave, making each little hair on their arms and neck stand poker straight.

'Look over there' yelled Elk, sending his voice echoing around the cave, a pair of gleaming red eyes appeared at the far end of the cave.

'There's another set of eyes over there,' gasped Rhoadan, pointing them out.

'It's not looking any better from what I can see. They're over here as well,' said Kadence; pointing to them.

Low growling and hissing filled the cave.

'What do you think they are?' Elk asked.

Rhoadan shrugged his shoulders.

'I'm not sure. Whatever they are, they're creeping me out. Listen to that horrific sound they're making.' replied Kadence.

'Elk, try to get that fire alight again, we're going to need to be able to see, if we are to stand any chance here,' ordered Rhoadan.

Elk got his lighter out again. He was thankful that the kindling lit up as quickly as it did.

'There's more above us,' yelled Elk.

Two more sets of glowing eyes appeared above them.

'Brightbane, you're okay girl, don't you worry,' yelled Rhoadan.

The creatures skulked along the ceiling of the cave, the firelight revealed them to be huge black lizards that were as dark as the shadows dancing on the wall.

They had a set of glowing eyes and they were about four-foot in length from their curved gnashing needle-like teeth all the way to their swishing spiky tail.

'That's five in total,' yelled Elk.

'Where is Delph? We need him here now.' Rhoadan roared.

The glowing eyes slithered towards them, another four sets of eyes appeared level to them on the chilly ground, close to where they stood.

'That's nine of them in total now,' screamed Kadence.

Brightbane stomped her hooves nervously, the sound echoed through the cave, and she would have bolted by now if Rhoadan hadn't tied her up.

'That's it. I'm not just standing around waiting for them to come to us. I'm attacking!' Elk roared.

Elk aimed and shot one of the lizards that was on the ceiling above them, it died immediately and fell to the ground, landing on top of another one that stood only a few feet away from them, crushing its head on the cold, wet ground.

'Wow, lucky shot.' thought Elk; grinning at himself.

Rhoadan ran over to where three of the reptiles were lurking, he raised both Brother and Sister up in the air.

When he reached the scaly fiends he brought them down on their heads, killing two of them instantly by splitting their skulls wide open with a bludgeoning almighty strike.

Rhoadan stared at them and their dead eyes stared right back.

The remaining fiend opened its mouth and hissed, spraying a shower of rancid saliva everywhere.*

Rhoadan took two large steps over to it and with his size twelve boot, he kicked it right in its face, it screeched supremely as it flopped to the ground and died.

'That's this lot cleared over here,' yelled Rhoadan.

'This one over here's dead.' yelled Kadence, she stood on its head and pulled her five-pronged arrow from it and blood shot out everywhere, like a ruptured water hose.

'I've just killed the other one on the ceiling, we're doing great.' roared Elk.

'That just leaves two of them. I'll take thi— woah—' Rhoadan screeched, as an arrow flew past his face.

* Much like a water feature that's gone wild.

'Watch where you fire those things, that arrow nearly skewered my face there.' Rhoadan yelled.

'If you look behind you, you'll see that I just saved you from having a set of curved and crooked teeth impaled into your skull.' replied Kadence.

Rhoadan turned around and looked at the ground behind him. The monster lay there with an arrow where its face would normally be.

'Thanks, Kadence, you drastically improved its looks at the same time. They are ugly aren't they.' laughed Rhoadan.

'That just leaves one,' Elk said.

'Can either of you see it?' asked Kadence.

They all looked around the cave for it.

'Did we get it?' Rhoadan asked.

Brightbane started going wild. She bucked, she snorted, and she brayed, the trio looked over at her and they found out exactly where the missing beast was.

Kadence's blood curdling scream bore through their ears

Rhoadan was horrified watching as the lizard swung from Brightbane's neck trying to pull her to the ground with all of its strength.

The fiend overpowered Brightbane, she misjudged her footing, and collapsed. It let go of her and hissed with victory like it had accomplished a great task when in reality, it was far from that.

Rage erupted within Rhoadan. His heart pumped blood around his chest so fast he felt like it was about to explode.

He watched his beloved horse and ally of many years fall to the ground, he roared supremely and ran at the huge lizard, he was hell-bent on causing as much damage as he could.

As Rhoadan neared it, he knocked the beast flying on its side and he reared Brother and Sister up into the air and smashed them down repeatedly until there was only a mass of red mush where it previously stood. Elk and Kadence ran over to Rhoadan.

'That's enough Rhoadan, it's dead,' said Elk, resting his hand on Rhoadan's shoulder.

'My poor Brightbane, please tell me she's okay,' Rhoadan pleaded.

'I'm afraid not, she's not moving and I can't find a pulse,' said Elk; who was down on his knees beside Brightbane.

'No!' Rhoadan screeched, his legs turned to jelly, and he dropped to the ground, all other concerns scampered from his mind and his main priority was Brightbane, he threw his head into his shaking hands.

'My poor girl, I've raised her since she was a tiny foal, I can't believe this has happened.' he wailed.

Kadence, also kneeling, stood up and comforted Rhoadan, she rubbed his upper back.

'There's nothing I can say to you, that will make you feel any better at this point in your life, other than I know how it feels to have lost someone you were so close to, I'll leave you be.' said Kadence, her voice trembled. She wiped a tear from her eye.

Rhoadan sobbed, his shoulders shook uncontrollably.

Secretly Elk couldn't believe just how much mush that the lizard had been reduced to.

He wasn't going to point it out to anyone though, he considered his audience and now wasn't a good time, sometimes his own span of distraction and thoughts worried him.

Rhoadan stood up. His face was pale white. The adrenaline that he was experiencing had gone, combined with the sudden loss of his prized companion. He felt faint, he slowly walked over to where Brightbane lay, his legs shook uncontrollably, he flopped to the ground beside her.

He stroked her soft black face gently and saw a lone tear sitting in the corner of her eye. His own eyes filled with tears as he wept into Brightbane's side.

Elk lovingly patted Rhoadan on his back: 'I'm so sorry' Elk mustered.

Rhoadan didn't notice Elks gesture of compassion.

Kadence wiped away another tear, she remained still, she looked down at poor Brightbane, not knowing what to say. She quickly lifted her head and gasped as she realised there might be a way she could help.

She ran over to her rucksack and ferociously searched through it, she pulled out the contents of one sack, after realising the item she sought wasn't in there, she abandoned the rummaging and carefully tipped another sack upside down and sifted through the items that rolled out onto the ground.

'What is it you're looking for Kadence?' Elk asked.

'Give me a second, there's something I need to find,' Kadence replied.

'Is there anything I can do to help? What is it you need to find?' Elk asked.

'Ah-ha I've found it' Kadence replied; as she held up a small ruby glass vial that contained a bubbling substance, she jumped up and ran over to where Brightbane lay.

'What have you found? What is that?' Elk asked.

'Please just watch, don't interrupt. I have to work fast,' said Kadence.

'Rhoadan, there might be a chance that I can bring her back to life, but I must act fast. I need you to move out the way and let me near her,' Kadence commanded.

'What do you mean?' Rhoadan asked, as he stood up and moved back.

'Please listen to what I ask and try not to interrupt too much. I need to be quick.' Kadence replied.

Kadence placed the small vial close to Brightbane's face and collected the glistening tear that lay there.

'I also need to capture one of your tears Rhoadan,' she put the vial to Rhoadan's cheek and caught one of his trickling tears.

'I need a hair from your head, Rhoadan. I will also need one of Brightbane's hairs as well,' Kadence ordered.

Rhoadan reached up to his head and pulled at his hair, in his rash attempt to grasp one hair, he painfully pulled out more than just one, checking his head to see if he had inadvertently given himself a bald patch.

Kadence knelt down and as respectfully as she could, she pulled out one of Brightbane's long sleek golden hairs and she put it with Rhoadan's hair; she entwined them exactly five times in a clockwise rotation.

Kadence carefully singed the ends with an ember that had escaped from the fire. She did it to make sure that the hairs held together in place securely.

She slid the hairs into the ruby vial that held the mixed tears and bubbling substance. She muttered something to herself, which was unheard by Rhoadan and Elk who just watched on in confusion.

She returned to the back of the carriage and continued searching for her next item; it was a few moments before she found what she was trying to find. She pulled a wooden box, she opened it and pulled out a bright orange and scarlet red feather, it shone magnificently and lit up their faces.

'This is the tail feather of the most magnificent bird that ever lived. The majestic phoenix.' Kadence gloated.

'Apparently, they haven't been seen for years. I don't know anyone that's seen one. I thought they were extinct. How do you have that?' asked Elk.

'Oh they're not extinct, they're still around, you just need to know where to find them.' Kadence replied, winking at Elk.

Elk looked at her with a strange expression then he glanced at Rhoadan.

'Where do you find them?' Elk asked.

'I'll show you one-day.' Kadence replied.

'What are you doing Kadence?' Elk asked.

'Just watch. There may just be a chance,' Kadence replied.

She pulled out a leafy stem of sage and snapped it in half, then separated the leaves from the stem and carefully crumbled them into the vial.

She twisted the phoenix feather around the stem in the same clockwise rotation and amount of times as she did before with the hairs.

'Rhoadan, could you check in that sack there for three white candles please?' she asked, pointing out the bag. 'The ones I'm looking for have a purple cross on the bottom of each of them,' she added.

'I'll keep watching in case more of those hideous lizards come back,' said Elk.

Kadence thanked Elk.

Rhoadan searched for the candles, he found six white ones, they all varied in size, so he pulled them out and turned them wick-side down so he could see which ones had a cross on them.

He found the three candles and handed them to Kadence, she was crushing a piece of burnt wood, she crushed it finely with her boot to make sure there were no parts still alight, she made a circular bed of burnt ash and placed the candles at three points, emulating the points of a triangle.

Rhoadan put the other three candles back in the bag.

'Thank you. I need some more light around here,' she said.

'Elk, Kadence needs light, let's get these torches lit back up,' Rhoadan loudly told Elk.

Elk ran around and lit the torches one by one, light filled the cave, the shadows returned to the walls to dance once again.

Kadence threw the last of the unused fire logs on the fire, she needed the fire to be as grand as it could be.

The flames were quick to engulf the wood, and it wasn't long till the fire was roaring. The wood crackled as the heat licked her face.

'That's better. I can see properly now,' Kadence thanked them both.

Rhoadan ran back over to where Kadence was. Unfortunately, he could now clearly see his beloved horse laying there still and lifeless, he gritted his teeth, his heart sunk again, his mind had been momentarily elsewhere in the sudden commotion of running around gathering the items for Kadence's task.

Elk was sure he had just heard a scuffling noise over in the shadows, he lifted a torch and slowly walked over to a quiet spot, away from the commotion for a moment and he remained silent and still.

He heard it again, this time it was followed by a low growl that quickly grew into a ferocious bark far-off into the darkness of the cave.

'Guys, did you hear that?' Elk yelled.

'I did' Rhoadan yelled back.

'Do you think that was Delph?' Kadence asked.

'That's got to be Delph, what is he doing?' Elk asked.

'I have no idea. I hope he's not in any trouble.' Rhoadan replied.

A torch at the far end of the cave flickered and went out, followed by the other torches.

'Oh dear Lord of Eshia, we do not need this again.' screamed Kadence.

Hissing filled the air. Even more lizards had returned. They were hell-bent on avenging the loss of their kin.

Multiple sets of glowing eyes closed in on the group, appearing all around them, they were everywhere, on the ceiling, the ground and on the walls, a few were even on the carriage, they were surrounded.

Kadence made sure the lid of the vial was secure. She put it down gently on the ground and slid it behind a rock to make sure it wasn't crushed by a misguided foot.

Elk and Rhoadan met Kadence by the fire, it was still burning tall and proud, more lizards kept coming.

They dropped from the roof of the cave like a fly after being hit with a newspaper.

The hissing was intense, making it hard for the group to concentrate.

'This is it, my time has come.' thought Elk.

They couldn't see a clear way out of this situation.

As the hissing lizards closed in, they found the air around them felt like it had thinned out, the heat of the cave increased, their agitation eased as a wolf howl filled the cave, it was like a heaven-sent welcoming warning.

The hissing grew louder, and a commotion erupted at the other end of the cave.

Rhoadan put his arms around Kadence.

A lizard lay in wait. It clung to the rocky stalactites with its razor-sharp claws stuck in tight, with all the commotion going on around them the group never even noticed it. This lizard differed from the others. Its scales were an olive-green colour with vibrant pigment green markings swirling along the full length of its body that reflectively shimmered against the light of the fire.

Its eyes were noticeably different compared to the others, they were emerald-green although just like the other lizard's eyes, they shone equally bright against the fire.

It was much bigger than the others. He was the leader of the cave lizards. It's not known if he had a name, his ferocity was obvious, clinging to the ceiling, just above their heads, with Kadence in his sights.

He opened his eyes wide and his jaws even wider, presenting his true prowess as to why this lizard, in particular, was the head of his clan. Each one of his teeth were like jagged needles.

He wrapped his tail around a stony spike that hung down from the cave roof and he extended his claws and stealthily lowered himself down towards Kadence.

Gloopy saliva hung from his tongue, gravity eventually took hold and as stringy as it was, it descended and landed on the back of Kadence's head and slowly drooped down to the back of her neck; he hissed quietly to himself.

Kadence felt a damp sensation on her neck, she reached up to feel what had just fallen on her neck.

She looked at her hand and separated her fingers, revealing a webbed array of gunk, disgusted, she tried to flick it on the ground although it just sprung back and wrapped around her hand, horrified; she looked up to find the lizard was directly above her with its mouth open wide.

As she screamed, the lizard's lowly hissing turned into a deafening screech. Elk and Rhoadan had no time to react.

From out of nowhere, Delph leapt through the flames of the fire with his mouth open wide, his sharp teeth shone through the darkness.

He clashed with the hideous lizard champion just as it was inches from her head. He grabbed it with his teeth and pushed it away from Kadence.

He tried to pin the lizard king to the ground. He struggled mostly because of the lizard's brute strength. He sunk his sharp teeth into the lizard's neck and clenched his jaw down hard and with one brutal tug he ripped the lizard's throat out and its struggling tail crashed to the ground.

Delph towered over the lizard and he spat out the remains of the lizard's throat out onto the ground.

Delph walked away from the lifeless lizard and joined the rest of the group. Elk and Kadence cheered, they were relieved to see their friend return in their utmost time of need. Having Delph back by their side gave them the rallying support they needed and this visionary sight made them reach for their weapons.

Kadence rubbed Delph's furry head, and she tickled behind his ear until one of his back legs started thumping off the ground, she realised just how surreal it was so she stopped.

Rhoadan reached for Brother and Sister and he roared something which sounded like he was chanting although the rest of the group couldn't understand it.

He ran with his hatchets held high and aimed for the lizards that were close by; he swung Brother and Sister around in no particular order and he sliced up any lizards he could reach.

He was determined to seek revenge on these relentless reptilians; he held no remorse; he did his best to cause the greatest damage, there were bits of legs and tail flying all around them.

Elk was equally committed to making sure these savage creatures paid for what they did, he fired several shots out into the cave with his gun.

Each direct hit was like a little piece of weight that magically lifted from his shoulders, it was like a little set of red lights were turned off every time he killed one.

Kadence released explosive arrows as fast as she could manage, she had rarely needed to use her explosive arrows in the past as she has only come across a horde of enemies like this once before, the explosions she caused were a grand feature, they showered the cave with red sparks.

Delph ran at high-speed, so fast that the stones on the ground jumped with the vibrations. He jumped up against the wall so he could use his padded paws to throw himself with force into a bunch of them, his impact knocked two flying, while Elk shot another one and Rhoadan sliced the last two, at long last the fighting was over.

Everything was still, there was no more ear-piercing high-pitched hissing in the air.

They were left with an eerie ringing in their ears, the sort you get when it goes from booming with commotion to silent.

There were no more manic grunts from Rhoadan as he had twisted around the cave with his arms out wide, gripping his razor-sharp hatchets in a deadly hurricane of destruction and there was no more growls or yaps from Delph as he bore his sharp fangs into the enemy.

Kadence and Elk dropped to the ground panting for air, they remained still as they came to terms with the deadly brawling that they had just committed and more importantly, regain breath.

'I'm so happy that it's finally over' panted Kadence, once she had her breath back.

'Same here' puffed Elk.

Rhoadan sat on a rock and shook his head. 'That was absurd, all that blood' he said.

'I don't want to think about how many lizards we killed there,' said Kadence.

'Not enough, as far as I'm concerned,' Rhoadan stated.

'I just hope that's the last we see of them,' said Elk.

Delph suddenly dropped to the cold ground, the familiar feeling of transformation had taken over, he howled loudly.

His howl progressively turned into grunts and groans as he transformed into his natural state. His stomach cramped up, he pulled his knees into his chest, his arms propelled themselves forward and his fingers stretched out on their own accord.

His silver fur retracted into his face, his skin was soon as peachy as it ever was, his eyes returned to their icy blue colour. The pain eased when his insides stopped twisting and churning.

He sat in silence for a few moments just staring at his hands. The others were also silent.

They stared at him without even attempting to make any conversation. Secretly none of them knew what to say.

Delph broke the silence: 'Pass me my clothes Kadence please' he said, sluggishly; picking up a rucksack to protect his modesty.

He stood up, however, his knees gave way, and he fell to the ground again. 'I guess I'm going to just sit down where I am then. I was in that form for a while, I guess.' Delph said.

Kadence stood up and walked over to where his clothes were, she picked them up and handed them to him. Delph thanked her.

'Delph, I never noticed that you were naked when you turned back into your human form in the forest. Why did it happen this time?' Kadence asked.

'Oh it happened then as well, I was ready for it and I hid out of your view, whereas this time, that change was a little unexpected and I had no idea I would be like that for as long, so I'm a bit ill-prepared this time around.' he replied.

'Delph, there's something we should tell you.' said Elk.

'What is it?' Delph asked.

'While you were in your wolf form, one of those bloody lizards killed poor Brightbane.' replied Kadence.

'Aww don't tell me that.' Delph replied sympathetically. He wandered over to Rhoadan and gave him a hug.

'I'm so sorry Rhoadan, she was a great horse, she'll be missed' Delph said.

Rhoadan lowered his head and grinned half-heartedly.

'I don't mean to sound horrible here, but I must get back to what I was doing, I won't have long now,' said Kadence, as she looked on the ground for the vial.

'What are you doing?' Delph asked; he was confused.

'Don't ask, she won't tell you.' Elk sarcastically added.

'Look, Elk, I'm trying to bring Brightbane back, what I'm doing is time-consuming and everything needs to be carried out in a certain way, if I do something wrong it's not going to work. I would have had plenty of time if those lizards hadn't attacked us.' Kadence snapped.

She paused for a breath.

'And now I'm under even more pressure, so please quit with your sarcastic tone,' snapped Kadence.

'I'm sorry. I'll give you peace and leave you to get on with it,' Elk sheepishly replied.

'Right, what can we do to help Kadence?' Delph asked.

'Rhoadan, can you grab some torches and make sure there is plenty of lighting around here again and Elk can you help me look for that vial?' she asked.

'Delph, you stay where you are and get your strength back, remember what happened last time you never gave yourself some time to recover,' said Elk.

'Yeah, yeah I remember it well, point taken.' sighed Delph.

'What happened last time?' Rhoadan asked.

'One day Delph was in his eagle form, he and I were larking about and I dared him to stay up in the air for as long as he could, it didn't go well,' explained Elk.

Delph cringed as he thought back.

'He was up in the air, putting on a right show, he was doing loops and he even tried to dive-bomb me on more than one occasion. He became tired, and he plummeted to the ground—'

Rhoadan's sudden gasp interrupted Elk.

Elk looked over at Rhoadan and paused for a moment; Rhoadan's gasp put him off his stride.

'So as I was saying, luckily for him, he wasn't all that high in the air anyway, he hit the ground. he got up way too fast and when he came around he got up and just went about his day. When he finally settled down for the evening, he tried to get up and found that he couldn't move at all and he was stuck in his sitting position until the next morning, so we can't risk that happening here.' Elk explained.

'Elk, Rhoadan, move. We don't have any time to spare!' ordered Kadence.

'I'm sorry that I can't be of more help Kadence,' said Delph.

'Don't be daft Delph, just sit there and regain your energy, we need you to be healthy,' Kadence replied.

'Pass me your lighter Elk.' said Rhoadan.

Rhoadan ran around the cave lighting the torches, then he fixed the fire.

Elk fetched one of the torches from Rhoadan and he brought it over to Kadence.

Kadence found her vial. She knelt down, picked it up and gave it a shake, watching it intensely.

'Phew, all intact.' she thought.

'Elk, could you get a small piece of firewood and crush it on the ground over here, but please can you make sure there are no lit parts at all,' she said.

Elk found a piece of wood and gently kicked it over to where Kadence had pointed, it was too hot to carry, so he crushed it with his foot to ensure that there was no light or heat coming from it.

'Could you draw a circle with it, please?' Kadence asked.

Elk grabbed a set of tongs from the rucksack and drew a circle, Kadence placed the candles exactly as she had done before at the three points and lit them, each one had a different coloured flame. The first one which sat at the north point of the triangle shone red, a blue glow shone from the one on the east point and the one to the west point glowed with a white hue.

The light from the candles rose like three lasers. They all coiled around one another producing a spiral effect as they made a whirring noise, starting with the north candle Kadence drew a line down to the east then over to the west candle, thus depicting the triangle completely.

Rhoadan was instantly infatuated by the lights. Elk noticed his wide-eyed stare and nudged him gently. Rhoadan was non-responsive.

Elk looked over at Delph, who had also seen that Rhoadan glared creepily at the lights.

'I need as much silence as I can get, I need to focus. Elk, please keep an eye out for any further interruptions,' she begged.

Elk nudged Rhoadan again and once again there wasn't any response.

'Kadence, I think Rhoadan is in a trance or something like it,' Elk said.

'It sometimes happens, or so I'm led to believe, anyway. Just leave him be for now, he must have been watching the lights as they spiralled.' she replied.

'Are you sure he will be okay?' Elk asked.

'I think so, I've never seen it happen before, although I have heard of it happening when rituals are prepared, I've heard it's normal and I'm sure he will snap out of it once it's complete,' replied Kadence.

'I hope so. I really don't think I could look at his blank expression forever.' laughed Elk.

Delph watched Kadence with confusion, whilst he regained his strength.

Kadence knelt at the candles, she sat the ruby vial in the middle and uncorked it.

A greasy, multicoloured smoke-like-remnant floated out from the vial and quickly surrounded Kadence. She clasped her hands into a praying position and bowed her head over the vial.

She began rocking back and forward slowly, her rocking soon accelerated until she was in an unstable motion. She closed her eyes and inhaled the smoke. She gasped and opened them again, revealing misty blue eyes. She began chanting loudly.

'Blood absorption, come forth to me.

Release Brightbane and send her from thee.

Bone and veins rise together as one.

Break this death and make it undone.

This newly presented soul was taken far too soon.

Her life must be returned, this vial contains the rune.

Take her as black, but release her as white.

Let her join me by travelling through thy light.

Thy phoenix feather will give thou thy life that thou need.

Oh, great lord of Eshia, please grant me this deed.'

As soon as she spoke her last word she stopped rocking, and she bolted upright onto her feet, her arms were poker straight down by her sides.

Her fingers were almost crooked like claws, her head was tilted back, her mouth was closed tight, but her eyes were open wide, her ruby red eyes were replaced with golden like orbs, producing an immense light.

The torches all around them flickered and waved about from left to right and then in a circular motion. Rhoadan snapped out of his trance. He blinked his eyes a few times and looked at Elk.

'Rhoadan, are you okay?' Elk asked.

'Yeah, why?' Rhoadan replied.

'Well, you looked dazed.' Elk responded.

'Did I?' Rhoadan asked.

'You don't remember?' Delph asked.

Rhoadan looked at Delph: 'I don't' and he shrugged his shoulders.

'Aren't you worried by that?' Elk asked.

'No I'm not, I try not to look too deeply into things' laughed Rhoadan: 'Those lizards better not be back,' added Rhoadan.

'I hope you're right' replied Elk, who was deeply confused.

Delph looked at Elk, they screwed their faces up at each other. Neither of them knew what had just happened to Rhoadan.

'Guys, look at Kadence,' yelled Delph.

Delph stood up and reached for his weapon. Elk, Rhoadan and Delph all shuddered at the sight of Kadence.

'What is she doing?' Delph asked.

'This isn't right. What's happening?' Elk asked hastily.

'I have no idea' replied Rhoadan.

'First, Rhoadan was dazed and now we have a freaky Kadence, we need to get out of this cave,' Elk said.

An icy cold wind gushed through the cave, miniature hurricanes rose from the gravel and mini lightning forks pierced through from the heart of the hurricanes.

Elk, Rhoadan and Delph all shuddered as they took a few steps back from Kadence.

The lights from the candles were rotating fiercely. The vial rose into the air and the lights all focussed on the vial which twisted ferociously. The hurricanes had surrounded Kadence and Rhoadan didn't like it, so he slashed his hatchets into the hurricanes, they went right through and he was thrown onto his back by an invisible force, he immediately got back up and had another go.

He found himself back on the spot he had just picked himself up from. Rhoadan stood up again and growled in frustration.

'Just leave it Rhoadan, Kadence knows what she's doing. It must be what's supposed to happen,' said Elk.

The golden colour that shone from Kadence's eyes focussed on the vial which glowed vibrantly. The hurricanes violently circled Kadence, the lightning sparked wildly in all directions, cracks of electricity lit up against the wall and thunder roared through the cave.

'What's going on here? I don't like it,' moaned Elk.

The torches were flickering wildly even though the wind roared through the cave the torches somehow stayed alight.

Whispering flowed through their ears and mist sneaked in from every direction joining the other elements. It wisped around the men and finally surrounded Kadence.

At first, the mist was white puffs of cloud which soon turned tar-black. The clouds rose whilst revolving around Kadence and then hovered over her for a few moments before they moved on to the rest of them.

They felt a damp sensation seeping through their clothes, little beads of water fell down from the rotating clouds. They now had to deal with horrendous hurricanes, mysterious mist, lethal lightning and whistling wind.

Everything suddenly went dark as though someone had turned the darkest cavern inside out and implanted it onto the exact spot where they stood.

Gusting winds roared and rumbled through the cave. It threw the carriage on its side, Rhoadan had to jump out of the way as the carriage hurtled towards him.

Screeching sirens pierced through into their ears. They grasped their ears tightly as they fell to the ground and curled up into balls.

The force of the sirens eased up, so Delph, Elk and Rhoadan clambered and crawled along the ground to get away from danger and get some shelter from the shock waves that the sirens produced.

A great light expelled from Kadence, who was still poker straight, a sonic boom of lightning surged from her and shot out into the cave, the light scorched the walls and everything else that it touched; they got behind a rock just in time.

Without any warning, everything turned black again, even if it was just for a few seconds. The torches flickered away, and the fire shone a bright amber glow once again. It crackled away nicely as though nothing had even happened, an eerie silence filled the cave leaving everyone with buzzing in their ears again.

They peeked up slowly from the rock and looked over at Kadence. She was no longer poker straight; she was lying down.

The three of them quickly made their way from behind the safety of the rock over to where their friend helplessly lay.

Her legs were bent to one side, she had one arm outstretched and her other one clutched the glowing vial. When Elk reached Kadence he sat down behind her and lifted her head up onto his legs to provide her with some protection from the cold ground.

'Talk to me Kadence, are you okay?' Elk asked.
He panicked and wiped away a tear that rolled down his cheek.

Kadence was lethargic, she just lay still.

'Elk' was all she could muster; her hand twitched.

Elk looked at her twitching hand and saw the glowing vial moving ever so slightly in her soft hand. He reached over and pulled the vial closer.

'What do you want me to do?' Elk asked.

'Bright—bane—' she groaned.

'Do you want me to give it to Brightbane?' he asked.

Kadence calmly nodded once.

'Delph, can you come here and sit where I'm sitting?' Elk asked.

'Sure' replied Delph.

Elk carefully moved his legs and held Kadence's head in his empty hand, while Delph made his way over and took Kadence's head into his hand and lowered himself down so she could get a soft place for it.

'If this involves Brightbane, then it involves me.' said Rhoadan, watching every move Elk made.

Elk took the glowing vial over to where Brightbane lay peacefully, looking down at her, sighing with sorrow, Rhoadan clasped his hands and he inhaled deeply.

Elk crouched down and uncorked the vial, sparks of rainbow colours flew up into the air, each colour illuminated in front of them, their eyes took a few seconds to adjust, leaving them with a green glow in their vision that remained there until it gradually faded away.

He could feel movement in the vial.

He laid it on its side and a tiny glowing horse galloped out onto his hand and reared up onto its tiny back legs and whinnied a confident neigh.

Elk and Rhoadan stared at Elk's hand in awe.

Maybe it was the fact that Kadence had produced this amazing little horse or maybe it was the fact that this amazing little horse was bellowing such an almighty neigh in his hand.

The tiny horse hammered its hooves against Elk's hand it then ran around in a tiny circle.

'Brightbane' Kadence whispered to Delph.

'Get the horse to Brightbane.' urged Delph.

Elk leaned in closer to Brightbane. Delph twisted his neck trying to get a better look. He embraced the pain as he didn't want to miss one moment of this magical event.

Chapter Four

-Gila Vision-

The tiny horse stood motionless on Brightbane's head, gently stamping its hooves as if it were testing the stability of an uneven surface. It reared up on its hind legs again and whinnied before vanishing and leaving an arrangement of falling golden sparks as though a golden bubble had just burst in front of them.

Rhoadan and Elk gasped.

'What's happening Elk? I can't see anything from over here, you're in the way. What's going on?' Delph asked eagerly.

Elk apologised and moved to the side.

'The tiny horse has only gone and disappeared,' explained Rhoadan.

'What do you mean, it's just disappeared?' Delph asked.

'It just vanished into thin air, evaporated in front of our eyes.' gasped Rhoadan.

'Keep watching' said Kadence, who was still sluggish.

'Kadence told us to keep watching,' Delph explained.

Elk and Rhoadan watched the spot which was previously occupied by the tiny horse before it vanished. A few moments passed without anything eventful happening.

Kadence told Delph that she was feeling itchy and fuzzy in and around her ears.

'Did you see that?' Rhoadan yelled excitedly, unsure if his eyes had duped him or not, he could have sworn that he just saw Brightbane's ear flicker.

'See what?' Elk replied.

'I'm more than positive that I just saw her ear move,' replied Rhoadan.

'Did you? I never saw anything.' replied Elk.

Elk joined Kadence. He wanted to make sure she was feeling better.

'Do you need anything Kadence?' Elk asked.

Kadence shook her head then rubbed her face and ears.

Elk nodded his head and rubbed her hand.

'Just let me know and I will get it for you,' said Elk.

'It happened again, although this time her two ears flicked,' Rhoadan yelled excitedly.

Rhoadan crouched down by Brightbane and lovingly held his head against her chest listening for a heartbeat, but unfortunately he couldn't hear anything, he rubbed her chest, running his hand up and down against her ribs.

'Come on my girl, you can do it,' he wailed.

Elk stood beside Rhoadan and impatiently waited to gain a glimpse of what Rhoadan had talked about.

Rhoadan grew disheartened.

'Give it time guys, have some patience,' said Delph.

'Are any of you hungry?' asked Elk.

They all shook their heads to tell Elk that they weren't.

'Elk fetch a blanket for Kadence please, she's shivering.' Delph said.

'Yeah sure, no problem' Elk answered, he grabbed a blanket from his rucksack and took it over to Kadence, he shook it out and laid it on her.

Kadence smiled at Elk and she patted Delph's hand.

'I'll make us some tea,' said Elk.

'And I'll fix the fire, it's just about out,' added Rhoadan.

'Have we still got enough water?' Delph asked.

'Yeah, there's still some left from what we lifted back at Rhoadan's Inn,' replied Elk.

'Delph, could you keep an eye on Brightbane for me, if there is any sign of movement, no matter how small, shout me over please.' said Rhoadan.

'Of course, let me position myself so I can see her better, my neck is still aching from looking around earlier,' answered Delph.

'Elk, can you help me for a moment?' Delph asked.

'Yes, what do you want me to do?' Elk replied.

'Can you come over here and hold Kadence's head for me whilst I turn myself around so I can see Brightbane?' Delph asked.

Elk walked over and gently lifted Kadence's head. Delph got himself into a comfy position.

'How are you feeling Delph?' Elk asked.

'I feel fine now that I've rested,' replied Delph.

'Good, I'm glad to hear it, I'll go and see to our tea,' Elk replied.

Elk walked back over to where Rhoadan was fixing the fire. He quickly helped Rhoadan gather the wood that had been scattered about and he placed it back on the fire bed they had made earlier.

Once they had finished setting the fire up and restoring it to its former glory, Elk set about fixing the pots to make some tea. The atmosphere was gloomy, so the thought of a cup of tea seemed to lighten their spirits a little.

Elk finished making the tea, and he brought a cup over to each of them, he sat Kadence's cup down beside her.

They all thanked him as they took their cup. Rhoadan walked back over to Brightbane and sat down beside her and drank his tea.

'Ahh! That's just what I needed. I hadn't realised how thirsty I was.' Rhoadan said.

'You're welcome, I put extra sugar in them, we need to get our energy back up, we haven't rested for a while now and we've had an eventful time in this cave.' Elk laughed.

Delph and Rhoadan both nodded their heads.

Kadence still had little to no energy, she shuffled herself up with the help of Delph, she leaned against him, she groaned and winced as she moved. She had been laying down in the same position for a while and she found that her legs had gone to sleep, which in turn caused the ache of pins and needles to come rushing in, she remained motionless to allow the numbing to disappear.

Delph was free to move his legs, he was no longer having to support Kadence as he had done before, the pins and needles had reached Kadence's feet, it caused her feet to twitch uncontrollably. She accidentally elbowed Delph in the face as she wriggled about.

Rhoadan rubbed his hands along Brightbane's mane, he saw her legs twitching, he jumped up in shock and accidentally spilt the remaining tea he had in his cup.

'She moved her legs.' he yelled* ecstatically; repeatedly pointing at Brightbane; startling the others.

Elk got up to his feet and by the time he had fully stood up, he had already taken out his gun out and had it pointed in Rhoadan's direction.

'Calm yourself, lad,' roared Rhoadan, with both hands held high.

'Sorry, I'm still nervous, I thought those lizards had returned.' Elk apologised.

'Yeah... I got that.' Rhoadan replied sarcastically.

Elk put away his gun and walked over to Rhoadan, he looked down at Brightbane, her legs were still moving. He was happy for both Rhoadan and Brightbane.

Kadence opened her eyes wide. They were itchy.

Brightbane's eyes flickered and then opened wide.

Rhoadan couldn't contain his excitement, his beloved true friend was showing signs of life when all was previously taken from her. He started dancing.

* You could say that it was more of a squeal than a yell.

It looked like he had an unreachable itch. There was a lot of crouching and celebrating, so much so that Elk backed up a little in fear of inadvertently being punched in the face.

Delph thought it must have been a dwarven dance because he had never seen anything like it before.

Kadence tried to reach down for her cup of tea, she sat up halfway. She felt herself falling forward, so, she put her arm out in front of her so she could protect herself from falling, as she did it, Brightbane's front leg shot out sidewards, kicking Rhoadan right on his behind, knocking him into a rock.

Elk saw what had just happened, he looked at Brightbane, then at Kadence, who returned his glance with a puzzled expression, he rested his eyes on Rhoadan, who was nursing his sore head after falling into the rock, luckily he never hit it at full speed though.

'Ouch' cried out Rhoadan, rubbing his head and laughing at the same time, he wasn't going to let anything dampen his mood right now.

'Did you see what just happened there, Delph?' Elk asked.

'Not really, I had to catch Kadence, she started falling towards the ground, but I felt something fly past me,' replied Delph.

'That *thing* that flew past you was Rhoadan.' Elk said.

'Yes that was me' groaned Rhoadan; still nursing his sore head.

'First Kadence put her arm out to stop herself from hitting the ground and then Brightbane's leg shot straight out at the same time, sending Rhoadan flying right past us. There's got to be some connection between Kadence and Brightbane.' explained Elk.

'Surely there can't be. Can there?' Delph asked.

Rhoadan flashed them a confused look. He was still a little fuzzy from bashing his head off a rock.

Colour returned to Kadence's face. She was no longer looking as pale as she had done and at last she started feeling better.

'Transitioning' said Kadence.

'What's that?' Elk asked, scratching his head.

'Transitioning is when a caster creates a spell, so he or she, she, in this case, I mean me, sorry I'm still a bit fuzzy.' said Kadence.

'Don't worry. Take your time,' said Delph.

Kadence took a large breath. 'Transitioning, means, that once the caster has cast a spell to return a life, their soul is temporarily conjoined with that of the formerly deceased.' Kadence explained.

'The deceased being Brightbane in this case?' Delph asked.

'Yes, once the life has fully returned, that's when the transition is complete and the conjoined souls then split and return to its original source, if you cast your mind back to the tiny horse, that was part of my soul flowing into Brightbane.' explained Kadence.

Elk watched Kadence and then he looked at Brightbane again.

'Can you make Brightbane move again?' Delph asked.

'I can. Watch this.' replied Kadence.

Elk and Delph focussed on Kadence, they watched her as she lifted her arm, she could lift it halfway before it flopped back onto the ground, they immediately looked at Brightbane.

They saw her lifting her front leg out halfway and it also flopped to the ground.

'Can you try to move something else?' Elk asked.

'She's not a performing monquat.' Delph added.

'How rude of me, sorry Kadence, I never thought' said Elk, who had secretly been drumming up the courage to ask Kadence to make Brightbane dance.

'It's fine, I just don't want to move anything else for a while, I do, however, feel a bit better, but I don't fully feel like my normal self and I don't want to risk anything going wrong because I'm moving about too much,' answered Kadence.

'If there's a chance that something could stop Brightbane from returning then please don't risk it,' pleaded Rhoadan.

Kadence nodded in agreement.

'Yeah let's just allow Kadence time to recoup her lost energy, let's get our things gathered, they were scattered about all over the place when we were attacked and I sincerely hope we don't get bombarded by those beasts again,' said Elk.

'I don't think we will, I reckon we've seen the last of them. It was their king that I killed and once the king falls the underlings fall along with it, or so the legend goes anyway,' explained Delph.

'Thank you very much for the support Delph, I think I will be fine from now on.' said Kadence.

'Cool, no problem, let me just move out of the way.' he replied.

Kadence backed herself up against a rock.

'Pass my tea over Delph,' she requested.

'I'm still surprised your cup survived that,' laughed Delph, as he handed it to her.

'So is the transitioning part of your training Kadence?' Elk asked.

'I think it is, that and the potionology I did when I was younger, I think it's all connected,' she replied, glancing over at Delph.

Kadence was thankful that she had listened to Delph and stuck in with her lessons when she was younger. She raised her cup to Delph, who also lifted his cup and joined her with her toast.

Rhoadan's head wound had finally clotted over and had stopped bleeding, so he stood up and walked over to the carriage. It had been thrown quite a distance by the elements, from where it stood before.

Rhoadan had to step over several lizards that were lying in a dead heap. He shuddered every time he stepped over one of them.

When he reached the carriage, he crouched down beside it and tried to lift it himself, soon realising that it wasn't going to happen, he was only able to lift it until the muscles in his legs started to burn, he felt pressure on his back, so rather than risk damaging himself, he decided it would be better to release his grip, after all, what use would he be to the group if he was hurt.

'Can someone come over here and help me lift the carriage? It's far too heavy for me alone.' he yelled.

'I'll be right over' Delph yelled back.

'It would be wise to bring a torch with you, it's dark over here, so watch where you step,' Rhoadan added.

Delph lifted a torch down from the wall and met Rhoadan, he placed the torch's base into a large crevice which was set within some rocks, allowing it to stand on its own. He bent down to help Rhoadan lift the carriage.

'On the count of three, we lift it.' commanded Rhoadan.

Delph nodded his head.

'One, two, three and lift,' ordered Rhoadan.

Even with the help of Delph trying they still couldn't lift it, the carriage did, however, reach higher than it had on Rhoadan's failed attempt, they got it level to their waists, Rhoadan noticed that there wasn't as much pressure on his back.

'Hey Elk, we will need your help over here,' Delph yelled.

'Right let me finish here and I'll be over in a second,' replied Elk.

'Should we try again?' asked Delph.

'Yes, on the count of three,' replied Rhoadan.

'One, two, three and lift,' Rhoadan said.

They struggled, their knees became weak and they trembled.

'Put it down, put it down,' Delph groaned.

They released the carriage, and it clambered back down to the ground.

'Let's leave it until Elk gets over here. I'll give him another minute before calling him again,' said Delph.

'Let me have a few minutes to catch my breath first before trying again,' panted Rhoadan.

Elk had just finished gathering items that were scattered all over the place, he stood up straight, realising that he had over crouched and felt his back twinge a little when he stood up.

'Elk, is there any way that you could hurry over here?' Delph yelled.

'I'm coming, calm yourself!' Elk yelled back, he muttered to himself, mostly grumps and curses.

He passed by Kadence and asked her if she was okay, she nodded her head, he looked over at Brightbane, who along with Kadence, also nodded her head.

'This is getting creepy' he shuddered. He made his way over to Rhoadan and Delph.

'I'm here, calm down,' sighed Elk.

'About time lad' replied Rhoadan with a smile.

'Let's get the carriage up. We're going to need it,' said Rhoadan. They got ready and lined up equally across the edge of the carriage, they bent down and prepared themselves.

'Let's try to get it on the first try. Are you two ready?' Rhoadan asked.

'On three... one... two—' Delph counted down.

'WAIT!' Elk interrupted.

'What is it?' Rhoadan asked.

'I'm just kidding, let's do this,' he said laughing.

'Three' Delph sternly counted out loud.

They gripped the roof of the carriage and lifted it up, they got it up to their knees with little to no bother, but as soon as it was level with their waists, they found out just how heavy the carriage was, their legs shook and their arms performed some sort of wing flap technique as if they could fly off at any given moment.

Three crimson red-faced friends stood there hunched over just heaving and puffing. Each of them scrunched up their faces making them look like they had just sucked on a sour fruit.

With one last heave, they got the carriage upright and standing on its wheels again.

Elk and Delph held their fists aloft in the air. They cheered and dropped down into a heap on the ground, Rhoadan slumped himself down against a rock and he simply grunted.

He was lucky the rock wasn't a sharp one.

The three of them sat there inhaling and exhaling air faster than a wild tri-tusk hog that's being chased by a hungry forest fox, their arms and legs were all jittery and aching, they decided it was best to take a few moments to allow their shaky legs and arms to stop quivering.

Delph was the first out of the three of them to move, he stood up, 'I'm just going to check on Kadence, she's quiet over there' he carefully stepped over the lizards as he made his way over to Kadence.

'I wonder what time it is just now. It feels like we've been stuck in this cave forever,' said Elk.

'It surely can't be far-off sunrise, I would have thought' replied Rhoadan. He stood up from the rock and walked over towards Kadence and Delph, he also watched where he was walking.

Elk decided that he no longer wished to sit alone in the dark, dingy part of the cave, he thought about his recent experiences with the cave dwellers and it made him shudder. He stood up quickly and ran as he imagined being chased by cave lizards, he never any attention to his surroundings or what was below his feet.

'Hey guys, shall I make us some more tea' Elk yelled, as he rushed towards them.

'That boy is obsessed with tea,' Delph laughed.

'Elk, when you make your way over to us, mind your feet.' yelled Rhoadan.

Rhoadan's warning came just a moment too late. Elk tripped over one of the lizards massive tails.

He hurtled towards the damp cave ground. Rhoadan and Delph heard Elk falling down with a great thud.

Elk stretched his arms out instinctively to break his fall and to protect his face, but because of the way his foot clipped the tail, along with his clumsy footing, he was launched sideways.

He hadn't even had time to finish his gasp, before crashing down and along the ground, on his side.

He continued to skid along the cold dank ground, the algae and mould prevented him from stopping and after what seemed like forever, he eventually came to a halt.

He rolled onto his back to relieve the pressure of the jagged stones sticking into his side, he lay there facing the ceiling, embarrassed as he realised what had just happened to him.

Elk gasped in pain, he held his arm up to his chest and nursed his elbow with his other hand, his hip also ached. 'Ouch.' was all that he could muster.

He finally opened his eyes to see Rhoadan and Delph towering over him. Delph tried hard to hide his giggle although not succeeding.

Rhoadan elbowed Delph in the ribs, which enticed Delph to apologise to Elk.

'What a team look at us. My head is all banged up, Delph's legs are still like jelly, you're on the ground half dead and Kadence over there is—well we won't even go there.' laughed Rhoadan.

They all laughed at the thought of them being a band of merry misfits. Rhoadan and Delph held out their hands to help Elk up to his feet.

Once Elk was upright, he felt the blood rush to his face, he could tell from the roaming heat circling his face, that he was, in fact, showing the others his embarrassment, so he turned his face away from them, they couldn't see the redness on his cheeks, but Elk still felt like his face was a giant beacon that could be seen for miles.

Full of frustration, he kicked one of the lizards and one of its eyes fell out and rolled onto the ground, making a clinking noise as it went. They all watched as the glowing eye danced around on the spot before it came to a halt.

'That's gross,' groaned Elk; crouching down to pick it up.

'You're the one that just picked it up,' Delph pointed out.

'I know, but it's so shiny' replied Elk, it slipped out of his hands and hit the ground, making another tinkling sound. Elk thought it sounded just like a ruby would sound if you dropped it.

Rhoadan crouched down to pick it up. He groped it for authenticity before passing it to Delph.

'I wonder if it really is.' Delph said.

'Wonder what?' Elk asked, stopping Delph mid-sentence.

'Surely not' replied Delph.

'Not what?' Rhoadan asked.

'Have you heard the story of the jewel lizards?' Delph asked.

'No' replied Rhoadan and Elk simultaneously.

'Well, legend has it that there are these massive horrific, cave lizards and when their hearts stop beating, rubies and emeralds replace their eyes.' Delph explained.

'Do you think those lizards are the ones the legend talks about?' Elk asked.

'It would be one hell of a coincidence that this ruby has just fallen out of the lizard's head, for it not to be true.' replied Delph.

'It's happening. She's just opened her eyes,' Kadence yelled.

Rhoadan and Delph rushed over to Kadence, Elk hobbled, remembering to watch where he was going this time.

A golden white light surrounded Brightbane and lit up the cave.

Rhoadan turned around and rushed over to her, he slid down onto his knees, almost smashing into her side, the light glared in their eyes, distorting their vision.

'This is it. It has to be.' he yelled with joy.

Brightbane flicked her tail, she snorted and tried to stand up, they all waited anxiously, she couldn't quite stand up, her legs shook and she fell back down to the ground.*

'Come on girl, you can do it, just take your time,' Rhoadan said excitedly, as he stood up and moved back to give her some room, shading his eyes with his hands.

Brightbane snorted again, her tail flicked angrily from side to side in frustration, she stretched out her front legs and then her back legs, she slowly lifted herself up, her legs shook again. Rhoadan noticed she was struggling, so he walked over and helped her up by holding his arms under her stomach he was able to take some weight off her legs, it proved successful and she could stand, although her legs were still a little shaky.

* From their experience with the carriage recently, the boys all knew exactly how this felt.

They all cheered, Rhoadan, however, cheered the loudest, he had tears running down his dusty cheeks, leaving a winding trail as they went.

Kadence felt a prickly sensation nipping her waist, and it warmed up as it worked its way down to her feet, by the time it had reached her feet they felt hot, she knew for certain that the transitioning was complete.

She held Delph tight for some support and she pulled herself up. Everyone erupted with joyful cheering.

Brightbane neighed and stamped her front legs followed by her hind legs, Rhoadan threw his arms around her neck all while keeping his eyes closed, the light shone bright, she nuzzled into him and a sparkling tear meandered down her soft face as if she knew what had just happened.

The rest of the group joined Rhoadan and gave Brightbane a welcome back hug, Rhoadan squeezed himself out of the clinch and made his way over to his rucksack. He rummaged through the bag till he found a carrot and a few sugar cubes.

'Guys, step back and let me in so I can give these to her' Rhoadan stopped where he stood. The light disappeared suddenly without any warning, leaving little flecks of light swirling in their eyes. He dropped the carrot and cubes when his vision returned: 'What the...' Rhoadan gasped.

The others, who were still hugging Brightbane, all turned around to look at Rhoadan, who was stomping towards them with his mouth open wide, his arms straight and hands with his palms outward.

'Why... why is... she white?' Rhoadan stammered. They all turned to face Brightbane.

'Kadence, why is she white, and why is her main and tail glowing red?' Rhoadan asked.

'It's all part of the transitioning process, she gets a second beginning, she's pure once again,' replied Kadence.

'Yeah, pure white.' laughed Elk.

Delph cleared his throat and glared at Elk.

'You certainly know when to choose your words.' Delph said.

Elk shrugged his shoulders, 'There's nothing we can do about it, what's happened has happened, I do like it though,' he replied and patted Brightbane's head.

Brightbane snorted at Elk.

'You'll get used to it' Kadence said awkwardly, squinting her face.

'I guess you're right, who cares what colour she is, it just shocked me because I wasn't expecting it, I'm just glad she's back,' cheered Rhoadan.

The rest of them cheered as well and Brightbane flicked her flame red tail.

Rhoadan walked back and picked up the carrot and sugar cubes and pushed them towards Brightbane. She grabbed them from his hand and almost bit his thumb off in the process.

'I notice you haven't left that bad habit behind.' Rhoadan laughed.

'Elk, bring me some water for Brightbane please,' said Rhoadan.

'Of course,' replied Elk.

Elk brought a pot of water over to Brightbane and placed it at her feet.

'We're running low on supplies, it won't be long till the water is gone. I used more than I meant to when I made our tea earlier. We'll have to get moving soon and make our way to Dirtbere before we completely run out.' said Elk.

As soon as she saw her water, she gulped it down fast, almost tipping the entire pot.

'Slow down girl,' said Rhoadan. He ran his fingers through her wiry mane: 'I'm glad you're back. I was so sad and angry' he said.

He rubbed her mane and Brightbane swayed her head from side to side, she used to do it when she was a foal, any time Rhoadan used to rub her mane, she also flicked her tail to match her head, Rhoadan smiled and another tear ran down his face as he reminisced of when she was a foal, his cherished memories flashed before his eyes: 'I'll let you drink that in peace' he said and he patted her side.

'Where's Kadence?' Elk asked.

Rhoadan looked around to where she had sat before. She was no longer sitting there.

'She's over there stretching her legs,' replied Delph.

'Kadence, are you okay? What are you doing?' Elk shouted.

'Yes, I'm fine. I'm just walking off this cramp,' she yelled back.

'We are going to have to start thinking about getting out of this cave,' said Delph.

'I like the sound of that,' said Rhoadan.

'I've seen enough in here to make sure I have trouble sleeping for a month.' moaned Elk.

'The bags are almost packed, we just need to let Kadence stretch her legs and let Brightbane recuperate, how about we set off in one hour, that way Kadence will be ready to go I'm sure,' replied Delph.

'Kadence, do you think you and Brightbane will both be ready to leave in an hour?' Delph yelled.

'The full transitioning process is complete and Brightbane is as good as she always was, with the exception of her colour, the same goes for me, so we can pretty much leave whenever we're ready, I've rested enough now.' she replied.

'Okay, that's settled then. Can you all make sure we have everything ready? Rhoadan could you see to Brightbane and the carriage, Kadence, could you make sure that all the bags are ready so we can just lift them up into the carriage before we leave and if it gets too much for you just leave it and we will get it. Elk and I will collect some of those jewels from those beasts and if the legend is true, then we won't have to worry about never having enough triarps to buy anything again as we will be rich.' said Delph.

Kadence started collecting all of her belongings, including the items that she could still use from the transitioning ritual, some of the things that she had used were no longer of any use to her, like the sage and the ruby vial she used to call the tiny horse spirit guide.

She knew she would just have to leave them behind, so she buried these in a small gravel grave, as a mark of respect and gratitude to the equestrian god above. She stood up and dusted herself down once she had finished.

Kadence searched around the cave for any items they could use for the rest of their journey, she gathered the dishes, blankets and any wood they hadn't burnt, she noticed some items were lying around over by the front of the carriage.

She bent down to pick up one of the rucksacks and she could hear a rustling noise coming from the other side of the carriage. She didn't fancy finding out what was making the noise, so she backed off silently and looked around for the others. She couldn't see any of them.

'Guys...' she whispered aloud.

She waited quietly for a reply and when no response came, she remembered that just like herself, they were supposed to be doing the jobs that Delph tasked to them.

Unfortunately, she knew she would have to face whatever gory creature was lurking around by the carriage, pilfering their remaining stock.

She was convinced it was more likely to be one of the cave lizards, although all sorts of ghastly images of unpleasant creatures invaded her thoughts, making her anxious.

She knew she had to do something other than stalling herself from confronting it; reaching for her trusty bow, she crept as close to the carriage as possible, quickly checking under the carriage to make sure there wasn't anything lurking underneath.

She stood back up and brushed the dust off her knees before cautiously making her way around the side of the carriage, peeking around the other side to see if she could find the horror. There was nothing out of the ordinary.

Anxiety flickered in her chest, knowing she would have to continue searching and she really didn't want to. She carefully peeked around the other side of the carriage, to no avail, it was also clear; she scratched her head.

She wondered if she had imagined the full thing; she shook her head and started picking things up again.

The rustling noise happened again, she was experiencing mixed emotions, the sudden threat was real again.

Her stomach churned and her mind whirred. Kadence hesitated for a moment, she tried to think of what she was going to do next.

She reached for her bow, she stretched the string back slowly and grasped the arrow tightly, she held it in place as she slowly etched towards the carriage one foot at a time.

Her fears had been confirmed, and she knew for certain that an enemy was lurking inside the carriage. She had only taken a few steps before the carriage shook in small bursts of movement. She made good use of the commotion to advance without the risk of drawing attention to herself.

Kadence crept on until she reached the rear of the carriage where she stopped and got ready to face the beast. Apprehension fluttered through her as she stood there in silence letting her breath out very slowly.

At least she had the comfort of knowing that she had her bow cocked and ready.

Without any warning, the beast jumped out of the carriage, Kadence received such a shock, that she tripped over one of the bags and landed on her back, she accidentally let go of the arrow sending it flying off into the darkness, she lay there helpless and unarmed.

The hideous creature and Kadence locked eyes, both of them were as shocked as one another, they stared at each other in silence.

Chapter Five

-A Crick's Temperament-

'What are you doing, lass?' asked Rhoadan.

'I'm sorry. I thought you were one of those lizards,' she replied.

'Do I actually look that bad?' laughed Rhoadan, helping her to her feet.

'That's some mess back there by the way,' Rhoadan said, nodding towards the carriage.

'Don't fret, I'll sort it out before we leave, I can't believe I nearly hit you with my arrow.' gasped Kadence.

She was glad the darkness hid her blushing.

'Forget about it, you're forgiven for being so jumpy, it's understandable, that's me got Brightbane's harness anyway, so I'm done over here,' said Rhoadan.

'I'll get these bags tidied up.' said Kadence, as she starting picking the items up that had spilt out of the carriage.

'Kadence, I want to thank you for bringing Brightbane back to me, you have no idea what that means to me, so thank you from the bottom of my heart,' said Rhoadan.

'You don't need to thank me. Just think of it as reimbursement for letting us use your carriage,' said Kadence.

Rhoadan nodded his head and smiled, he took the harness over to Brightbane and placed it over her head and secured it in place, he did the same on her back and down under her stomach and looped it back up into place.

He was smitten that his favourite companion was once again standing in front of him and enjoyed every time Brightbane nuzzled into him.

Elk and Delph were still collecting gems. Some gems had to be prised out of the dead lizard's head. Some came out fairly easy whereas some required a little force. They filled a sack with the gems.

'This is gross.' moaned Elk.

'I know it is, just think of the fortune we'll have when we work out how to cash in this bag of treasure, however, that's if the legend is true mind you.' replied Delph.

'Let's hope it is true' said Elk.

Delph nodded.

'It just feels wrong. I know they attacked us, but I feel sorry for them. Just think of all the lives that were taken by our hands and now we are planning on using their eyes for our own wealth.' said Elk.

'I don't feel as bad as that, they attacked us for no reason after all, so it was either kill or be killed and I've grown rather fond of living you see,' laughed Delph.

Elk nodded.

'All we were doing was escaping the cold of the night, looking for a place to rest and don't forget what happened to poor Brightbane, let's grab a few more gems, then surely we will have enough, if we ever run out of wealth in the future, we can come back and see if there are any left lying about' said Delph.

'I guess you're right, they did attack us first. Do you think we should bury them?' Elk asked.

'We don't have the time to do that, we will need to be leaving soon, I reckon this is about as much as we will need,' said Delph, as he popped the last gem out of the lizard's skull with a knife.

Elk recoiled, horrified by the sound.

'Don't worry about it. That's me done now,' Delph sighed.

Just then, something whizzed past Delph's head and pierced into the lizard that Delph had just removed a gem from.

'Wow, I have no idea what just happened there, but that was much closer than I would have preferred' said Delph.

'Look, that's an arrow,' screeched Elk.

'Let's get back to Kadence and Rhoadan. They might be in trouble,' said Delph.

They both grabbed their bag of treasure and rushed back to Rhoadan and Kadence.

Delph and Elk reached the camp, they saw Kadence clearing up the bags beside the carriage, they looked for Rhoadan, he was busy seeing to Brightbane.

'Would either of you know anything about an arrow that nearly impaled my face?' Delph asked.

Rhoadan and Kadence both stopped what they were doing and turned around to look at Delph.

Rhoadan remained silent. He decided Kadence would be the best person to provide an explanation.

'Guys, I thought Rhoadan was a lizard, so I got my bow ready, although he gave me a fright and I tripped up and it flew out of my hands, it didn't harm anyone did it?' Kadence asked.

'Almost. It nearly hit me. I was nearly skewered,' Delph replied.

'We thought you were in trouble so we rushed back.' added Elk.

'I'm sorry' replied Kadence.

'I'm just relieved that it missed me,' laughed Delph.

'Me too' replied Kadence.

'Right, I'll stick the bag in the back of the carriage shall I Del—?' Elk asked.

'I've almost collected everything that we need, all that remains is a few bags, I just have to get them and put them in the back as well and then we're done,' interrupted Kadence.

'We'll get them,' said Delph.

'I can understand why you thought Rhoadan was a lizard you know,' laughed Elk.

Rhoadan growled at Elk.

Elk decided it was best for his own safety to stop laughing.

'That's great, thanks Delph,' said Kadence.

'Elk, can you come and give me a hand with the rest of these bags please?' Delph asked.

'I'm just about finished tightening this harness. Then I'll get Brightbane attached to the carriage and then I'm done,' said Rhoadan.

Delph and Elk had finished picking up the remaining bags, and they threw them into the back of the carriage.

'Right Elk, we need to move some of these lizards out of the way to clear a path,' said Delph.

'Okay, let's do this!' Elk said loudly. He beat his chest and laughed, making Kadence and Delph laugh with him.

As they walked over towards the first lizard, they pondered over which was the best end to grab first.*

'You grab its head.' ordered Delph.

Elk crouched down and accidentally stuck his thumb into one of the empty, bloodied eye sockets. He shuddered as soon as he felt his thumb being encapsulated with red mush.

'Stop messing about Elk and get it done!' warned Delph.

'I don't think so, I'm covered in enough lizard blood as it is, I'm not touching its head again, in fact, look, *eww*, that one over there doesn't even have a head, that must have been one of Rhoadan's trophies.' groaned Elk, wiping his thumb on his trousers.

'Guys, just get on with it will you, and quit your moaning,' Kadence yelled.

* They bickered about who would grab which end. They couldn't decide which was worse. When you think about it, they didn't really have much of a choice, they could either go for the eyeless head or the other end and we know what lay at the other end under that tail.

'Let's just both grab the tail and drag it and try not to focus too much on what's under it,' said Delph.

'Okay, good idea.' replied Elk.

They decided together that it was the better course of action, so they adopted this technique and approached each lizard this way, and if they found one that didn't have a tail, well—they would just improvise. Once they had cleared enough space for the carriage, they joined the group.

'While I was following those tracks before, I saw a path that could lead us out of here, if we head out from here and head into the darkness over in that direction, we can follow the path and it should be wide enough for the carriage to get through,' explained Delph.

'That's us all ready to leave. I'll grab a few torches to light our way, then I'll extinguish the fire and any torches that remain,' said Elk.

'What are we going to do about sleep?' Kadence asked.

'How about we take it in turns in the back of the carriage?' Rhoadan suggested.

They all nodded in agreement.

Kadence climbed into the back and the rest of them clambered up to the front.

'Let's move girl. It's time to get out of this wretched cave' Rhoadan said, as he directed Brightbane into the darkness.

As they made their way through the rest of the damp cave, they saw countless magical wonders. They passed an underground pool, with every splash that dropped from the jagged roof and splashed on the pool's surface, produced a magnificent array of luminous coloured swirls.

They also passed all sorts of little creatures and critters and thankfully none of those creatures were lizards.

'Stop for a moment and be quiet. Did you hear that?' Delph asked.

Rhoadan clicked his tongue at Brightbane, she slowed down and came to a halt. They remained silent for a few moments until an abrupt, but cheerful chirp invaded their ears.

They scanned the area, but couldn't pinpoint where the noise originated from.

'That noise is made by a cricket. I'm sure they're called shooter cricks,' explained Delph.

'How do you know that? I can't see a thing, I love crickets.' said Rhoadan.

'I know you can't see it, but it is there,' added Delph.

Rhoadan thought it would be a good idea to try to capture a few of them, so he could keep them as a pet.

'Why are you getting off the carriage Rhoadan?' Elk asked.

'I'm going to get me some cricks, pass me two jars out from the back please Elk,' Rhoadan replied.

'I wouldn't do that. If I were you!' warned Delph.

'Why not?' Rhoadan asked.

'I just wouldn't. You'll regret it.' Delph replied.

'Delph stop being so cryptic' moaned Rhoadan; still determined to catch one.

Delph shrugged his shoulders and smirked.

Elk fetched the jars and handed them to Rhoadan.

Rhoadan stopped briefly to see if he could work out where the cricks were hiding.

'Watch this,' said Delph, nudging Elk.

Kadence was still sleeping in the back of the carriage.

Elk and Delph continued watching Rhoadan.

Rhoadan heard the noise again, so he slowly crept in its direction, he opened the lids on the jars so he was ready.

'I'm getting bored with waiting around,' moaned Elk.

'Just watch, if he finds one it'll be worth the wait, trust me.' replied Delph.

Up till now, Rhoadan hadn't had much luck, although it soon changed when a little red and white crick unluckily took a misjudged jump and landed right inside one of the jars.

Rhoadan saw it and immediately seized the moment and closed the lid on the jar. 'Hah, see that was easy' Rhoadan cheered.

'I thought you said it would be worth the wait, Delph?' Elk asked.

'He got lucky, just keep watching,' replied Delph.

Rhoadan was greedy you see, so one crick alone wasn't enough for him, he had to have more, he crawled through all sorts of sludge and grime, he didn't care, he just wanted another crick, regardless of what it took to get one.

The only noise that broke the silence was the odd droplet of dirty cave water dripping from the ceiling spikes on to the equally wet ground below that and the odd chortle from Delph. Another crick chirped; alerting Rhoadan to its whereabouts.

Rhoadan stealthily* crawled up behind the unsuspecting crick and the closer he got, the lower he got, until he was just a few inches behind it.

Delph and Elk were surprised that Rhoadan and his massive bulk had got as close to the crick without it noticing or indeed scaring it away. Just as Rhoadan lifted the jar to capture the crick, Delph could no longer contain his laugh, he snorted a little too loud and alerted the crick.

* **Well as stealthily as his bulky frame would allow.**

It defended itself and shot red ink all over Rhoadan's face, Rhoadan had amazingly caught another, although this time it came with consequences.

Elk and Delph both burst out laughing and the hysterics had taken over them so much that Elk rolled out of the side of the carriage and landed on the damp ground, Delph laughed even harder at Elk's misfortune.

'Eurgghh' said Rhoadan, as he tried wiping the gunk away, although he failed and smeared it over his face. His hands were covered with what he had just wiped from his face. He tried removing it by wiping his hands on the ground, it didn't help, his hands were stained and you can imagine what his face looked like.

'I... told... you... it... would... be... worth... it...' Delph giggled hysterically, through broken breaths.

Elk stood up and laughed even harder when he saw that Rhoadan's face was bright red.

'Oh by the lord of Eshia, have you seen your face,' laughed Elk.

'How would that even be possible, there is no reflective glass in this cave and what is this stuff on my hands and face.' grunted Rhoadan.

'If you had been listening to me, that stuff on your face wouldn't be there.' said Delph.

'I hear what you're saying Delph, but now is not the right time for a lecture,' Rhoadan grumbled.

'I tried to warn you,' Delph added.

'Like I just mentioned, now is not the time' Rhoadan scolded Delph, as he shook his head.

Elk looked for something in the back of the carriage that Rhoadan could use to wipe his face.

He searched as quietly as he could so he didn't wake up Kadence although he wondered how she was could sleep through their laughing.

'Here you go, try to clean yourself with that' said Elk, as he handed the rag to Rhoadan.

'Thanks, lad' Rhoadan said.

It was only when he wiped his face that he discovered that the stuff stunk to the high heavens, now that it had had some time to dry in a little.

Delph and Elk, unfortunately, discovered this at the same time. Brightbane even snorted and shook her head when she smelt Rhoadan, the smell was putrid.*

'Rhoadan, you smell so bad' said Elk in a squeaky voice; he was trying hard not to vomit, he held his nose tightly shut.

'Do you... honestly think... that I'm... not aware of that?' Rhoadan asked—through uncontrollable boaking.

'Let's just get out of here. I've seriously had enough of this hellish cave.' sighed Rhoadan.

'Yeah, we haven't had the easiest of times in here have we?' laughed Elk, he felt his right eye twitch a little.

'I'd stop laughing if I were you Elk, grow up.' growled Rhoadan.

* The only thing possibly similar to the stench, was a decaying bokbit lying in a swamp pit on a hot day. It was horrific.

They climbed back up onto the carriage.

'I don't want to risk anything happening to us whilst I have this stuff on my face, Delph could you steer?' asked Rhoadan.

'Sure, no problem' Delph replied.

Delph gently whipped Brightbane's reins: 'Let's get moving girl' he ordered, and they set off again.

They were unsure of how long they had been travelling since last setting off, Elk and Rhoadan had almost nodded off with the continuous motion of the carriage wheels against the bumpy ground below them, they noticed a light breaking through the darkness, which got them excited because their torches were close to dying off.

They had been in the dark for some time with only torches and a fire for light, so the sunlight was immense. As they reached the sunlight, their pupils contracted to match the light, it was so bright.

'Easy girl, slow down' ordered Delph, signalling for Brightbane to come to a halt.

'What are you doing?' Rhoadan asked.

'I can't see, the light is so bright, give me a moment or two,' Delph replied, rubbing his eyes.

Rhoadan and Elk did the same. Rhoadan disturbed the smell which meant it flowed through their nostrils once again. Once their eyes and noses stopped irritating them they moved out into the broad sunlight, Delph pointed out a small stream running alongside the entrance to the cave, he told Brightbane to stop.

'Why don't you try washing your face in there Rhoadan?' Delph asked.

'Anything has to be worth a go' Rhoadan said as he fumbled his way off the carriage and down to the stream.

He crouched down, cupped his hands and scooped the water up and splashed it on his face.

'Ahhh, that's cold' he shuddered. He was taken aback at the bitter temperature of the stream as he circled his hands around his face.

Unfortunately, it didn't make any difference, the slop was as stubborn as Rhoadan was and it wouldn't budge.

He made his way back to the carriage with his head hung low and with the help of Elk, he climbed up. Delph ran down and threw their torches into the stream.

A cool breeze brushed against their faces, heightening the stench of the sludge on Rhoadan's face, they didn't like the smell one bit.

Delph and Elk both pinched their noses again as they could no longer take it. Rhoadan decided not to, no matter what he did, there was no way he would escape the smell.

The sun shone a magnificent heat, making them feel good. They breathed a sigh of relief, knowing they were past the trouble and torment of the cave.

'How long have we been travelling now?' Delph asked.

'I have no idea' replied Rhoadan.

'We've been travelling for hours.' moaned Elk.

'It's hardly been hours Elk, just be patient,' Delph replied.

'I'm so bored, can't we go any faster?' Elk moaned again.

'Can you stop moaning, just for a second,' Rhoadan, ironically moaned.

They were thankful the cave was now feeling more of a distant memory, one they were hopeful of never repeating.

Rhoadan's crimson face was, however, a current nightmare, not only for him but for the full group, the smell had been attracting some unsightly insects for some time now, the unlucky bugs that had escaped Rhoadan's hand swipes, met an unpleasant demise by being stuck on Rhoadan's face and then incurred a horrible crushing death as Rhoadan took great pleasure in striking each one with a well-targeted slap.

'What's that horrible smell?' yelled Kadence from the back of the carriage. She had just woken up.

'That smell is coming from Rhoadan, he needs a bath' yelled Elk. Rhoadan just mumbled some unintelligible words, more grumble than words in fact.

'I wish he would stop that' thought Delph, who winced with every slap Rhoadan made.

'Are you trying to knock some sense into that head of yours?' Elk laughed.

'I can easily knock some sense into yours you know, I can't help it. These blasted bugs are driving me crazy' growled Rhoadan.

'I warned you' Delph reminded Rhoadan.

'I never heard you' replied Rhoadan.

'I said it, I think you ignored me,' replied Delph.

'Well, now I wish I hadn't,' replied Rhoadan.

'Hopefully, we will be stopping soon. I'm getting hungry,' said Elk.

'You can't possibly be, you just finished nearly a full quart of that crisp loaf recently.' replied Delph.

'That was ages ago,' replied Elk. His stomach rumbled.

'It actually wasn't, you know.' Delph laughed.

'The fact remains that I'm still hungry. I can't change that you know,' explained Elk.

'Elk, you're always hungry and no, we won't be stopping anytime soon. I want to get to Dirtbere before the night is upon us,' explained Delph.

Elk sighed.

Delph lashed at Brightbane's reins to make her gallop.

'C'mon girl, let's get moving' directed Delph, and they set off along the chalky, dusty road.

Kadence had long grown bored with travelling and was trying to get back to sleep, even though she had only been awake for a short time, she was so bored that she counted the trees from the back of the carriage as they passed them.

As uninteresting as this was, it seemed to take her mind off of her boredom.

Kadence counted various trees from minuscule saplings to mighty towering trees that were waving high into the air, she was soon getting bored with this as well, then something caught her attention, by the time she looked to see what it was, there was nothing there.

She immediately stopped counting the trees and focussed her attention on what she thought she saw. Just then a dark shadow caught her attention again. Kadence thought she saw it disappear leaving a cloud of purple smoke, it happened quickly so she couldn't be sure of what she saw.

'UM GUYS' she yelled, blindly tapping the carriage to alert them, whilst keeping her eyes on the road behind them: 'We have a few guests.' she yelled.

'Not again' groaned Rhoadan, clenching his fists.

'Easy girl, stop' said Delph. He pulled on Brightbane's reins, she halted, the four of them jumped down from the carriage and drew their weapons and waited with eager eyes.

'Keep watch over here it'll happen again at any moment,' said Kadence, pointing down the road.

They waited in silence.

Purple, wispy smoke appeared in front of them and just hovered, it circled them and then it disappeared again. They waited for what seemed like an eternity before anything happened.

All they could see was the leaves of the trees waving in the wind and the occasional slap from Rhoadan killing whichever insect landed on his foul-smelling face.

Without prior warning, the purple mist reappeared, it hovered in front of them, just as it had done before. Delph raised his sword and sliced right through the purple fog, as quickly as his sword cut through the smoke, it separated and spiralled into two.

Once Delph had lowered his sword, the two clouds merged back into one and a body materialised out of the purple vapour, it spiralled upwards and disappeared as quickly as it appeared.

With all the surrounding commotion, they never had any time to focus properly on what was going on in front of them. A set of wide, piercing green eyes and a set of pearly white fangs was all they could make out was.

'Did you see that?' Kadence yelled.

'I saw it' Delph replied, just as loud as Kadence.

'Brace yourselves!' yelled Elk.

The smoke appeared again, this time it circled above, it hovered again before slowly floating away from them, it darted from left to right and suddenly stopped and hovered in the air once more.

'Do not attack. I am a friend' a voice echoed from the cloud of smoke. 'Do not attack. I am not a foe,' it echoed a second time.

The group remained still, taking in the spectacle that was unfolding in front of them, each with an expression as puzzled as the next person.

The beast showed itself again: 'Do not attack. I am not a foe' it repeated. It wisped away as quickly as it had come into view.

The only thing they could concentrate on was a glimpse of its arrow tipped tail, swishing about like an angry cat's tail through another cloud of smoke.

'Should we believe it?' Rhoadan asked.

'Do you really think it would have taken the time to give us that warning?' Elk replied.

'I believe that it would have just attacked us if it truly wanted to,' replied Delph.

'I think we ought to give it a chance, I agree with what Delph has just said,' Rhoadan replied.

Brightbane, who had been forgotten about, was becoming edgy, she was restless with all the porting the creature was doing, it darted about too fast for her liking.

'I can't help thinking it's a trap,' replied Kadence.

'Only one way to find out I suppose,' added Elk.

'I think we should lower our weapons and find out,' suggested Delph.

They all lowered their weapons, not fully though, just in case it was indeed, a trap. Elk's gun dropped to the ground, clattering on the stones below their feet. Kadence twisted around quickly to face the noise with her weapon drew high she realised the noise was made by Elk's gun hitting the ground.

'Elk, what are you doing?' Delph asked.

'What a fright you gave me,' sighed Kadence.

'I didn't do it on purpose, it fell, I had a firm grip on it, I just lost grip. I'm not sure how that happened,' replied Elk, scratching his head.

The smoke appeared in front of them again and the mysterious figure materialised from it as though it had just twisted and spiralled from out of nowhere.

It landed gently on the ground without making any sound.

They all had to look up to see it properly.

'Look at the size of you' thought Delph; as it stretched itself to its full height.

'My name is Ooseriz, I have come to aid you like I said before, I am not your enemy,' Ooseriz said.

She stood at seven foot tall, staring out at them from piercing green eyes. She was as skinny as a root bean plant and covered in preened, velvety purple-berry coloured fur which went from her pointy ears right down to her long paws and all the way along to the tip of her arrow pointed tail.

Her tail flicked and waved about menacingly through the air from left to right in a swishing motion.

Much like an irritated cat's tail would sway, although, she was far from angry.

'I'm Delph. This is Elk, this is Kadence, and this is Rhoadan' explained Delph, pointing at each of them and as he said their name.

Ooseriz nodded her head to acknowledge them.

'I know who you are. I've been watching you for a while now,' explained Ooseriz.

'You've been watching us, what do you mean?' Delph asked, secretly wondering if it would be wise to reach for his weapon.

'Can you remember back when you reached the cave?' Ooseriz asked.

They all cast their minds back to their journey.

'Remember those creatures kept disappearing, well that was me, I got rid of them,' explained Ooseriz.

'What did you do with them?' Rhoadan asked.

Her tail flicked up behind her.

'I ported them to another place. Miles away from you or anyone else in fact, to a place they could cause no harm to anyone,' answered Ooseriz.

'I knew something strange was happening' proclaimed Kadence. Ooseriz just smiled.

'I continued doing it until I could do it no more. I only have a limited number of ports that I can perform before I'm drained of energy and have to rest. I found a spot, and I settled down to wait for you whilst I regained my strength. I saw you appear on the road where you first saw the cave and I waited until I had enough energy to throw my voice to you, giving you a warning not to go into the cave,' Ooseriz explained.

Delph thought back to the cave: 'You know what? I heard something before we went into that cave, I heard a voice, but I couldn't make out what it said,' replied Delph.

'My voice would have been clearer if my health had been stronger,' Ooseriz explained.

'What are ports?' asked Rhoadan.

'Ports are short for teleports. See just now when I was disappearing and reappearing, that was a port, I can vanish into the air, I can become the wind, the leaves and mostly anything that is around me,' explained Ooseriz.

'Aren't you able to port into a wolf and tell them not to attack us?' Kadence asked.

'Unfortunately not, even if I could do that, they wouldn't listen to me. I'm sure I would need to be a port master, although I've never really bothered with further training on ports, I'm quite lazy that way you see, so I can only change into non-living things for now,' Ooseriz replied.

'I thought you just said you can port into the leaves?' Kadence asked.

'I can, but only ones that have dropped off the branch, like the ones you would see dancing in the surrounding wind,' Ooseriz replied.

'Did you tamper with my gun at all?' Elk asked.

'I did' replied Ooseriz, with a sly smirk.

SLAP.

They all turned to look at Rhoadan, he had just sentenced a few insects to a flattening death, with an almighty slap.

'Could you by any chance do something with this gunk on my face, port it away or something, I mean it's not living at all, the only living thing about it is that it's annoying the living life right out of me,' pleaded Rhoadan.

'Sure, let me take a look at it' said Ooseriz, as she bent down to take a closer look, immediately wishing she hadn't as she screwed up her face and grimaced at the smell.

'What is it?' Ooseriz asked.

'Rhoadan got too close to a shooter crick, and it shot that stuff on his face,' laughed Delph.

Rhoadan didn't appreciate Delph's laughing.

'I will help you, those slaps sound sore and I can't stand back and watch you slap yourself, you are going to need complete focus for the times ahead, as they will be dangerous,' said Ooseriz, disappearing into a puff of purple smoke, which engulfed Rhoadan completely.

Delph, Elk and Kadence all stood back to give Ooseriz plenty of space to work. Ooseriz surrounded Rhoadan. She spiralled around him like she was a purple vortex, sucking in any loose leaves around her.

Once she finished taking care of Rhoadan, she disappeared again leaving a very confused Rhoadan and a small tornado of leaves.

Once the leaves stopped spinning, they dropped into a little pile on the ground.

'You never twisted up that time,' said Kadence.

'Oh that's just for first impressions,' laughed Ooseriz, as she returned to them.

'What a relief, you did it! You removed the gunk from my face. No more red, no more flies and no more slapping,' yelled Rhoadan ecstatically, almost dancing with joy.

Only almost though, dwarves aren't the nimblest of people, and if you were ever to watch a dwarf dance, you would be forgiven for thinking he was writhing in pain, the sound almost matches it as well, although, they got a tiny sampler back in the cave.

'And more importantly, no more stench,' Kadence laughed.

'I wouldn't say all the red was gone.' Elk joked, laughing at Rhoadan.

'That smell is still there, though, oh no wait, that's Rhoadan's natural scent,' laughed Delph; leaning in for a smell.

'Oh no, hasn't it worked?' Rhoadan stressed.

'Oh it's worked fine, but the red in which I'm referring to is where you have left a massive, red hand-print right across your cheek, from all the slapping that you've been doing,' laughed Elk.

'Why do you have to try to ruin everything Elk?' Kadence sighed.

'I'm just pointing it out,' replied Elk.

'He hasn't ruined it for me. I can handle having a red cheek, for the time being, at least it won't attract the beasties and it'll soon be gone,' replied Rhoadan.

Delph, Elk and Kadence cheered.

'Please focus your attention on me. I must stress the importance of the little time you have left, you must go, there is a vast number of those wolves heading in our direction, I can sense they won't be long in reaching us, you must be in the safety of the next city by the time they reach you, or I fear you will not survive,' explained Ooseriz.

'We can take them,' growled Rhoadan.

'There is simply too many of them to fight. I will make my way back to them and try to port as many as I can out of the way and by doing that, you should hopefully have a fighting chance to make it. You must travel fast and don't stop and I will see you again at the right time. I will answer any questions you have when I see you next, you need to move now,' stressed Ooseriz. They watched as Ooseriz disappeared into a puff of purple smoke and vanish for the last time.

'What a way to kill our happiness,' said Elk.

'Right, you heard her. We need to act now,' ordered Delph.

'Let's move, I'd rather not take any chances,' replied Kadence.

'I'll jump in the back with Kadence, in case those fiends manage to reach us and that means we'll have protection from the back,' said Elk.

'I'll stay up front and keep an eye out and we should be covered from all angles that way,' replied Delph.

They secured their weapons and jumped up on the carriage. 'Right girl, let's get moving.' yelled Rhoadan as he snapped Brightbane's reins, signalling for her to leave.

Brightbane, however, had other ideas, she never moved, not even an inch, Rhoadan snapped her reins again and still, nothing happened.

'What's she doing? Why isn't she moving?' Delph stressed.

'Brightbane lass, we don't have time for this. What are you doing? Why aren't you moving?' Rhoadan yelled.

'What's happening guys, why aren't we moving?' Elk yelled.

'Brightbane won't move,' Delph yelled back.

'Ooseriz said we should hurry.' Kadence yelled.

'I know she did, I was there remember.' yelled Delph.

'Can everyone just stop yelling for a moment, I need a minute to think and I can't do it when everyone is yelling!' Rhoadan ironically yelled back, he held his head in his hands.

'I thought you said you stop yelling.' yelled Elk.

Rhoadan shook his head and flashed a dispassionate look of disbelief at Elk, whilst mumbling something.

Kadence briskly struck Elk's ribs with her elbow.

'Has she done this before?' Delph asked.

'Yes, but not for a long time, I'm just trying to remember what it was that I did to get her to move on.' replied Rhoadan.

'She's just being stubborn,' thought Delph.

'Oh, I remember what it was now,' Rhoadan said as he jumped down from the carriage and quickly made his way around the back towards Elk and Kadence.

'I'll keep watching from up this end,' said Delph.

'What is going on up there, we need to move. Can't you sort Brightbane out? What is wrong with her?' Elk asked.

'Elk, can you keep your lips closed and remain silent or you are the one that I will be sorting out!' scolded Rhoadan, as he appeared in front of Elk and Kadence.

'What a fright you gave me,' gasped Kadence.

Elk said no more about the matter, or in fact any other matter, with emotions of fear and embarrassment he quickly moved away from Rhoadan's reach. Delph jumped down from the carriage and walked around and he met with the others.

'I don't want to rush you, but we need to get moving,' stressed Delph.

'Kadence quickly pass my orange bag over,' said Rhoadan.'Where is it?' she asked; as she looked for the bag, 'Got it,' she yelled from the back of the carriage.

'Can you pass it to me?' Rhoadan asked.

Kadence threw the bag to Rhoadan.

Rhoadan took out a clear jar, and he threw it back in the carriage then he ran back to Brightbane, followed by Delph.

'What is it?' Delph asked.

'It's sweet water, Brightbane likes it, it gives her energy and makes her move fast, I think it'll do the trick, it worked before.' Rhoadan explained.

Delph jumped back up on the carriage while Rhoadan opened the jar and patted Brightbane's neck.

'Right girl, take some of this and show us how fast you can go' he said. He poured some into her mouth, Brightbane's eyes widened. Her ears pointed forward, and she whinnied with joy.

Rhoadan put the jar in his pocket and jumped back up onto the carriage.

'Guys, we need to move now, we have company' yelled Elk; who was half hanging out the back of the carriage.

In the distance behind them, black wolves were descending in their direction, yelping and snarling as they came.

'Hold on guys,' yelled Rhoadan, he snapped Brightbane's reins, Brightbane lifted her two front legs up into the air and whinnied again.

She started off like a rocket.

Elk stumbled backwards with the sudden speed, luckily Kadence was paying attention, she grabbed on to Elk's arm and pulled him back into the carriage.

Delph looked behind them and saw the horde of wolves rushing towards them. With every stride that Brightbane galloped, she picked up speed until they were in full motion and they were travelling as fast as a steam train.

'Wow, that was a close one' Elk laughed nervously; clinging on to the carriage like grim death, not wishing to repeat what just happened.

'I don't know why you're laughing, that could have gone so wrong.' Kadence gasped.

'Let's just look at it this way—it didn't, I'm really glad you grabbed me though. I appreciate it,' Elk said.

'Just don't do it again, stay in the carriage please,' laughed Kadence.

Elk gave Kadence a one-armed hug, expressing his appreciation and still grasping the carriage with his free hand.

'What's that for?' Kadence asked, she blushed.

'Just for. Thanks again for saving me,' Elk replied.

With every powerful thud of Brightbane's hooves on the ground below, it sounded like a roar of thunder.

They felt a few droplets of rain land on their faces and in no time at all it was lashing down, they were getting soaked, but they didn't care. The rain didn't last long, but it was enough to clear away the musty air that had been lingering since they left the cave.

Brightbane felt free again, she flared her nostrils and breathed in as much air as she could; powering along the path, she had beaten her temporary lull and was soon thundering along the dusty road to escape the wolves.

Chapter Six

-Press To Dirtbere-

Kadence tried shouting up to the front of the carriage, but the wind kept catching her breath, making it difficult to speak. Leaves that floated uncontrollably in the wind kept getting tangled up in Kadence's dishevelled hair.

Elk stood up to speak at the precise moment a sodden wet leaf hit him on the face: 'MRPHLLL MRPHLLL MPH' he grabbed Its stem and flicked it off the side of the carriage.

'I'll try saying that again' he thought, wiping the residual wetness from his face.

'They're catching up to us. We need to do something,' yelled Elk.

'We need to lighten the load. Have we got anything in the back that we don't need?' Delph yelled.

'I think we need everything' Kadence yelled back; she managed to take control of her hair and had removed any leaves.

'Plan B' Rhoadan stated.

'Plan B?' Delph asked.

Rhoadan nodded.

'Plan Brightbane, take the reins and I'll show you' Rhoadan said loudly. Rhoadan wearily stood up, he stumbled and grabbed onto Delph's head, almost poking Delph in his eye with his thumb.

'Oops,' Rhoadan said loudly.

'Watch what you're doing,' screeched Delph.

'What?' Rhoadan yelled.

'I said, watch what you are doing please' Delph yelled louder this time, the increasing wind muffled his initial response.

'Sorry' replied Rhoadan.

'What are you doing?' Elk yelled.

'What?' Rhoadan yelled back, cupping his hand up to his ear.

'Yes, what' roared Elk.

'I can't hear you over this wind,' cried Rhoadan.

'What?' yelled Elk, holding his hand up to his ear to obtain a better grasp on what Rhoadan was saying.

'I can hardly hear a word he's saying' Rhoadan yelled at Delph whilst he shrugged his shoulders.

'What are you doing?' bellowed Delph.

'Just watch' Rhoadan yelled back.

Rhoadan reached into his pocket and brought out the jar of sweet water and he clambered over the front of the carriage.

Rhoadan climbed down onto Brightbane's back and grabbed her harness tightly, the last thing he wanted to do was to fall to his death and be trampled by anything, let alone by his beloved horse.

As he edged his away along Brightbane's back, he patted her on the neck telling her to remain calm, he didn't want to startle her although because of Rhoadan's bulky weight, Brightbane was fully aware that Rhoadan was making his way across her back.

'Right girl, I'm just going to give you more sweet water, take it nice please and don't go bucking me to the ground,' Rhoadan yelled.

He edged along a bit further and grabbed the lid with his teeth, he twisted it open. He managed to remove the lid without too much hassle. He held the jar to the side of Brightbane's mouth.

She opened her mouth and drank the rest of the water and again just like before, Brightbane whinnied and bucked Rhoadan. Luckily he grabbed onto her reins and just in time.

He lifted right off her. He was practically flying, possibly becoming the first of his kind to be aerodynamic even if it was short-lived, much to Rhoadan's relief. He landed on his bottom facing the carriage which was handy as it was the direction in which he was about to make his way back.

Delph watched him with a few emotions, first, it was shock, then it was amazement. He was amazed that Rhoadan had succeeded.

'Woah girl, woah,' Rhoadan yelled to Brightbane, as he patted her side with his free hand: 'Just give me a couple of minutes until I get back to my seat before you go crazy and dash off,' he added.

Rhoadan clambered back over to the carriage, he shuffled along a little bit before realising he was being tugged backwards, he couldn't get his arm free, he was stuck.

Brightbane eagerly whinnied again, she ignored Rhoadan, and the excitement took over.

She thundered down the road; it was almost as if she was drunk on the sweet water, and the instant rush caused a euphoric feeling to take over, there was no way she was going to respond to Rhoadan at all.

'Woah girl, my arm is caught, slow down!' Rhoadan yelled, he knew himself that she couldn't even if she wanted to, there was no stopping her once she had drunk the sweet water.

Delph looked on in horror, he reached over the edge of the carriage to try to grab Rhoadan's free hand. He pulled Rhoadan towards him, but it wasn't any use, Rhoadan's arm was caught.

'It's no use lad I'm stuck,' Rhoadan yelled.

Delph sighed with empathy.

Every time Rhoadan tried to loosen off the rein strap, he lost the little bit of balance that he had. Brightbane was thundering so fast it caused Rhoadan to lift up into the air again.

'Argh!' Rhoadan yelled.

'Hold on Rhoadan,' yelled Delph.

'Oh I intend to, don't you worry.' Rhoadan yelled back.

'There are two wolves gaining on us,' yelled Elk.

'We keep missing them.' yelled Kadence.

'Your aim is awful Kadence' laughed Elk, trying to make light of the situation.

'I don't see you hitting any of them either' Kadence scolded Elk, and she rolled her eyes.

Elk and Kadence aimed at the pursuing wolves, trying to push the chase in their favour.

No matter how many times Elk fired his gun or Kadence released an arrow, the wolves kept dodging them.

Rhoadan tried to shuffle forward again, and the closer he got to the carriage the tighter the reins felt around his wrist, he knew he had to endure the pain and ride it out because if he didn't, there was a chance the rein strap would snap and he would go hurtling to his death, so he just went with the flow and clung to Brightbane's harness as tight as he could.

'Rhoadan, hold on tight, we're going around a corner, there's a cliff edge up ahead, you will need to hold on.' yelled Delph.

Rhoadan couldn't do anything except close his eyes and pray to the lord of Eshia that he survived.

'I just hope Brightbane isn't too juiced up to realise the corner is there, or we will all be in trouble,' yelled Rhoadan.

'I'll whip her to check,' yelled Delph.

Kadence and Elk were still trying to target the wolves, but the mutts kept dodging the shots.

Brightbane thundered on, Delph whipped her to make sure she was focussed.

She shook her head as though she had just come out of a trance.

The two wolves that had been evading Kadence and Elk's shots had just spotted Rhoadan, they sped up and ignored Kadence and Elk completely and were focussed solely on an easier target which came in the form of Rhoadan.

They ran alongside the carriage, one in front of the other, neither of them noticed the corner that was ahead, their eyes were fixated on their prize and that prize was a struggling Rhoadan.

'Corner ahead, hold on tight,' Delph yelled.

Kadence and Elk grabbed the side of the carriage, to make sure they were as secure as they could be. They held on tight as Brightbane almost ran right off the edge, they manoeuvred around the corner, much unlike the two wolves who hadn't been as quick-witted as Delph.

One of the wolves lunged at Rhoadan's feet. Rhoadan's eyes met the determined wolf's eyes, his heart fluttered as the fiendish wolf snapped its jaws.

Rhoadan swung his foot around and kicked it in the face with his heavy boot, the wolf yelped and tumbled over the edge, the remaining wolf had been running too fast and had no time to stop.

It skidded as it tried to stay on the path, the wolf rolled over the edge and tumbled to its death and just like its friend both wolves plummeted to the sea below.

Rhoadan swung over the edge, luckily for him he was still attached to Brightbane and that the carriage was sturdy enough to support his broad frame.

He watched as the wolves hurtled to their deaths below him. He shuddered and breathed a sigh of relief that he wasn't joining them. They made it safely around the corner, much to everyone's approval.

'We made it' Delph cheered.

'Thankfully, that wasn't a sharp corner because if it was, we would never have made that turn and the speed we were going,' yelled Elk.

'Where are those wolves? I can't see them,' yelled Kadence.

'They went for a swim,' replied Delph, chuckling at his own joke.

Kadence was confused.

The group continued along the crooked path they were on. They were travelling slower as there was no need for speed because they were no longer being pursued by those wolves.

They relaxed a little, however, they still wished to continue at a reasonable rate of speed as they didn't want the wolves to catch up to them.

'Throw me a knife Delph, I'm going to have to cut it,' Rhoadan said.

'I don't have one. I have my sword though,' Delph replied, signalling for Brightbane to stop.

'What are you doing?' asked Elk, peeking over the side of the carriage.

'We're setting me free, lad,' yelled Rhoadan.

Delph jumped down and did just that.

He dragged his sword over the reins, and Rhoadan jerked backwards when the tension released, rubbing his wrist he nodded at Delph and jumped down from Brightbane.

Rhoadan and Delph climbed back up onto the carriage and they set off.

'Will we ever get off this wretched road?' Elk asked from the back of the carriage.

'I'm happy that the wind has died down and we don't have to yell any more,' said Rhoadan.

'Yeah, me too, my throat was beginning to feel strained,' Kadence replied.

'How's your wrist Rhoadan?' Delph asked.

'It's still tender lad,' Rhoadan replied, rubbing his wrist again.

'It looks swollen' said Delph, pointing it out.

'I'll survive' laughed Rhoadan.

They travelled for over an hour without facing any other danger and they were enjoying the relaxation until a familiar sound filled their ears.

'Uh guys, we need to get off the road.' shrieked Kadence.

'Don't they ever give up?' Elk moaned.

'Look down there, let's just get down there, that's got to lead somewhere' said Delph as he pointed towards what looked like the perfect way off the road.

'That's got to be at least two miles away, even with that slope. Do you think we can make it in time?' Kadence asked.

'Only one way to find out, I don't think we have any other choice,' replied Delph.

'Right I'll move over and you take control,' ordered Delph. They both switched places.

'It's good to be back.' roared Rhoadan.

He cracked Brightbane's reins, instantly regretting cracking them as hard, when the pain from his wrist kicked in, and with that, they set off with a jolt and thundered down the slope.

They reached the bottom of the slope with a thud.

They skidded around the slight bend and navigated along the path without any sign of the wolves, the decline on the hill gave them a warm welcomed head start.

'There they are now,' screeched Elk.

'I count four of them,' yelled Kadence.

'Right guys, prepare yourself,' Delph roared.

'Sheesh, I'm sick of these blasted wolves. I wish they would just pi—' Rhoadan moaned.

'That's another two coming from the left over there, look there's two more over there,' yelled Elk, pointing them out, interrupting Rhoadan.

'Damn, that's eight of those blasted beasts now,' Kadence yelled.

'Just be ready, focus,' Delph yelled.

'We're not far away now. We can make it,' yelled Rhoadan.

'Make it where?' Delph asked.

'I'm not sure, we're just going to have to keep pushing on until something comes up,' replied Rhoadan.

'ARGH!' Kadence screamed.

'Elk, what's happening back there?' yelled Delph.

Elk kicked the wolf's face, sending it hurtling off the back of the carriage. He heard it yelp as it rolled back to the ground where it belonged.

'Elk, what's happening?' Delph yelled a second time.

'A sneaky wolf tried to jump up here, he thought he could hitch a lift, the cheeky beggar. I've sorted it so we're down to seven now,' yelled Elk.

'Elk, grab one of those crick jars and throw it at the wolves,' ordered Delph.

Elk did as he was asked and grabbed the first one he could.

'Did you see that?' Kadence asked Elk.

'See what?' Elk replied.

'A wolf just ran past us, right along the side of the carriage,' said Kadence.

'Delph, a wolf is close to you, so watch out,' yelled Elk.

Elk threw the crick jar at the wolves. It hit the wolf nearest to him and cracked open and the crick sprayed ink everywhere as expected.

There was an almighty red cloud, almost like a small explosion, covering four of the pursuing wolves from head to tail.

Those wolves stopped chasing and they dropped the ground clambering their paws over their eyes, almost clawing them out, trying to get the gunk off.

The others that had escaped the ink spray stopped and backed off from the ink covered wolves, they noticed the smell and decided that they didn't like it, or want to be covered themselves.

Elk, Kadence and Delph all cheered at the sight of the ink splattered wolves.

'What's happening back there?' Rhoadan asked.

'Elk just threw one of the crick jars at the wolves,' said Delph.

'Did he get any?' Rhoadan asked.

'Yeah, four of them,' replied Delph.

'That's great n' all, but don't use my other jar, I need that other one!' Rhoadan warned.

'If we need to use it, we will use it, we can always go back and get more,' said Delph.

'That's five down,' yelled Elk.

'Two of their mates are backing off, so that's seven in total,' cheered Kadence.

'Where is that other wolf that ran past us, Delph?' Kadence yelled.

They had forgotten about the other wolf, the commotion that was happening at the back.

Delph searched for the missing wolf. He saw it up ahead; it wasn't alone; it had a friend, however, its friend was much bigger.

'There's another two up in front of us, look!' Delph yelled.

'Look at the size of that other one,' Rhoadan gasped.

The two creatures, stood motionless on the path in front, and as they got closer, they realised the biggest of the two wasn't a wolf.

'What is that?' Delph yelled.

'Is that a tree, surely not, it can't be, can it?' Rhoadan asked.

'It certainly looks like one, we will soon find out,' Delph replied.

'Right girl, you know what to do' yelled Rhoadan, as he whipped her reins.

Brightbane was focussed, she snorted her nostrils, lowered her head and charged. She thundered towards them.

'Looks good from this end,' yelled Kadence.

'It's not so good up front,' Delph yelled back.

Kadence and Elk both clung to the back of the carriage and hung over the edge to get a better look at what Delph was referring to.

Elk gripped his gun in his free hand. Both beasts just stood there, neither of them flinched.

Brightbane sped up, and she ran as fast as she could, she powered herself to all, but a few feet from them. The biggest of the two swirled up into a huge black cloud which was much bigger than the one Ooseriz had conjured earlier and as it disappeared, the other wolf jumped through the cloud of smoke.

It snarled confidently as it surged towards them, its wild eyes concentrated solely on Brightbane and bringing her down.

The group, of course, wasn't going to allow this to happen. Elk raised his gun and fired a shot into the wolf and with immense accuracy, he hit the rampaging wolf on the forehead. The wolf's head exploded right in front of them, spraying blood in every direction. Elk's quick thinking saved them from what could have been potentially lethal.

The wolf dropped to the ground and because there was no time to manoeuvre Brightbane trampled right over the wolf, crushing it into the ground.

The carriage jolted and shook as they rolled over the wolf and with every bump they grimaced as they knew what they were running over.

'Wow Elk, what a shot,' cheered Delph.

'It was, wasn't it' replied Elk, blowing the top of his gun, trying to look cool, but unfortunately, far from it. Elk and Kadence both swung back around into the safety of the carriage.

'Look, guys, we've made it' yelled Rhoadan. They all cheered again.

'Kadence, look down and see what those other two wolves are up to, will you?' Delph asked.

'They must have backed off Delph, I can't see them,' Kadence replied.

'Brilliant, I'm glad to hear it,' Delph said.

Rhoadan gestured for Brightbane to slow down as they were nearing the forest's edge, they continued along the last part of the road, until they could go no further.

'Rhoadan and I will have a look around here. Kadence, Elk, can you both keep an eye out for any other wolves?' Delph asked.

'Yeah sure, no problem,' Kadence replied.

'One question though. What was that thing back there?' Elk asked.

Kadence and Rhoadan shrugged their shoulders.

'I have no idea. I've been wondering that myself,' Delph replied.

'Hopefully, it wasn't those blasted J'yoti again,' Elk responded.

'I sincerely hope not' said Kadence as she shook her head.

'Let's not mull over it too much just now, let's just find a way into that forest,' said Delph.

'How are we going to get through that?' Elk asked.

'Can everyone keep an eye out for any wolves please?' Delph asked.

They stood in front of a tremendous wall of trees. It was full of huge vines which were knitted together tightly. They studied the hindrance for signs of an entry for what felt like an eternity, much to Elk's annoyance.

'Any luck guys?' Elk enquired impatiently.

'Not yet' Delph simply replied.

'We need to find a way in now,' yelled Kadence, panicking.

'Right, there's only one thing for it, stand back,' Delph bellowed.

Wolf howls quickly filled the air.

Delph stood with his sword at arm's length, he scanned the vines for the thickest one and made the first swipe.

It took a few swings to get through the vine and as soon as it was cut, the rest of the vines separated and slithered apart like serpents.

They receded as if something wanted the group to pass through this way and enter the forest.

'Quick get in. Those wolves are getting closer,' cried Elk.

Rhoadan climbed back on the carriage and lifted the reins.

'Kadence, get in there and Elk, you stand guard,' ordered Delph.

Kadence ran in, slowly followed by Brightbane, not fully understanding the urgency, so Delph gave her a swift smack on her behind.

Gently enough so not to hurt her, but hard enough so she knew she had to move quickly. Brightbane didn't like it and galloped in, almost bucking Rhoadan off the side of the carriage.

'Easy girl, less space, less speed,' yelled Rhoadan, as they galloped past Delph and Elk at an unappealing pace.

'Those wolves are getting closer, should I fire at them?' Elk asked.

'No just get in before those wolves make you their lunch,' replied Delph who was standing at the entrance.

As soon as Elk placed his second foot through the entrance, the barbed vines saw fit to spring back into action and seal the thorns back into place.

They swung around to see what was happening, just in time to see the entryway they had just passed through seal before them.

'Oh well, we won't be going back out there then,' laughed Elk nervously.

'Why would we want to anyway with those wolves out there,' Kadence added.

'Let's just keep moving,' said Delph.

They turned back around and made their way further into the forest, Delph went first so he could lop away any vines and thorns that hung and congregated, making it easy to pass through.

This went well until the newly hacked vines came back thicker than they were before, they stopped when they could no longer go on with the carriage.*

Delph continued to hack and slash at the branches and vines, most of them broke easy, some, however, required brute strength. 'This is going to take forever,' moaned Delph.

* The thicket became too... thick.

'Do we really need to push through? Should we try going back and find an alternative route? Maybe we could try to head along and around the forest?' Kadence asked.

'There's no way we can head back through the way we came, have you forgotten about the struggle we had getting this far and even if we manage to hack our way back through, what about those wolves at the entrance, surely they would be waiting for us,' Delph replied.

'We have to keep pushing on, unfortunately. My arms and hands are sore from those thorns,' added Elk.

'Mines are as well, look' Delph showed his damaged hands to the others.

Elk helped Delph with the more manageable branches, shooting them and being careful not to have his bullets ricochet and hit one of the group.

'There is no way we can continue to cut through enough branches to squeeze the carriage through. It will take us long enough to fit ourselves and Brightbane through,' said Delph.

'Delph's right. If we are to make any sort of progress through the forest and its horrific branches, we're going to have to ditch the carriage,' groaned Rhoadan.

'It feels wrong just to leave it here to rot after it's gotten us this far,' said Kadence.

'I know, I've had it for so long now, it's served me well over the years, it's past its best now anyway,' Rhoadan replied.

'Hopefully, we won't have far to go. We can replace everything once we get to Dirtbere and we can buy a whole lot more,' said Rhoadan.

'Elk and I will continue making our way through these branches and could you and Kadence unload what we need and try to somehow attach it to Brightbane. Remember just to take the essentials as we won't need everything,' said Delph.

Kadence and Rhoadan took the essentials out of the carriage while Elk and Delph continued clearing a suitable walkway.

Rhoadan put Brightbane's saddle on her.

She didn't like it and felt trapped with it on. He detached her from the carriage.

'We're going to have to leave most of our things behind,' sighed Kadence.

Kadence jumped up into the carriage and started searching through the bags, she made sure she got her prophesy supplies, of course, she handed the bag down to Rhoadan.

'Is there anything in particular you need?' Kadence asked Rhoadan.

'All I want is gems and that crick jar,' replied Rhoadan.

Kadence found the gems, she separated the larger bag and filled one of the other backpacks with gems, she found the crick jar and handed them to Rhoadan.

'That's not all the gems. I had to split them and put them into that backpack to make it easier to carry and lighten the weight for Brightbane,' Kadence explained.

'Great idea, we can always come back again another time, if we need to,' said Rhoadan.

Rhoadan checked that the crick was fine, luckily he'd put air holes in the lid earlier or the crick wouldn't be alive, he put the jar into the backpack and placed it on his back.

'Is there anything you two need?' Kadence yelled over to Elk and Delph.

'No, I have all I need on me,' replied Elk.

'Nothing in particular for me,' Delph replied.

'Right' replied Kadence.

'That's me got everything,' Kadence told Rhoadan.

'Right lass, you go on ahead, I've still got some stuff to fasten on Brightbane's saddle, I'll catch up.' replied Rhoadan.

Kadence handed Rhoadan her prophesy bag and left him to finish what he was doing.

She followed the path that Delph and Elk had cleared, although every few steps, there was either a big vine to climb under or climb over and after what felt like an assault course she finally caught up to them.

Delph and Elk were that busy hacking through branches and vines that they failed to notice that she was even there.

'I thought you were clearing a way through?' Kadence asked.

'We were. I mean we are,' said Delph.

'What does it look like we're doing, why don't you help us rather than criticising,' Elk snidely suggested.

'That's not why I'm asking,' replied Kadence, screwing up her face at Elk.

'Well if that isn't the reason, then why are you asking?' Delph asked.

'On my way to you, I basically had to fight my way through the vines and branches, they looked like they had always been there,' Kadence explained.

'That doesn't sound right at all' said Delph, scratching his head.

'Look behind you. We've just cleared them and now they're back,' Elk said.

Vines had sealed them into a makeshift prison. Delph hacked at them again, but to no prevail.

'They're just coming back, thicker than before. What is going on?' Kadence yelled.

THUD.

They were thrown on their backs.

'RHOADAN... RHOAD... HELP... HEL—' Kadence screamed, her final word was silenced before she could finish it. The thick foliage dulled her scream.

Their arms were bound tightly around their bodies, they couldn't move no matter how hard they tried.

They were being pulled further into the forest, the last thing they saw was a mass of green hurtling towards their faces, then... there was only darkness.

Rhoadan thought he could hear scuffling, he stopped to listen.

'Come on girl, let's get moving then' he said to her, as they followed the path that mysteriously appeared in front of them.

Rhoadan and Brightbane had been walking for a short time before Rhoadan wondered why he hadn't caught up with the others yet, he found it strange at how clear the path was.

'Delph, Elk, Kadence,' he yelled then waited for a response.

'Guys, where are you?' he yelled.

'Well that's weird,' he told Brightbane.

Brightbane halted, she shook her head, she didn't want to go on.

'Come on girl, we need to find the guys, we need to keep going' Rhoadan gave her a gentle reassuring pat on her side, they continued to walk on.

It wasn't long before Rhoadan saw something lying down on the ground, they walked over to it and stopped, it was Kadence's bow.

'What is happening? First, there's no sign of them and now, I find Kadence's bow lying on the ground,' Rhoadan said out loud.

Branches and vines rapidly parted over on Rhoadan's right.

Rhoadan picked up her bow, and he secured it on Brightbane's harness for safekeeping, they continued walking until he found Elk's gun and Delph's sword, he scrunched up his face and bent down to pick them both up, also securing them on Brightbane's harness.

A walkway appeared in front of them, he warily peered down it. He wasn't keen on just heading straight in without checking it out first. He could have sworn he saw a dark blur running past right at the far end of the walkway, although giving the current conditions, he couldn't be one hundred percent certain.

Rhoadan searched for another way through the thick foliage, almost feeling around for some sort of switch or lever that would open a different way for them to pass through.

He quickly looked on the ground around his feet just in case he had unknowingly stood on something that opened the walkway a few minutes ago, his search proved futile.

He decided his safest option was going to be safety, he walked over to Brightbane and lifted Brother down and gave Brightbane a loving rub on her neck.

'Come on girl, I want to go down there as much as you, it's the only way we can go, we can't go back I'm afraid we must go on, we have to find the others,' he said. Brightbane wasn't keen on this idea, she nuzzled into Rhoadan for comfort.

Unknown to Rhoadan and Brightbane, the forest had been slowly creeping up on them, a wall of vines was gradually advancing on them, they were first alerted to the wall when Brightbane's tail unintentionally swished and brushed up against it giving Brightbane a fright. She threw her front legs up and out into the air recklessly, almost smashing into the back of Rhoadan's head.

Rhoadan turned around to see what the commotion was although what he saw was blurred and he couldn't make it out. Brightbane's hooves narrowly flew by his head, Rhoadan could feel the air whoosh past his face.

He was just glad it was only the air that he felt passing his face and not Brightbane's hooves.

'Woah girl, calm yourself down!' Rhoadan yelled. Brightbane snorted.

'Come on girl, let's get moving,' said Rhoadan.

With every step they took, they heard the forest press on behind them in sync with each step they took, the quicker the step meant the faster the wall of vines moved, Rhoadan stopped and in turn, the wall of vines stopped.

A strange feeling rushed over them, it almost felt like a gust of wind brushing over their skin and right through their body, a static rustling sound rung in their ears, Brightbane became unnerved, Rhoadan shuddered. The new sensation lasted for only a split second, but it was enough to make Rhoadan nervous.

'What in the name of Eshia was that?' Rhoadan wondered.

Rhoadan was sure he saw a little body laying on the ground, the pulse of energy he and Brightbane just experienced had knocked the little being on its back. It picked itself up off the forest ground, it quickly glanced at Rhoadan, but it didn't stick around long enough for him to get a decent look at it.

One thing Rhoadan noticed was the sound the creature made as it darted away he tightened his grip on Brother.

The pulse caused the sinuous wall behind them to start twisting and meandering its wild vines. Some of the vines struck out in many directions. Rhoadan turned around to see the great wall of vines vibrating magnificently only a few feet behind them.

'This isn't good Brightbane, not good at all,' he groaned.

He climbed up onto Brightbane's back quickly, but conscientiously making sure not to harm her with Brother. Brightbane grunted as his bulky, broad frame pushed down on her.

He had only just sat his full weight down on Brightbane's back when the writhing wall behind them shook vigorously.

'MOVE!' he yelled. Brightbane didn't hang around, she was off like a shot.

'Follow that creature girl,' he roared.

Brightbane bustled after it like lightning as the mass of unruly weeds thundered after them. Brightbane sprinted as fast as she could with Rhoadan on her back, there was no way they were willing to let the pursuing barrier catch up to them only to have it then trample over them, that would without a shadow of a doubt be an end to them both.

'Can you see it girl? Can you see where it went?' Rhoadan yelled.

Brightbane was quick enough to dodge under the many branches that were striking out in all directions.

The creeping vines were close to smashing into Rhoadan, and it required all of his strength just to stay on Brightbane's back.

Luckily for Rhoadan he still had Brother in his free hand, so he could strike any vines that came close, he even managed to cut a few back, some of the other vines retreated each time he did.

'This place is crazy' thought Rhoadan. He gripped on tightly as they navigated through the dangerous and ever-changing forest.

Without warning, another pulse of light surged through the forest and everything in it. The pulse shot through Rhoadan, so much so that he almost rolled off the back of Brightbane, she quivered and almost came to a halt. After they regained their senses, Rhoadan checked behind him and even with the high speed that Brightbane ran, it seemed to have had little impact on the speed that the wall of vines followed. Rhoadan caught sight of the creature again. He tugged on Brightbane's reins and pointed it out to her.

'Over there girl,' he yelled.

'WAIT' Rhoadan yelled to the creature. The creature ignored them and continued running. It ran to the left around an old decaying tree, Rhoadan and Brightbane followed it around to the left, dodging under the tree's distorted branches. Whichever way the creature ran, Rhoadan and Brightbane were close behind it.

A further surge boomed through them, this time it revealed a new blockade of vines in front of them, although this one stood still, even though it was still way ahead in front of them, Rhoadan knew it would still be a problem sooner rather than later.

Spiked vines continued lashing out from every direction, some even tried to lasso Rhoadan right off Brightbane's back, although they dodged every one. The forest was becoming a gauntlet for them, with all the ducking and diving they were having to do. A Barbed vine struck out at Brightbane, she didn't see it and she lost her footing whilst trying to jump over a second one that has appeared. Rhoadan was thrown a few feet in front. He skidded across the ground, scattering broken twigs and soggy leaves everywhere.

The creature stopped at the motionless wall and silently watched Rhoadan and Brightbane, it tried to camouflage itself against the vines, it was as still as the wall it stood in front of. It remained calm until the massive, bulky frame that was Rhoadan started barrel rolling towards the little creature, swiftly followed by Brightbane hurtling in a non-controllable undignified manner, sending their belongings everywhere.

An almighty pulse vibrated through them, this particular one was more powerful than the last, it destroyed most of the thrashing vines that were bombarding them all.

When the little guy saw that Rhoadan and Brightbane had finally stopped rolling towards it and realised that it had nowhere to go, panic-stricken, it tried climbing up the wall, but to no avail, kept slipping back down again, so it just crouched down and cowered in the corner.

The last pulse slowed down the wall of vines significantly and it was thankfully no longer following them at a hefty speed. It was, however, still pursuing.

Brightbane clambered up onto her hooves, Rhoadan got up and dusted himself down, he checked to see where the wall was and when he realised it wasn't coming as fast; he checked to see that Brightbane was okay, and quickly picked up as much of the belongings that he could, making sure he picked up Kadence's prophesy bag.

He secured them back on Brightbane's harness and he turned his attention to the cowering creature.

'Will you help us? We need a way out of here and we need it quick. We've been stuck in here for longer than I would care to imagine and we desperately need to find our friends,' Rhoadan pleaded.

The silent fellow glared at Rhoadan without saying anything at all.

'My name is Rhoadan' he said referring to himself and then pointed to Brightbane as he said her name.

'We will not harm you' Rhoadan added while holding out his other hand.

The creature reluctantly held out his hand and took hold of Rhoadan's hand, he looked at Rhoadan and said, 'Yak' pointing to himself whilst wearily looking up at them both, they were gigantic compared to him. His eyes lingered on Brightbane.

'How do we get out of here?' asked Rhoadan.

Yak pointed back to the wall that was right behind him.

'We need to get out of here or we will soon be squashed into these walls. That way is sealed, look,' Rhoadan yelled, pointing towards the wall.

Yak cringed at Rhoadan's raised voice.

'Sho Sho' Yak sheepishly said.

Rhoadan couldn't understand what it meant.

There was a massive wall of vines in front of them and behind them. Rhoadan looked along the length of the one in front of him, searching for a break that they could escape through, but each wall looked as though they went on forever, so they couldn't even get around it, there was physically nowhere they could go.

The wall still proceeded towards them. They backed into the motionless wall that towered behind them. Rhoadan decided he would not die like this.

He let go of the Yak's little hand, grabbed both Brother and Sister hatchet from Brightbane's harness and hacked at the oncoming wall, it seemed that it was a little too late.

Unfortunately, Rhoadan couldn't even make a dent in the wall, any time he that hacked a vine or branch it just grew another one back in its place. Just as the wall was mere seconds away from squashing the life out of them, the most powerful surge soared through them, knocking them all on their backs, smashing the two walls into smithereens in the process.

There were massive vines, branches and thorns flying everywhere and a surprising amount of dust and liquid from the explosion, spraying sticky dew everywhere.

The three of them lay there startled not knowing exactly had happened. They waited until the ringing in their ears subsided before they tried to get up. They all groaned as they struggled to get up.

Rhoadan had to crouch on his knees and use Brightbane to help pull him up and then he helped Yak up to his feet. They surveyed the immediate devastation that surrounded them, not saying anything at all for a few moments.

'Sho Sho' Yak excitedly said, whilst pointing to the clearing that appeared in front of them.

Rhoadan turned around, still unsure of what "sho sho" actually meant.

His jaw dropped when he saw what it was that Yak was referring to. He stood there dumbfounded and in disbelief, he shuddered as every hair on his body stood on edge and what he saw would stay in his mind for a long time to come.

Chapter Seven

-Tribe Amora-

Rhoadan was astounded, he remained still, his eyes were wide open and his mouth was even wider. He couldn't tell if his eyes were deceiving him or not.

'Could it really be?' he thought, turning his head to the side.

Delph, Kadence and Elk were in front of him, hanging upside down. Vines had wrapped right around them, Rhoadan envisioned a snake that was crushing its prey before devouring it.

The vines coiled all the way from their ankles and spiralled right up to their shoulders, constricting every movement.

'Guys, are you okay?' yelled Rhoadan. They didn't respond, vocally or physically.

'Sho sho' yelled Yak. He jumped up and down on the spot excitedly.

Rhoadan was on the higher ground, so he climbed down into the clearing and walked over to the others, he warned Brightbane to stay back.

He couldn't see any movement as he approached them, he was unsure if they were dead or alive at this point.

'Elk, what is going on?' Rhoadan reached out and prodded him, it didn't result in any change, he still didn't receive an answer.

'What are you doing Delph? Are you okay Kadence?' Rhoadan asked.

Rhoadan looked up at them as they hung there motionless, he followed the vines with his eyes up to the branch they were hung from, he pointed up to the branch and Yak ran over to the great tree and began to climb it.

'I'm sick of these blooming vines. They've caused me nothing, but bother since we came into this forsaken forest,' muttered Rhoadan.

Yak climbed up to the sturdy branch and edged his way along until he came to the vines that were curled up and supporting the others.

He pulled his knife out from his little belt, and began cutting into the vine; hoping it would help free them.

As Yak sat there slicing back and forth through the rugged vine, he came across a knot that was proving to be tougher than the rest of the vine, rather than holding on with one hand and sawing with the other, like he had been before.

He positioned his legs around the branch he was sitting on and used both hands to go at the knot, this procedure was going okay at first until he nearly rolled right of it backwards, he was able to steady himself just in time.

Black mist rose from the base of the tree that Elk, Kadence and Delph hung from. It circled up around the tree and along the branch and flowed right down to Kadence, Elk and Delph and then circled them.

It swirled up around Rhoadan, Brightbane and Yak, they shuddered as they were shrouded in an eerie chill. Rhoadan backed up trying to get away from the smoke, there was no point, it just wisped around him even more, he stood still and watch on with confusion, not knowing what to do. Yak caught his eye. Yak tried waving the surrounding smoke away, he nearly fell off the branch again, but he caught hold of it just in time.

Rhoadan heard branches snapping in a bush close to where he and Brightbane stood. He looked up at Yak, who also heard the noise. He unhooked Brother and Sister and crept over to the bush to investigate.

Rather than face the consequences of being attacked first, without any hesitation, he threw Brother into the bush.

The bush shuddered and shook violently. He heard squealing and grunting. A tri-tusk hog* ran out of the bush.

Rhoadan backed up a little, he wasn't exactly sure what it would do or indeed what it was capable of. He held his hands out in front of him, still gripping Sister.

* A tri-tusk is bigger than a normal hog. They have three tusks, two at either side of its snout and another just at the tip which points away from its body. The colour of that tusk usually indicates if it's ready to attack, red will warn you to get out the way, blue generally means you're safe, although they have been known to be unpredictable at times. The male's fur is usually black and white with a blue stripe, and the females have a red stripe, this one was a male and his horn was red, therefore he was enraged and had his sight set on Rhoadan.

The tri-tusk charged at Rhoadan, Brightbane didn't like this, she charged towards the rampaging hog and butted it on its side with her head, Brightbane used a lot more force than was required, she didn't like anything attacking Rhoadan and she punted the hog, sending it hurtling into a tree, once it had composed itself, it got up and changed its focus to Brightbane.

It snorted and flared its nostrils. Rhoadan threw Sister at the hog, his aim was perfect and Sister struck the hog's head, it dropped to the ground; it was all over so fast. Yak watched on in horror from up in the branch. The dark hazy mist swooped on the hog and engulfed it.

Rhoadan couldn't concentrate because of the continual droning that came from the mist as it flocked around the dead hog, Rhoadan and Brightbane quickly backed away and watched from a distance as the mist rapidly revolved around it. When the mist eventually disappeared all that remained was Sister laying on the ground, the tri-tusk had vanished. The mist had devoured it.

Rhoadan walked over and picked Sister up, she was bitter cold; he got a fright, he hadn't expected her to be cold; he dropped her on the flattened grass.

'I think I'll just let her sort her temperature out, that was pretty sore,' he said nursing his ice-cold hand.

'Why did that just happen?' Rhoadan asked out loud, looking at Yak for an answer.

Yak looked down at Rhoadan and shrugged his shoulders, with a blank expression spread across his face, it wasn't the first time that Yak had seen the black mist, he knew it was trouble. Since Rhoadan didn't get a response from Yak, he knelt down and cautiously picked Sister up.

Sister wasn't as icy as before, she was, however, still cold, Rhoadan still didn't know what had happened, he understood that it was the mist of course, the evidence of that was astounding.

He heard rustling coming from a distance and by the commotion, it was making, Rhoadan thought it must have been big, it could have been a pack of angry tri-tusks for all he knew, he rather hoped that it wasn't though.

He found a suitable hiding spot for Brightbane and him, Brightbane, however, was reluctant to go into hiding, she kept stamping her hooves in frustration and it took most of Rhoadan's strength to get her in.

Yak cautiously ran along towards the main trunk of the tree and climbed up into the leaves so he remained out of sight and they both waited anxiously to find out what it was that was heading in their direction.

Rhoadan grew nervous. He was sick of the drama and fighting he had endured since leaving Bramwich. He was ready for an easy life, he just wanted to get out of the forest. Whatever was making the noise was surely taking its time. It seemed like forever before it revealed itself. Brightbane was just as nervous as Rhoadan, she showed it more than he did.

'Keep yourself calm lass, I hope whatever it is that's making that noise will just pass through and won't come anywhere near us' whispered Rhoadan as he petted Brightbane lovingly, trying to settle her.

They could hear it was getting closer, and saw some smaller trees move, as though they were parting to let whatever it was through, and the closer it got, the more noise it made. They noticed that the mist had started stirring again, it had stopped when the tri-tusk vanished, which they were thankful for, but it was now swirling violently.

The mist clouded their view, Rhoadan tried blowing it away, but it just came back, he tried waving it away again, this was no use at all, it kept coming back.

The brute was close to them, its snarling growls gave it away, they knew roughly which area it stood because of the noise it was making. Brightbane couldn't take the suspense any longer, she stood up, giving away their hiding spot.

'Dammit girl, I asked you to wait.' growled Rhoadan.

The mist evaporated into thin air, revealing the wretched horror that was making all the noise.

Something behind them rustled, Rhoadan saw two little hands touching Brightbane.

They were only there for a few seconds before they vanished. Brightbane bolted out of the bushes and headed straight towards the beast. It watched Brightbane and tried to grab her tail when she got close to it.

Its aim was off and fortunately for Brightbane, it missed her and was now facing away from Rhoadan; she circled around it and bolted off into the forest without a trace.

Rhoadan gasped unintentionally; choking on his own breath.

The monster slowly spun around until it was fully facing Rhoadan, it creaked with every movement; it fixed its eyes on him.

They both remained still, just staring at each other, the monster's swamp ridden hair looked as if it was vegetation, the type you would expect to be hanging from a willow tree, it draped over its half rotten face, holes situated where its cheeks once were, displaying intimidating jagged wooden teeth, or what was left of them.

The fiend was hunched over, it was made from wood; but not your normal strong type of wood, this wood was the type of wood that had been laying water for a long time, it was bloated and rotten, the disgusting smell that secreted from it invaded Rhoadan's nostrils.

The waterlogged beast's eyes lingered on Rhoadan, trying to stare him down. Neither he nor the tree freak was showing any signs of backing down, Rhoadan tightened his grip on both Brother and Sister.

It curled its thick hands. Black balls of mist encased them. Rhoadan heard a faint whine, he recognised it. It was the same grunt the tri-tusk made.

'That thing must have somehow consumed that tri-tusk, well I ain't gonna let it do that to me,' he thought, as he launched Brother at the attacker.

The foul beast was as fast as Rhoadan was and it fired one of the black mist balls at him, encasing Brother. It showed Rhoadan that it could control things with its mist. It raised its arm up and the black ball of mist also raised.

The monster sent Brother soaring into the tree that Elk, Kadence and Delph hung from. Rhoadan gripped Sister and threw her at the monster with extra force this time.

The fiend didn't like it and it repeated what it had just done with Brother and threw Sister into the same tree.

Rhoadan panicked, he had nothing left, Brother and Sister were implanted into the tree, he didn't know whether his friends were dead or alive and his sacred Brightbane had decided she would rather be anywhere except here.

He didn't know what he would do next, then he remembered that Yak was still hiding up in the tree. The creature focussed on Elk, Kadence and Delph. Rhoadan knew that he alone was no match for it.

It hobbled over and sniffed the surrounding air when it detected their scent, it raised its arms up and screeched with delight at finding its prey.

The tree thug lifted its hands up towards Elk, Kadence and Delph. It moved the vines that constrained the guys; swinging them from left to right. The creature glanced again at Rhoadan with a creepy, crooked grin.

It hadn't noticed that the momentum of the swings had caused another pulse; which came from Kadence and it caught the monster unaware sending it stumbling backwards, wiping its crooked grin from its face in the process.

Rhoadan saw the pulse emit from Kadence. It gave him hope that she was alive and indeed still with him in his uneven fight.

Yak watched on from a safe distance up in the tree and decided it was time to make his move. He jumped down from the tree with his knife held high above his head. He landed on top of the monster and fought his way through the beast's rotten withering willow hair, slicing and slashing as he went, he was fast and nimble and the monster couldn't grab him.

Yak made his way down to its decaying shoulders and flipped himself backwards and stabbed the monster in the face, his knife went right into its head, it screeched with pain.

It grabbed Yak and threw him to the ground; he landed with a thud, a few feet in front, knocking the breath from his lungs, he lay there coughing.

While the monster was preoccupied with Yak, Rhoadan ran behind the monster, he knew he had to be quick; he reached down and took the crick jar, out of the gem bag.

'Look at me,' roared Rhoadan.

The fiend turned around, Rhoadan was ready with the jar, he threw it as hard as he could at the monster.

The jar exploded on the monster's chest, it lost its balance and stumbled backwards again waving one of its arms about uncontrollably.

The other arm flailed by its side, there was crick ink everywhere, some ink even splattered on Elk, that was definitely karma because he laughed so hard at Rhoadan receiving the same inky fate earlier.

As the creature was pre-occupied trying to wipe the ink from its face, Rhoadan grabbed Sister and pulled her out of the tree, he was surprised that she came out without too much bother, he threw Sister without any hesitation or aim and it landed perfectly in one of the beasts decrepit shoulders and shattered it.

The beast's shoulder broke away, and it took the rest of his arm with it, the monster howled in agony and spun around to face Rhoadan.

Rhoadan reached over to Brother and struggled as he tried to pull his hatchet from the tree. The monster charged at Rhoadan and grabbed him with its remaining arm; squeezing him tight.

Rhoadan struggled to catch his breath as the creature clutched him with a vice-like grip. It lifted him up until he was level with its own face, it roared, the sound hurt Yak's little ears and the smell offended Rhoadan's big nose, it was putrid.

The beast turned around and threw Rhoadan over towards Yak. Yak was lucky Rhoadan hadn't landed on him as the little guy would have been crushed.

The monster cherished the thought that it was on the verge of killing them both at the same time. The beast hobbled over to them writhing as it went; it growled with pain and it clutched its shoulder.*

It roared at them again, raining spit and bits of broken, sodden wood and the odd worm that had been lurking in its saturated insides. It raised its remaining arm once more and curled its clawed hand up into a fist.

It forced itself down towards Rhoadan and stopped just in front of his face; it leaned back to where it was before, quickly rushing down to Rhoadan, each time covering them both in festering saliva again.

* Or rather, more like where its shoulder used to be.

It unwillingly repeated this a few times although almost as if it did it in a stop and start strobing motion. Rhoadan and Yak looked at each other, both equally unsure of what was happening.

'It's twisting and turning in ways it shouldn't be able to twist and turn. What is it doing?' Rhoadan said out loud. He thought it looked like a defective machine, the crunching sounds that came from the creature's joints made Rhoadan and Yak cringe.

The monster screamed again and lifted its foot up to stomp on them, it put its foot back on the ground and lifted it right back up, then down again and up again, something clearly wasn't right.

'It could be a death ritual or it could physically be failing,' thought Rhoadan. He and Yak backed off.

The monster bent back over. It held its remaining arm up in the air behind it. Its wooden crooked fingers were writhing back and forth. It watched them, its mouth was open wide, this time nothing fell out. Small puffs of dark mist excreted from the gaping hole where it's shoulder once was.

The warped brute crunched its hulking hand into a fist and speedily brought it down towards Rhoadan and Yak, with its mouth still open to the world, ready to consume them.

Suddenly a huge metal sword protruded from its gaping mouth, stopping only inches from Rhoadan's face. The monster bellowed, and it's scream intensified into a blood curling hack, black sludge oozed down the full length of the sword and landed at Rhoadan and Yak's feet.

Its remaining arm went limp and dropped. It fell to its knees, revealing a welcoming sight beyond it.

A smiling face was the first thing that Rhoadan set his eyes on. The mysterious newcomer used his foot to pin the dead beast down to the ground as he extracted his sword from the back of its head.

The sword-wielding stranger then extended his hand out to Rhoadan.

Breathing a sigh of relief, Rhoadan stretched out his own hand to accept the help. Yak's eyes widened, and he smiled magnificently, he stood up ran straight over to the saviour and hugged him.

'Sho sho, sho!' Yak yelled with joy as he danced around the hero.

'Thank you' Rhoadan hesitated. 'Sho sho' he nervously added as he stood up, he ran his eyes over Yak then met the stranger's eyes.

'I'm Jinx-Amora and this is my tribe,' he said, stepping aside to let Rhoadan see the tribe.

'I'm glad we found you, we sent Eaki-Trin out to see what the bedlam was, we sensed there was trouble, so we decided we would come and see for ourselves what it was that caused the disturbance,' Jinx-Amora explained.

Rhoadan introduced himself to Jinx-Amora.

'I'm so glad you arrived when you did Jinx-Amora, or else I wouldn't be standing here in front of you now,' Rhoadan said thankfully.

'Just call me Jinx,' he said.

Rhoadan nodded and Jinx smiled. Rhoadan smiled back as he watched the tribe momentarily.

There were lots of little beings, all similar to Yak and indeed Jinx, except the difference between them was that Yak a bit taller, his markings were bolder and prominent and he had a tail.

Jinx was taller than the rest, he also had a pointed tail and two little horns that stuck out from just above his eyes. The most distinct difference with Jinx was that he could speak.

'Can you help me with something else?' Rhoadan coyly asked.

'If I can, then I will,' replied Jinx.

'My friends are over there. They're trapped in that tree, is there anything you can do to get them down?' Rhoadan asked; as he pointed over to Kadence, Elk and Delph.

'My tribe will get them down safely, don't worry about it, we will take them home and make sure they are safe, we have many spells that will do the trick, I'm sure,' Jinx reassured Rhoadan.

'Tribe' Jinx yelled, raising his right hand up into the air.

Rhoadan thanked Jinx again. The tribe stopped what they were doing and each of them turned to face their leader.

'Tribe, I ask you to help get our new friends down from this horrible trap tree and then take them home,' Jinx commanded.

'I would also like some of you to scout the surrounding area to make sure there are no more of those blasted Rootsmogs lurking about' Jinx ordered some of his tribe. The tribe did as they were asked. They made progress to get Elk, Kadence and Delph down, a few of the others scouted the area to make sure they weren't going to be ambushed by another Rootsmog.

'Would you mind answering something else Jinx?' Rhoadan queried.

'Carry on' replied Jinx.

'Why do you speak and Yak doesn't?' Rhoadan asked. 'Come to think of it, I haven't heard any of the rest of your tribe talking either, I know it's only been a short while that you have all been here, but for the vast amount of them, I would have thought there would have been some nattering,' he added.

'It's only the members of heritage that can express vocal ability,' replied Jinx.

'Heritage? What do you mean?' Rhoadan asked.

'We have a heritage structure in our tribe, a pecking order if you will. Within our structure we have four levels, we have our king, one guardian, one scout and the other level are the rest of the tribe, the only ones that can talk in fluent languages are the king and the guardian, the scout is able to speak a little, but is limited,' Jinx replied.

'Where do you and Yak fit into this class of society?' Rhoadan asked.

'I'm the guardian of the tribe and Yak is our scout,' Jinx explained.

'That explains why "sho sho" is all I've heard Yak say,' said Rhoadan.

'Ah yes, sho sho, that means friend,' explained Jinx.

'How does the rest of your tribe communicate?' Rhoadan asked.

'Watch them for a moment and listen,' replied Jinx.

Rhoadan observed the tribe members as they helped to get his friends down, he was momentarily fascinated by the clicking and grunting noises they made, it reminded him of a group of monquats.

'Yak is in training to become our guardian, he will replace me,' explained Jinx.

'What will become of you?' Rhoadan asked.

'I will become the king to the throne,' replied Jinx.

'What will become of your king?' Rhoadan asked.

'It pains me to tell you this, sadly our king is not long for this world. He is ill and there is unfortunately very little we can do to save him,' replied Jinx.

'What's wrong with him?' Rhoadan asked.

'That is a tale for another time, we must focus on getting your friends down and back to my home if we are to save them,' explained Jinx, becoming agitated.

'Set the horror alight.' Jinx slyly ordered his tribe.

'Why are they setting it on fire?' Rhoadan asked.

'In our culture, we believe that every living thing has a soul, once that living being has passed on, we honour its death by setting it on fire, regardless of whether it was good or bad in its living years, we set its soul free, that way it's returned to our lifestream and it returns to the ground and enriches our forest,' Jinx replied.

'That's a nice way to think about it, even though it tried to kill us.' Rhoadan replied with a slight bit of anger still breaching the surface.

'As you can see, your friends are down safely now. You can come back to my home if you're ready to leave, we will get your friend's home and make them better,' said Jinx.

'I appreciate your offer, however, there is something I must take care of here first,' replied Rhoadan.

'Very well, we will push on. Eaki-Trin, you stay with Rhoadan and help him with his task and then show him the way to our home,' replied Jinx.

'Sho sho' Yak giggled as he beat on his chest and roared. Jinx ordered the tribe to bring out their carriage, they did as he asked.

The faithful tribe came back with their towering golden carriage, every part was golden, from its huge wheels to the roof supports. It also had glass windows all the way around it with one big double door. Rhoadan was in awe of the carriage, wishing his abandoned carriage was something like this one.

Two massive, beautiful deer pulled the carriage, both were pure white from their hooves to their tail, they had glowing purple eyes and magnificent golden antlers, the antlers had a golden hue illuminating from them, and wisps of what can only be described as a glitter effect spiralled from them. Thin willow leaves drooped down from their antler tines.

A red light shone out from the tip of each of their antlers. Both deer were silent as they walked over to Jinx, without making a sound on the forest ground below, it was as if they glided, although their legs moved with a walking motion.

Jinx raised his hand up to them and they stopped just short of it, both calmly lowering their heads.

The tribe got Kadence, Elk and Delph into the carriage and they managed it with finesse and ease. They worked to ensure they took care when they placed the guys into the carriage. They were guests of the forest after all.

Jinx introduced his deer to Rhoadan. Mala and Mika allowed Rhoadan to pet them. He rubbed them behind their ears.

'Come closer,' commanded Jinx.

'This is Mala and Mika. They go everywhere with me, I adore them. One day I found them wandering together through the forest when they were just little fawns, there wasn't any sign of an elder deer to care for them so I took them into my care.' Jinx explained.

'I have a horse, her name is Brightbane. She's white, her mane and tail both glow red. She bolted just as that wretched creep stumbled upon us. I have to find her, we've been together since she was a little foal, I need to find her soon,' explained Rhoadan.

'I'm sure she will be fine,' Jinx replied reassuringly.

'I hope so,' said Rhoadan.

'Is that what your task is?' Jinx asked.

'Yes, it is,' replied Rhoadan.

'We need to get to shelter before it's dark, we don't want to be out here when the night falls,' explained Jinx, as he looked around and shuddered.

'What happens at night?' Rhoadan asked.

'You don't want to find out, just don't stay out longer than you need to, just get yourself to our home before nightfall or you will wish that you had,' explained Jinx.

Rhoadan looked down at Yak, who met his gaze and nodded his head in agreement.

The tribe had finished securing Elk, Kadence and Delph into the carriage.

'We are ready, I wish you farewell and we will see you when you get back home. If you pass me your bags, we will take them with us that will lighten the load for you and Eaki-Trin,' Jinx said.

Rhoadan fetched Kadence's prophesy bag, he knew how important it was to her.

He passed the bag to one of the tribe members who loaded it onto Jinx's carriage, then he searched for the gems. He momentarily forgot where he had put them and there was no way that he wanted to leave them behind, they were important to him and they would secure his future in Dirtbere. Much to his amazement and happiness, he found the bag fairly quickly.

'I don't have a lot of bags left, but this one means a lot to me, would you take it for me, please?' Rhoadan asked. He handed the bag up to Jinx.

Jinx nodded and held his hands out.

'If you believe that it is of importance, then I do as well and I will take care of your bag for you and personally ensure that it's put away safe when we get back home,' replied Jinx.

'Thank you, I'd appreciate that,' Rhoadan quickly replied.

'I suggest you keep your weapons handy, as I said before, nightfall isn't far off and if you are unlucky enough to get caught by the night, then find a safe place to lay and follow on in the morning. Eaki-Trin knows every part of the forest so you will be safe with him,' explained Jinx.

'Oh aye, my weapons are staying by my side, keep an eye out for Brightbane on your travels please and can you take my friend's weapons please, they're no good to me,' Rhoadan pleaded.

'If we see her we will make sure she gets to safety, we bid you farewell,' Jinx assured Rhoadan.

Jinx and the tribe left the area and everything turned silent, Rhoadan and Yak's ears rung, it felt surreal. Rhoadan silently stood still watching the spot where Jinx and the tribe made their exit.

The silence chimed in Rhoadan's ears. He was quickly brought back to reality when he felt something tugging at his shirt. Rhoadan shook his head. Yak stared at Rhoadan wondering what he was doing.

'Right Yak, we best be off. Let's have one last check around and make sure we haven't forgotten to lift anything, then we can get going and search for Brightbane,' said Rhoadan.

Rhoadan looked around for any spare bags, Yak followed closely behind him.

Rhoadan could feel himself clipping something with his heels every time he moved his feet to step forward. He looked around and saw Yak behind him.

'Yak, why don't you look over there and I'll check over here, you don't need to follow me as closely,' laughed Rhoadan.

Yak did just that and when Rhoadan was satisfied that everything had been picked up they walked through the opening that Jinx and the tribe left through.

The carriage was so heavy that it left tracks on the soft ground, so all Rhoadan had to do was follow them, he knew he would get to Jinx's home in doing that if he and Yak became separated, this provided some comfort to him.

Rhoadan soon discovered that Yak was an excitable little being, he kept having to remind Yak to slow down as he zipped around the forest, sometimes up into the trees and out of sight, often coming back and bumping into Rhoadan as he went.

It was Yak's way of searching for Brightbane, even though Rhoadan found his style a little manic.

Yak imagined that he would get a better view from all directions and it meant that Rhoadan could stay on the path and that way he wouldn't have to stray far and end up getting lost, Yak preferred to focus on searching for Brightbane, without having to look for a wandering Rhoadan too.

They kept on walking, it felt like they had been walking forever, Rhoadan wanted to slow down, but Yak kept pushing on.

'BRIGHTBANE' Rhoadan bellowed.

Silence followed.

Rhoadan watched Yak as he rushed about, he was amazed by Yak's stamina.

'BRIGHTBANE,' Rhoadan yelled again.

Yak was up on one of the sturdier tree branches above, he had paused for a moment and stood poker straight, he held one hand high and yelled, 'Sho sho.'

Rhoadan looked at Yak, with hope in his eyes, he ran on till he reached the tree.

'What is it Yak?' Rhoadan asked.

'Sho sho,' Yak replied.

'What can you see?' Rhoadan asked.

'Sho sho,' Yak repeated, he pointed a little up into the distance.

Rhoadan, couldn't see anything because of the dense surroundings on the ground.

Rhoadan then heard a commotion in the distance. Yak climbed down from the tree and jumped up onto Rhoadan's shoulders.

'Right Yak, hold on tight.' Rhoadan yelled.

Rhoadan ran in the direction of the noise, hoping and praying that Brightbane wasn't in danger.

Chapter Eight

-Mossguard-

The screams quickly became silent forcing Rhoadan to slow down as he was using the sound for guidance and after a momentary lull the screaming started again.

Rhoadan and Yak continued following the noise, they had to jump over and duck under vines; it was like something wanted to slow them down on purpose and stop them from getting to where the commotion was, Rhoadan wasn't going to let anything stop him, it grew morbidly silent. They hurtled towards an opening.

Rhoadan suddenly stopped and sent poor Yak hurtling off his shoulders.

Yak picked himself up and shook himself down and grumbled something unintelligible. Just then an array of lights flashed before their eyes. The dwindling light illuminated them that bit more than it would have done before.

Rhoadan could make out that there was a massive cliff edge that curved over to his left and halfway around the curve was another rampaging Rootsmog.

'For the love of Eshia, there's another of those infernal beasts,' moaned Rhoadan.

Rhoadan and Yak were mesmerised with the array of purple and they were momentarily transported in their minds to a peaceful place, and everything going on around them was pushed to the back of their mind.

Life briefly stood still until an almighty pulse brought them hurtling back to reality. The silence ended, and the commotion began.

'That must be the guys down there, we need to get down there now,' yelled Rhoadan.

'Shosh,' yelled Yak, while he pounded on Rhoadan's head.

'Easy, calm down, that's sore,' yelled Rhoadan.

'Shosh,' Yak repeated.

Rhoadan ran down the rest of the hill, ignoring everything that went on around him. As he was nearing the bottom of the slope, he saw that the Rootsmog was much larger than the one they met earlier.

He stopped momentarily to catch his breath, Yak looked small, but he weighed a fair bit.

'My word, will you look at the face on that, it's even uglier than the last one was.' said Rhoadan,

'Now if I can just get down there and crack it over the back of its head, then it's not going to know anything about it,' said Rhoadan.

Yak nodded in agreement.

Rhoadan spotted a ramp at the bottom of the slope. He ran, and aimed for it: 'Right Yak get ready,' he roared.

The vile creature used its vine tentacles to whip the tribe. It wrapped its vines around some of the tribe and then it threw them over the edge of the cliff.

No matter how fast the tribe cut these vines down, the monster rapidly grew another in its place.

Rhoadan ran to the edge of the ramp and he leapt. As he made his descent, he roared to Yak that it was time.

'Now Yak!' screamed Rhoadan.

Yak leapt off Rhoadan's shoulders and ran down and met his tribe, he began rounding them them up to safety.

Rhoadan waited until he was right above the fiend before smashing his hatchets right into its head and then down through its body, it crumbled under the weight of Rhoadan's bulky frame, it made no sound as it fell and was dead before it hit the ground.

Rhoadan lay awkwardly among the mutilated and flattened Rootsmog.

Rhoadan groaned as he untangled himself from the mass of tree leaves and vines, he stood up and wiped himself down as best he could, he was covered in what can only be described as sodden, tree slime.

It was as sticky as the cricks ink he was covered in earlier, but it wiped off effortlessly, much to Rhoadan's pleasure.

The full tribe watched on in apprehension, they cheered and each of them hailed Rhoadan as their hero. Rhoadan was embarrassed, he was a proud soul and didn't know how to embrace gratitude towards himself. Jinx walked over to Rhoadan and thanked him.

'If it wasn't for your quick thinking and heroic embark, we could have lost many of our tribe,' said Jinx.

Jinx knelt down on one knee in front of Rhoadan. Yak followed and then the rest of the tribe did as Jinx and Yak were doing.

'The guys in the carriage once told me something and I'll always remember it. It's called the debt toll and mine has now been repaid,' said Rhoadan.

Jinx stood up and looked at Rhoadan. Yak and the rest of the tribe followed suit.

'The debt toll, what is that?' Jinx asked.

'The debt toll is something that we have, it means, if you save my life, I then repay the favour and save yours,' explained Rhoadan.

'What do you gain from this?' Jinx asked.

'What we gain is that the aura restores within Eshia's karma, realigning the balance between the light and the dark, the good and the bad, us and them, I think,' Rhoadan laughed nervously, pointing at the defeated tree monster.

'We need to set it on fire,' said Rhoadan; quickly changing the subject.

'Well-remembered Rhoadan,' said Jinx.

Rhoadan pulled his lighter out from his pocket and knelt down to set the fiend alight, it caught flame faster than the last one did and was immersed in flames before Rhoadan had even managed to stand up.

The flames almost engulfed Rhoadan's beard and face, he hadn't expected it to go up in flames as fast as it did.

'Woah' was all he could muster in his panicked haste to tap out his smouldering beard.

Luckily for him, his beard was a fair length or his face could have been burnt. Rhoadan stood there slapping his face like a madman with the smoke nipping his eyes.

The smell surrounding them was horrific, it was the mixture of Rhoadan's singed beard and the smell of the Rootsmog's corpse that lay smouldering before them.

'I won't be doing that again, that's the last time I set one of those foul beasts a flame, I nearly joined it in death,' groaned Rhoadan.

Jinx couldn't contain his laughter and a giggle escaped, the rest of the tribe joined in laughing, even Rhoadan had a little chuckle once he saw the funny side of it.

'I'm sorry, I lost myself for a moment' explained Jinx; hushing his tribe to stop.

'No problem. I'd probably have done the same if it happened to you,' laughed Rhoadan.

'I learned the hard way when I was younger in the same manner you did, I used to have longer hair, I keep it short for that very reason,' replied Jinx.

'Did you?' asked Rhoadan.

'Yes, so I can sympathise with you,' replied Jinx.

'I still remember when that happened,' laughed a familiar voice.

Rhoadan and Jinx turned around to face the speaker.

'Ahhh Ooseriz, my old friend,' Jinx replied.

Rhoadan and Jinx both held out their arms to hug Ooseriz.

Jinx and Rhoadan looked at each other.

'Do you two know each other?' Rhoadan asked.

'Yes, Ooseriz and I have known each other for years,' explained Jinx.

'Yes, have you heard of The Guardia—' asked Ooseriz.

Jinx nudged Ooseriz to stop her from revealing too much.

Rhoadan hadn't heard what Ooseriz said.

'How are my friends doing?' asked Rhoadan. He couldn't understand why Jinx had nudged Ooseriz.

'We stopped to allow me to summon a slumber enchantment; or a chant if you like, on them and we were attacked by that vile creature and when—' explained Jinx.

'What's a slumber enchantment?' Rhoadan interrupted Jinx.

'I was about to tell you,' Jinx sternly replied.

'Sorry, go on,' said Rhoadan.

Jinx sighed rudely, he wasn't used to being interrupted by anyone.

'So as I was saying, we briefly stopped before being attacked, a slumber chant is a spell that when it's cast on someone, it keeps them in slumber until the caster removes it and I will remove it when we get home,' explained Jinx.

'Why would you do that, wouldn't they have been better-off being awake?' Rhoadan asked.

'No, definitely not Rhoadan, there will be a good reason,' Ooseriz added.

'Well, the reason I performed the chant is because one of my tribe told me that your friends had started stirring and if I didn't do anything, then we could have run the risk of your friends being harmed, it would have been dangerous for them to awaken whilst we were on the road because of the extreme pressure to their heads due to them being held upside down for so long earlier,' explained Jinx.

'Well, thanks for doing that. I can't imagine that they would have been able to defend themselves from that monster in their current state,' said Rhoadan.

Jinx called for Mala and Mika to come over to him and in tow, they brought the carriage with a peacefully sleeping, Elk, Kadence and Delph.

Jinx's faithful deer were now by his side, Jinx climbed up onto Mala's back and called for them to be off, but before they did leave, Rhoadan had a quick peek in at his friends, just so he could see for himself that they were okay. He saw condensation on the glass from their breathing.

'We will be off, follow on,' Jinx said as he and the rest of the tribe left.

'Come on, let's go,' said Ooseriz.

'I'm going to follow on. I need to find Brightbane,' explained Rhoadan.

'Where has she gone?' Ooseriz asked.

'She bolted when we were attacked earlier by one of those horrific Rootsmogs,' Rhoadan replied.

'You follow Jinx and his tribe and I'll find Brightbane, I can easily do it in half the time you can,' Ooseriz said.

'Are you sure Ooseriz?' Rhoadan asked.

'Yes, of course. I wouldn't have suggested it if I wasn't,' replied Ooseriz.

Rhoadan turned and walked away, with Yak closely following him.

PFFT.

Rhoadan turned around to see what the noise was, just in time to see the final flick of Ooseriz's tail before it disappeared through the purple smoke from Ooseriz's port.

Yak was startled.

'I forgot she made that noise when she ported,' laughed Rhoadan.

Yak stared in silence; at the space where Ooseriz just was. It was the first time he had been this close to Ooseriz when she was porting.

'You'll get used to it Yak, don't worry my little friend, let's get moving.' Rhoadan said.

Yak shuddered, turned around and kept walking until he caught up with Rhoadan.

It didn't take long for them to catch up with Jinx and the others because the tribe's legs were so small, they couldn't travel very fast.

As Rhoadan and Yak approached the others, the closest tribe members spun around with their knives pointing upwards at Rhoadan. Every one of them flashed their teeth and fixated their eyes on Rhoadan and Yak.

In turn, each of the tribe members behind them mirrored what the line in front had just done. All of their eyes were illuminated.

'Woah guys it's us, lower your weapons, it's just us!' Rhoadan yelled as he backed off.

Rhoadan looked down at Yak, whose eyes were the same, he was holding his knife up towards the tribe, ready to protect Rhoadan. Yak jumped in front of Rhoadan. He was all the more determined to protect his friend than he was himself.

Rhoadan and Yak saw movement up towards the front of the tribe and it made a wave motion as it came towards them.

They could see that it was Jinx pushing through the tribe towards them. The tribe moved aside to let Jinx through.

'Stand down' commanded Jinx.

All except Yak stood down, their eyes returned to their original colour, they put their arms down to their sides and lowered their heads when they realised that it was just Rhoadan and Yak and not another Rootsmog. Yak remained vigilant and didn't stand down.

'I won't ask you again, Yak. Stand down!' Jinx scolded.

Yak looked up at Rhoadan, his eyes still glowing. Rhoadan didn't know what to do, he nervously nodded his head at him.

'Step down Yak' Rhoadan said awkwardly.

Yak did as he was asked. Rhoadan watched him, unsure of what had just happened. Yak glanced awkwardly at Jinx and back to Rhoadan. Everyone stood in silence.

'I'm confused, what just happened here?' Rhoadan asked.

'I can explain' Jinx replied.

'I would be grateful if you would because that was intense,' Rhoadan replied.

'After being set upon by that monster at the cliff's edge, I thought that would be the best time to cast the prepdef enchantment,' Jinx explained.

'Prepdef enchantment, what's that?' Rhoadan asked.

'The prepdef enchantment is one of my favourite chants, it's a spell that I can cast over my tribe, so they are prepared and ready to fight should even the smallest chance of an ambush happen, although I'm sorry that you had to experience that, it was definitely necessary,' explained Jinx.

'It's definitely a good idea, I would rather not be on the receiving end of it again if that's possible,' Rhoadan laughed nervously.

'Although, I'm confused as to why Yak didn't perform in the way I expected,' Jinx said.

'Yeah, I wonder why he did that. Why would he turn against his own people like that?' asked Rhoadan.

'He must now be under your command Rhoadan. It's the only explanation I can think of,' explained Jinx.

'Why now though?' Rhoadan asked.

Jinx and Rhoadan both looked down to Yak and Yak stared back at them both. The three of them all looked over at the rest of the tribe and scratched their heads.

'I reckon it's because you saved him earlier, back when you were attacked by that first Rootsmog. This is excellent news for you Rhoadan and at the same time, truly heartbreaking news for me, it means that Yak is no longer part of our tribe,' explained Jinx.

'No longer part of your tribe. What do you mean? Has he been cast out or something?' Rhoadan asked.

'It means that Yak is ready to follow you until his final day, or in fact your final day, whichever comes first, from here on in, you are Yak's tribe,' explained Jinx.

'My very own protector,' smiled Rhoadan. Yak looked up at Rhoadan and smiled.

'That sounds like slavery and I don't think I like that,' explained Rhoadan.

'It's not like slavery, nothing at all like it, you would be his main priority and he would protect you, I'm sure you would also protect him,' explained Jinx.

'Of course, I would. I'd make sure that no harm came to him, it's all very overwhelming, I can't quite believe it though,' Rhoadan replied.

Yak looked up at Rhoadan and smiled.

'It is in our genetic build, if we are lucky enough and manage to evolve into the next step of the tribe, like Yak and I have done, then we can go on to greater things, it sounds harsh to say, but only the gifted ones can achieve it and believe me when I say this, it doesn't happen often,' explained Jinx.

Jinx nodded his head at Rhoadan, who also replied by nodding his head.

'Tribe, gather some wood and then light us some torches, the night has approached, we will need to be able to see easily on our way back home as there are still some uneven paths which are close to the cliff's edge, much like the one we have just passed and we don't want to risk losing anyone,' ordered Jinx.

His kin began gathering wood for the torches.

'Now if you would like to follow me over to the carriage Rhoadan, you and Yak can climb up onto Mika's back and I shall take my place on Mala,' Jinx added.

Rhoadan and Yak followed Jinx over to Mala and Mika. Both deer knelt down so that they could be boarded. Rhoadan and Yak climbed up onto Mika, they both patted her lovingly, this seemed like a rare treat for Yak, he was so used to only running alongside them.

Jinx was already seated on Mala.

'Let us be off then, shall we?' Jinx asked, circling his hand, signalling for Mika and Mala to turn around so he could make his way through the tribe. They all parted and allowed them and the carriage to pass.

As soon as the carriage had passed each row of the tribe, they tucked themselves in and followed.

'Could we have a few lights up front, please? I can't see where we are going,' yelled Jinx.

A commotion of clicks and grunts sounded from the back.

Some of the tribe members from the back ran in single file up to the front and as they ran towards the front, the carriage and Mala and Mika, Jinx, Rhoadan and Yak, came into view.

'Let's move on,' yelled Jinx.

They started moving as Jinx had instructed to do.

The forest surrounding them was eerily silent, the only sound that broke the silence, was either the patter of tiny feet the ground below or a creaking turn of the carriage wheel.

Rhoadan yawned and rubbed his itchy eyes.

'You must be tired, sleep will be gripping at you. Just look at little Eaki-Trin, he's been sleeping for a while now, he's had a busy few days,' Jinx added.

Rhoadan looked down at Yak and smiled, then he yawned again.

'You're right Jinx, I'm tired. I haven't slept right for a while now, I reckon I could easily sleep through a herd of stampeding Taurox,' said Rhoadan.

'How long have you been travelling for, on this journey of yours?' Jinx asked.

'I don't even know, I've lost all track of time, I don't even know what day it is anymore. We've been travelling for a long time and I don't even know how long we all still have to go,' sighed Rhoadan.

'What's the aim of your journey, if you don't mind me asking?' Jinx questioned Rhoadan.

'No I don't mind at all. I'm not entirely sure what Kadence, Elk and Delph's purpose or destination is. The purpose of my journey is to reach Dirtbere, and that's where I plan to settle down,' Rhoadan replied.

'What makes you want to bide in Dirtbere?' Jinx asked.

'When I was a little lad, my family, and I used to go there and we would go for a walk along the shoreline and watch the merchant boats coming in for the night,' Rhoadan replied.

Jinx nodded and closed his eyes.

'We would sit there with our fried tuber roots and sizzling hot snapper fish, there was always events going on, I remember a massive festival as well, where you could get cotton-cloud, ride all sorts of magical rides that would go up and down and all around,' said Rhoadan.

'I like to remember Dirtbere that way also, I couldn't even imagine it any other way,' added Jinx.

'They also had a big market, it was always vibrant and bustling with the citizens of Dirtbere and visitors who were passing through, I have many fond memories of the city and after a long day with our tums full of wonderful food, we would take our carriage home,' Rhoadan recollected.

'I remember when it was just a small village, I've heard people call it a city like you've just done, I think it expanded into a city over the years,' said Jinx.

Rhoadan nodded. 'People call it different things,' he replied.

Jinx smiled.

'I remember my pop telling me "If you can't get it in Dirtbere then it isn't worth having" he used to say that all the time,' Rhoadan said, mimicking his father's voice, smiling to himself as he remembered his father.

'Where is your home?' Jinx asked.

'I live, well I used to live in Bramwich,' answered Rhoadan.

'I haven't heard of that name in a long, long time, you just said you used to live in Bramwich. Have you left your town for good?' Jinx asked.

'Yeah, I used to live there, I left recently,' replied Rhoadan.

'Why did you leave?' Jinx asked.

'I left to set up a new life in Dirtbere. I've had a passion and need for a long time to settle down there,' Rhoadan explained.

'You intend to do this in Dirtbere?' Jinx asked.

'That's correct. I do,' Rhoadan answered.

Jinx fell silent, as did Rhoadan, they both glared into the darkness. The tribe's torches provided the only light they had.

Jinx could hear muttering towards the back of the tribe.

'What makes you ask that?' asked Rhoadan, breaking the silence between the two of them.

'Well I must tell you, the Dirtbere that I know is different to the Dirtbere that you've described in the fond memory of when you were a child, a lot of changes have happened in recent times you see,' answered Jinx.

'Aww don't tell me that. It's been my dream for many years.' Rhoadan replied.

'Disheartening you wasn't an intention of mine. I feel that because I know different from you, therefore, I must tell you and then when you get there, you are under no disillusionment,' Jinx explained.

'I don't think I'm going to like what I see. What happened to Dirtbere, do you know?' Rhoadan asked.

'Corruption is what I consider to be the reason. It was overrun by shadows of darkness a few turns of the three moons ago—' Jinx said.

Rhoadan loudly sighed, disturbing Jinx.

'The darkness came in looking for something, they never found it—as far as I know. The darkness killed off many of the inhabitants of Dirtbere, ever since then, the trade slowly dwindled and stopped, the markets broke down, civilisation as you once knew it, ceased to exist.' Jinx explained.

'What were these shadows looking for?' Rhoadan asked.

'As far as I'm led to believe, it was an individual they were seeking, rather than looking for a *something*,' Jinx answered.

'An individual, that sounds similar to what happened back in Bramwich, it must be linked, it's too much of a coincidence to be anything other than linked. Do you know if there is anyone left?' Rhoadan asked.

'Yes, although not many I would imagine, well I say not many, but I don't know exact numbers of course, but it's nowhere near what it used to be, as you know yourself, it was once bustling and vibrant, now there is just despair, corruption and grief. Security was increased when crime levels reached an all-time high and it's unfortunately been that way ever since,' Jinx explained.

'That's unfortunate,' Rhoadan replied.

They both grew silent again, they embraced the stillness of the forest along with the rustling of leaves and the odd howl of a hidden creature far off in the distance; bringing a relaxing state of mind to Rhoadan's weary head. He was long overdue a good sleep.

'It shouldn't take us long to get home,' confirmed Jinx.

'I'll be glad to rest my eyes without the worry of an ambush or attack,' Rhoadan replied.

'Well that is one thing I can guarantee, our home is safe, we have a protective aura all around it, so there is no need to worry,' Jinx replied.

Yak stirred, he stretched out his little legs; it felt like he was prodding little sticks right into Rhoadan's stomach. Rhoadan had to move them to the side, the lack of food in his stomach seemed to make it a tad more painful.

Grglgglglglglgggll.

Jinx quickly looked over at Rhoadan, a confused expression appeared on his face.

'Sorry about that,' laughed Rhoadan. He pointed down to his stomach, slightly embarrassed.

'I was about to get my sword out and slay whichever foul creature was attacking us,' laughed Jinx.

'It was my stomach. I'm starving, it makes that noise when I'm hungry you see,' replied Rhoadan.

'When we get home, I will have a meal prepared for us,' said Jinx.

'I can't wait,' replied Rhoadan.

'It won't be long till we're there, it would be best to wake Eaki-Trin, I'm sure he will be delighted when we get there,' said Jinx.

Rhoadan nudged Yak.

Little blue lights fluttered all around them as soon as Jinx had spoken his final word.

Rhoadan was puzzled as he watched the tribe members up toward the front become encased in a lilac light, and one by one the light made its way back towards him.

True to Jinx's word, they had arrived. Vast huts towered above them, way up in the canopy. A violet hue surrounded Rhoadan whilst little sparks of light danced all around them.

A sweet aroma filled the air. Every plant was in full bloom. Rhoadan could hear faint trickling coming from a river that flowed somewhere close to them, he just couldn't see it. Birds of the forest whistled a magical tune, Rhoadan embraced the welcoming sight and sounds.

'Let's begin,' commanded Jinx.

The tribe got to work. They had started unloading the carriage before Rhoadan had even thought about climbing down.

He decided to just sit down and take in the spectacular scene that was unfolding in front of his eyes. He was in awe, taking in every part of this beautiful and peaceful place was mesmerising, he nudged Yak.

'Yak, Yak, you have to see this,' forgetting it was nothing new to him, this was Yak's home.

Yak took a few nudges before he fully awoke.

As soon as he saw the colour of his home, he inhaled a big breath and embraced the familiar scent and with a massive toothy grin, he immediately sprung up from Rhoadan's lap, inadvertently kicking Rhoadan in all sorts of places as he jumped down to the ground and ran off into his beloved home.

Rhoadan clambered down from Mika's back and landed on the ground with a thump. Jinx jumped down, but since he was tall, he didn't have very far to go, he landed with grace, unlike Rhoadan had.

'Welcome to Mossguard,' Jinx proudly announced.

'Thank you' said Rhoadan.

'It's been the home of my people for longer than I can even remember, if you would care to follow me, we will make our way in,' Jinx said.

Rhoadan saw the tribe taking his friends inside.

'Will they be okay?' Rhoadan asked.

'Yes, they will be fine. I have asked the tribe to take them to Aedin-Kaori, and she will remove the slumber chant and will ensure that they are fine,' Jinx said.

Rhoadan was following Jinx when two little tribe members ran up to Jinx and hugged him, making a commotion.

Jinx crouched down to listen to them, he glanced over at Rhoadan and then back towards his tribe members and he gave them a stern look. He told them something in their native tongue and off they went although to Rhoadan's uncultured ears it was just a series of clicks and grunts.

Jinx spoke to Rhoadan, who was preoccupied. His attention was averted over towards the corner of the courtyard.

His eyes were drawn to a purple glint that flickered through the crowd of the tribe that had gathered over by an outbuilding in the corner of the courtyard.

'It has to be Ooseriz' Rhoadan thought excitedly.

Rhoadan ran over towards the light. He was correct it was Ooseriz and by the look of it; she was glowing magnificently.

Jinx jumped in front of Rhoadan, startling him.

'Rhoadan, can I have a quick word before you go over there, my tribe told me something they feel bad about and would like to say sorry,' Jinx explained.

'Sure, go on' replied Rhoadan.

'Back in the forest just before we arrived, I sent in a couple of scouts to find out what was happening, they have just informed me they are the ones that frightened Brightbane and made her run off, I can assure you that it wasn't their intention and I will see to it that they are punished,' Jinx explained.

'I hope you do punish them... I'm only kidding,' laughed Rhoadan.

Jinx laughed nervously.

Rhoadan smiled at Jinx and then walked over to Ooseriz. Brightbane popped her head up from the crowd to search for Rhoadan, she saw him and then lowered her head as though she was in trouble.

'Brightbane, my girl!' Rhoadan yelled ecstatically. The tribe stepped aside to let her through.

Rhoadan and Brightbane were reunited at last.

'Come hither. Let's get in and get some food fixed' commanded Jinx, the tribe did as they were asked.

'I missed you girl' said Rhoadan, he hugged Brightbane, she was loving the attention and the fact that she wasn't in trouble.

'Ooseriz, thank you for finding her,' Rhoadan said.

'My pleasure' replied Ooseriz.

'I'll leave you and Brightbane alone. I have a few errands I need to tend to inside,' Jinx explained, pointing to his house.

'Ooseriz, if you would like to come with me please,' Jinx added. Ooseriz elegantly nodded.

'I'll check in with Aedin-Kaori and explain our situation. That's the first task on my agenda,' said Jinx.

'Great, thanks very much,' Rhoadan replied.

'Before I go, please hand your weapons to me, I don't like them around Mossguard, I will ensure that they are placed away in our storage room,' Jinx said, holding out his hand.

Rhoadan gathered up his friend's weapons and reluctantly handed them over along with his. Rhoadan looked over at Ooseriz who seemed to be as confused as he was.

'When will I get them back and where will they be held?' Rhoadan asked.

'I will show you where they are whenever you want to see them and you can get them back when you want them,' replied Jinx.

Jinx called for his tribe to take Mala and Mika into their stable.

'Brightbane can stay in the stable tonight. My tribe will look after her for you and don't worry this time she will be fine. I'll have my master handlers see to her, just come in when you are ready,' said Jinx.

Jinx and Ooseriz started making their way inside.

Chapter Nine

-Anti C-

Ooseriz and Jinx left Rhoadan to rekindle with Brightbane.

Draped vines separated, revealing a heavy wooden door as they ascended the stairs and when they reached the top, they walked through.

'Brightbane lass, I missed you' said Rhoadan, wiping away the tears that he had been holding back for a while, the grief he was feeling vanished as the salty tears rolled down his cheeks.

Rhoadan rubbed her neck and placed his head on hers, she was as happy to be back as much as Rhoadan was to have her back. Mala and Mika both slowly walked over to their stables. Their coats glistened magnificently against the ambient purple of Mossguard's hue.

The cleanliness of the stables wasn't lost on Rhoadan, they were cleaned out every morning and the food and water refilled throughout the day if required.

Mala and Mika made quick work of their straw-hay and root-shunts. The tribe was orchestrated and didn't like breaking away from their routine, they nudged Rhoadan and sighed repeatedly until he moved out of their way and let them get Brightbane into the stables as well.

'I'll see you in the morning girl,' said Rhoadan as he moved aside.

Brightbane was led into the stables and given fresh water. The tribe refilled the food trough, so she had all the straw-hay and root-shunts she could eat.

Rhoadan walked over to the stairs, he stopped before he reached the base and he turned around. Comforting lights whizzed around him projecting a welcoming, tepid hue. He felt warm, but most importantly he felt safe.

His eyes were drawn to the luminescent lilac light that surrounded the outer part of the stronghold, he wondered what it was and then he remembered that Jinx told him that Mossguard had a protective aura.

A faint buzzing noise emanated from it. Smiling, he turned around and glanced up at the opening of Mossguard; which was still open, and with mixed emotions, he climbed the stairs, he reached the top and walked through the opening of the massive tree.

Rhoadan found himself inside a big hall. In front of him was two grand sets of stairs that went up and joined into one, which then split around to the left and the right.

There were three open doors, the widest of them was the one directly in front of him, set underneath the stairs and there was a door to his left and a door to his right spongy moss covered the floor and walls and floating lights danced around him, much like the ones outside except these were green.

The stairs in front of him comprised of static lines. They lay still and intertwined to create the stairs, Rhoadan embraced in how natural and calming they looked, almost frozen in time.

'Jinx, I'm here' wailed Rhoadan.

His loud voice thundered through the room and flowed off around Mossguard, the vibrations from his voice made the little lights swirl and shoot across the room.

He heard the buzzing noise again. It was the same sound that he heard outside except it was a little louder, he wondered what it was.

He waited in silence for a response from Jinx, but no response came.

He could hear distant voices, but couldn't figure out which direction they came from, curiosity got the better of him and he wandered into the room to his left, which was also full of moss.

He crouched down and ran his hand through the warm moss on the floor, he stood back up and did the same with the moss on the wall, it changed colour from dull green into vivid orange as he touched it and he was startled by the clamorous noise it made.

He was mesmerised by the vibrant display of colour, he traced the orange pattern with his eyes as it shimmied across the walls and up onto the ceiling, the noise stopped when he moved his hand away from the wall.

Rhoadan etched a little further into the room so he could get a better view of the magnificent patterned display. He watched it until it became still.

It turned green again once it had reached full circle, he couldn't help himself so he touched the wall again, loud droning the room once more. He was confused and couldn't understand why the wall lit up and buzzed.

He was astonished as he watched the same wave of orange race across the wall and up onto the ceiling and back again.

Once he had finished experimenting with sound and visuals, he had a quick look around the rest of the room. The room was bare and dim and looked like it was more of a walkway than a room.

He noticed another door in the far corner to the right, but he was too scared to explore further and remained where he was.

Muffled voices caught his attention, they sounded like they were coming from behind him, so he walked back into the empty hallway so he yelled for Jinx again.

'Jinx, hello, it's Rhoadan,' he bellowed.

The sudden boom of noise made the tiny lights whirl erratically around Rhoadan and then they darted off and separated into the two rooms. Some floated off up the stairs towards the next level.

He waited patiently for an answer that didn't come, he was left standing in silence once again.

The lights slowly returned to the room and continued to bob around like the did before.

He crouched down and ran his hand across the ground.

It felt nice against his rough hand. He was expecting another light show to appear in front of him however, he was left feeling slightly bemused when nothing happened so he grinned, shrugged his shoulders and he stood back up again.

'Jinx, where are you?' he yelled, he didn't receive any response. 'Have I come through the wrong door?' he thought as he turned around and walked out towards the courtyard and quickly scanned his surroundings to check for another entrance.

He soon realised that it was indeed the correct door he had walked through earlier, so he walked back in and with an almighty roar he bellowed, 'Jinx it's me Rhoadan.'

'For the great lord of Eshia, you don't have to yell. I'm here,' replied Jinx.

'Oh, I'm sorry. I didn't realise you were there,' replied Rhoadan; feeling rather embarrassed.

'I've been yelling on you for a while now,' Rhoadan added.

'I was down in the kitchen and I heard a ruckus, so I came up to see what was happening. There wasn't anybody here, so I went back down again and—' Jinx said.

'We must have just missed each other,' Rhoadan interrupted.

'And then I heard it again, so I about turned and walked up the stairs and you were just coming in through the main door here, just now.' Jinx smiled and continued with what he was saying.

'So, it was you I heard before. I don't know how we kept missing each other,' laughed Rhoadan.

Jinx simply smiled.

'Why didn't you shout back?' Rhoadan asked.

'In Mossguard, we like to keep placid and serene,' explained Jinx.

'I wish you had told me that before we came in, I can be quite loud-mouthed at times,' said Rhoadan.

'Going forward, if you could try to keep your voice at a peaceful level please,' said Jinx.

'I'm sorry, of course, I will,' Rhoadan replied.

'Don't worry about it. You didn't know and now you do,' smiled Jinx.

Rhoadan smiled.

The aroma of dinner floated through Mossguard, the invigorating odour was comforting and homely and reminded Rhoadan of just how hungry he was. Jinx watched Rhoadan as he embraced the scent.

'If you would care to follow me, dinner will be ready shortly, I see you noticed the heavenly scent coming from our kitchen, I asked my tribe to prepare the finest of delicacies for our guests,' said Jinx.

Rhoadan didn't need to be asked twice. He followed Jinx as he walked through the door to the right.

He now understood why Mossguard is named Mossguard. The room had an open door at the other end which was situated at the top of some stairs that led down into the kitchen.

As they descended the stairs, Rhoadan couldn't help run his hands across the wall to create a swirling motion and once again the room was filled with a loud babble.

The sound was exceedingly loud as it echoed throughout the enclosed stairway, Rhoadan and Jinx both covered their ears as orange swirls spiralled up the walls and across the ceiling and then slowly back to where it began.

'It's beautiful, isn't it?' Jinx said.

'It is indeed. It's magical,' replied Rhoadan.

'It is... although...' Jinx said, becoming silent.

'Although what?' Rhoadan asked.

'Don't you think the sound is disturbing?' Jinx asked.

'The lights are almost hypnotising, but the noise is soul destroying. How does it work? Is it some sort of display projection?' Rhoadan asked.

'Not quite no, it's actually sacred little creatures that are on the wall. They help protect Mossguard by keeping enemies away,' explained Jinx.

'Are you serious?' Rhoadan nervously asked.

'To the inhabitants of the forest, the creatures are sacred,' Jinx explained.

'What are they?' Rhoadan asked.

Jinx stopped where he was: 'Stop here for a moment please' Jinx commanded. Rhoadan did as he was told.

'Did you see those little lights flying about?' Jinx asked.

'Yes, the ones upstairs and I also seen them outside,' answered Rhoadan.

'Well, those are camoglows,' said Jinx.

'What are they?' Rhoadan asked.

'They are little insects and when they're relaxing or tired, they nest on the walls and camouflage themselves to look like something in their surroundings, in this case, it's moss and I'm sure you will have seen by now that we have an abundance of moss,' explained Jinx.

Rhoadan nodded his head.

'Camoglows don't like contact, so when you wave your hand across the wall, you're actually threatening them and when they're scared, they light up. It's their defence mechanism, and it's used to blind their enemy and cause confusion. It gives the glow-bug time to assess their situation and get away from the enemy; your hand in this case.' Jinx explained.

'Have I been harming these little mites?' fretted Rhoadan.

'Oh I don't think you will have, they're tough. They have a hard shell and have no bones, so they can withstand a hefty amount of pressure,' explained Jinx.

'I feel bad now, sorry' Rhoadan apologised, cringing at himself.

'Don't worry about it, just don't go threatening the camoglows any more,' laughed Jinx, as he walked through the door.

'Have you been terrorising those poor little camoglows?' Ooseriz chuckled, she was already seated at the table.

'Yeah, unknowingly of course,' Rhoadan replied.

'Don't worry about it, you didn't know. Take a seat Rhoadan and I will go and see how dinner is coming along,' said Jinx.

Rhoadan pulled a seat out from under the table and sat down. Jinx disappeared through the kitchen door.

'I feel bad for those poor little blighters. I'm amazed at how much they actually resemble moss,' Rhoadan said.

'They're covered in hundreds of little hairs and it's the hairs that change colour. They truly are amazing little creatures,' Ooseriz answered.

'I hope Jinx doesn't think of what I did as bad manners,' said Rhoadan, lowering his head into his hands.

'Of course, he doesn't. We've all done it at one point or another. How do you think we found out what they were?' Ooseriz laughed.

This cheered Rhoadan up a little, he looked around the room, it was the most brightly lit room he had ventured into since his arrival at Mossguard, there were candles everywhere.

The walls weren't covered in camoglows and the ground was free of moss.

There were several cupboards and shelves spread along the walls.

He was intrigued by all the pots, potions and many other mysterious items that filled the shelves, he envisioned himself investigating them when there wasn't anyone else around.

'Why aren't there any camoglows in here Ooseriz?' Rhoadan asked.

'Jinx simply doesn't allow it, this is his thinking room, and he needs peace and quiet down here. This is where he does any business that's required to run the forest and ensure of its upkeep,' Ooseriz explained.

'Surely he would still be disturbed by those little bugs. I mean they're right outside the door. How does he get any peace and quiet from the noise they make?' Rhoadan said.

'You're correct with what you're saying, however, they only make that noise if they are disturbed or threatened.' Ooseriz said.

'How does Jinx make sure that the little blighters stay out of the room?' Rhoadan asked.

'Well, see those pots and potions up there on that shelf,' Ooseriz said pointing over to the pot.

Rhoadan got up out of his seat and he walked over to the shelf for a closer inspection. 'I noticed these pots a few moments ago. Does he cast some sort of spell on them?' Rhoadan asked.

'Kind of, see that green one there,' said Ooseriz.

'This one?' Rhoadan asked as he lifted it down from the shelf.

'Well that's crushed camoglows,' said Ooseriz.

Rhoadan couldn't believe what he just heard and nearly dropped the pot. 'That's terrible, I thought they were sacred yet there they are, crushed to their death and stuffed inside a jar,' said Rhoadan, he was confused.

'No, no it's not that, these are ones that have died naturally,' said Ooseriz.

Rhoadan carefully placed the pot back on the shelf.

They could smell the dinner floating through from the next room.

'It smells like dinner is ready. Let's take a seat,' said Ooseriz.

Rhoadan walked back to the table and pulled out a seat and sat on it. 'So, what do you do with those?' Rhoadan asked.

'Well, it's a paste that's been spread thinly onto the walls and it seems to keep them out. I wouldn't like to imagine what the noise would be like if there was no paste to keep them out,' Ooseriz said.

'That would be noisy,' Rhoadan replied, screwing up his face.

'You're right, imagine if the room was filled with them and they were on that door there. Can you just imagine the noise they would make every time it opened?' Ooseriz asked.

'I can imagine the noise would give you a headache, but then the light show would put you into a trance and then the noise would bring you back out of it,' said Rhoadan.

'So, you can see why Jinx likes to keep them out, I'm sure I heard him say at some point he was going to extend the paste right up into the stairway there so that there is no noise at all,' said Ooseriz.

The kitchen door swung open, creaking as it went.

'Dinner is served.' Jinx proudly announced, and he bowed.

Jinx walked to the head of the table and pulled out a seat and sat down. He was closely followed by his tribe as they brought out the delights from the kitchen. Steam whirled up from the food that the tribe paraded around the table. Some of the tribe carried plates and utensils, whilst others brought out cups and an array of different sauces and pickles.

Jinx and Ooseriz were hungry, Rhoadan, on the other hand, thought he was nearing starvation, which he wasn't of course. As the food was placed down in front of them, Rhoadan had to refrain from showing how non-graceful he was when it came to food, yet he somehow waited until they all had plates in front of them. Jinx thanked his tribe as each of them walked back into the kitchen.

'Where has Yak got to?' Rhoadan asked. He had surprisingly taken his mind off this lovely and mouth-watering food that was laid out in front of him for a few seconds.

Jinx asked one of his tribe to go fetch Yak to come and eat.

'We will wait a few moments for Eaki-Trin to join us. I trust you are fine with that?' Jinx asked.

'Of course,' answered Ooseriz, bowing her head.

'Yes, fine by me' replied Rhoadan, secretly wishing that Yak would move his tiny behind and join them at the table.

Rhoadan looked around the table, there was only four plates laid out, one for Jinx, Yak, Ooseriz and of course one for Rhoadan.

Jinx watched Rhoadan as he mentally counted the plates to himself.

'The tribe doesn't eat at the table, it's for the higher ranks of the tribe, being Eaki-Trin, myself and any guests of course, and even if they did, we don't have a big enough table to seat them all,' explained Jinx.

'I see, will Kadence, Elk and Delph be joining us?' Rhoadan asked.

'Unfortunately not, they're still resting. They have had root pulse and dough bread. They need to rest after being in that trance and this meal would be too rich for them at the moment and don't worry about it there's plenty of space for them to have a meal when they are ready,' explained Jinx.

'Can I see them tonight?' Rhoadan asked.

'They aren't awake yet, but yes you can check in on them after dinner if you like,' Jinx answered.

'Great I would like that, thank you.' Rhoadan replied.

Loud buzzing erupted from the stairway, followed by a bright light. Yak appeared at the door grinning to himself. Jinx and Ooseriz stood back up, Rhoadan copied them and did the same.

'Eaki-Trin, do you really have to do that every day of your life.' Jinx sighed, staring sternly at Yak.

Yak immediately stopped grinning and ran over to the table, he pulled out a chair and jumped up onto the seat part of it. He had to stand, so he was level with the table, he nodded his head.

'Okay we may begin, help yourself,' Jinx said, as he sat back down, Ooseriz and Rhoadan followed suit and also sat down.

Rhoadan wasn't used to such formalities when it came to eating a meal, he preferred his usual style, which most of the time involved messy hands, a greasy chin and a midden of mess.

Yak had to climb up onto the table to reach the food that was laid out in the middle of the table.

Rhoadan watched on as Yak stretched over the table to reach the food, he saw that Yak's knee was heading for his own plate, so he stood up and brought the food closer to Yak, to save any accidents happening.

Rhoadan laughed, Yak's style of table manners was much to his liking. Once Rhoadan had finished helping Yak, he helped himself to some of the lovely delights that lay in front of him.

Ooseriz helped herself to a healthy bowlful of root pulse and three dough bread rolls. She cut into the dough bread rolls and finely spread butter on it. Yak chose crispy fried river fish and some thin cut tuber shreds, along with wheat-beans. Rhoadan liked the look of what Yak had.

The smell and sight was astonishing, so much so that Rhoadan couldn't decide on what he wanted, he had never seen food like it before, not one to pass on such a grand opportunity, he sampled everything from the root pulse to the spicy diced bokbit shreds, later returning for a second helping of crispy fried river fish.

Jinx opted for the fish and tuber shreds. Ooseriz had already started tucking into the fish before Jinx had even placed his plate down on the table.

'Fish is popular tonight' sputtered Ooseriz, hurrying to catch the bits of fish that spilt from her mouth.

'It's the best fish in the area and it was caught by my tribe this morning,' Jinx proudly replied.

'Where did they catch it?' Ooseriz asked, after finishing her mouthful.

'If you head out of the gate of the courtyard and look to your left, you will see a little arch,' replied Jinx.

'There are two arches there, which one is it?' Ooseriz asked.

'The one with the lilac root-shoots hanging from it. Well, you go through there and keep walking until you reach the old wooden bridge,' Jinx replied.

'Ah yes, I know where you mean, that's where I found Brightbane funnily enough,' Ooseriz gloated.

Rhoadan looked up from his dinner and smiled at Ooseriz.

'Well, once you cross the bridge, you will pass through a tunnel, just watch out for the low hanging vines, once you pass them you will come to a split road, take the path that curves to the right, just make sure you never take the path that snakes to the left,' explained Jinx.

'Why, should we stay clear of the path to the left?' Rhoadan asked.

Bits of food fell out of his mouth and landed on the table drawing Jinx's attention to it.

'The road to the left will get you no fish, the road to the left is where Chinqwacho bides' replied Jinx; bringing his eyes up to meet Rhoadan's.

'Chinqwacho is just a legend of the old days, isn't it?' Ooseriz asked.

'Chinqwacho, sho sho.' said Yak.

Rhoadan, Jinx and Ooseriz all turned to look at Yak.

'Eaki-Trin, you've been warned before to stay clear of Chinqwacho. It isn't your friend!' Jinx scolded.

'Sho, sho.' Yak muttered quietly to himself.

'I believe Chinqwacho is real, sometimes you can hear its shrill screeching when the forest is quiet at night, it sounds like a herd of Tikibleks* all roaring at once. The noise alone is frightening and is the main reason I have Mossguard safeguarded,' explained Jinx.

'I don't like the sound of it one bit. What is it?' Rhoadan asked.

* A Tikiblek is a huge, two-headed bear which has shimmering scales and it can breathe underwater.

'I'll come back to it. Ooseriz is eager to find out where my tribe catches the fish,' Jinx said, trying to brush off Rhoadan's question.

Rhoadan, nodded as he helped himself to some red mushrooms, tipping loads of them onto his plate.

'You will like those Rhoadan, they're my favourite,' said Ooseriz.

'What are they?' Rhoadan asked.

'They're bloodshrooms my friend, it's a type of mushroom,' added Ooseriz.

'They're good, Ooseriz was right' Rhoadan thought as he piled them into his mouth.

'So, once you walk down the path to the right, you come to an opening that's surrounded by massive mushrooms, those mushrooms should be left well alone, especially the red ones. If you touch one of them, your vision is the first to go, then it's your hearing, then shortly after that, you won't be able to feel your legs. You will become numb all over and within a matter of minutes, you will die,' explained Jinx.

Watching eagerly as Rhoadan abruptly stopped eating the bloodshrooms.

Rhoadan glared at Jinx, he was horrified.

He couldn't comprehend why Jinx would let him eat the bloodshrooms.

His fork clattered as it dropped on his plate, giving Yak a fright. He turned round to see Rhoadan making a mockery of himself. Rhoadan flung his mouth open wide, spraying bits of bloodshroom everywhere.

Yak mimicked everything that Rhoadan did, he dropped his little fork, and he opened his mouth wide letting his food fall out of his mouth.

Jinx threw him a stern look again. Jinx had mastered this look as he had used it more times than not with Yak.

Panic gripped at Rhoadan, laboured breathing left him gasping for air. He felt a dull numbing feeling ride up his arms. Ooseriz stood and rushed over to help Rhoadan.

'How — could — you!' Rhoadan panted as he tried to yell at Jinx.

Rhoadan got up from his seat with so much haste that his foot clipped the leg of the chair and he stumbled right into Jinx's sideboard and was knocked onto his back.

He writhed on the floor clutching at his throat. He ached all over. His vision became blurry and his ears rung.

No matter how hard he tried, he couldn't move his legs. Pressure crushed down on his body as everything went black and fell silent.

Rhoadan lay still unsure of what was happening. He could hear muffled yelling all around him, but couldn't make out whose voice it was.

The pressure eased, releasing the unbearable tension that was pushing down on his stomach, as he felt the pressure lifting from his body, the voices became clearer and his harsh breathing eased up.

A blurred light filled his vision.

'Get off of him you fools. Get out of the room at once!' Jinx roared.

The tribe scurried through the door, muttering some unrecognisable words to themselves.

Jinx was livid with his tribe.

Rhoadan squinted as the light pierced through the darkness. Miniature glittering lights slithered through his vision.

His arms and legs throbbed as they were freed from their confinement.

Something shuffled towards him, he couldn't make it out at first, but as it came into his range of view, it was clear that it was a hand. The hand belonged to Ooseriz.

Yak kept dipping in and out of his vision.

Rhoadan extended out his own hand and Ooseriz clasped her other hand on Rhoadan's and helped him up to his feet. Yak helped push Rhoadan up from behind.

Ooseriz smiled, Rhoadan smiled back. He was bewildered. The tribe's eyes were glowing again. They had sneaked back into the room.

'I've already told you to get out! He had an accident, he wasn't attacking me you fools,' Jinx bellowed at his tribe, he turned to Rhoadan and apologised profusely.

'What's going on?' Rhoadan asked. He could feel a sting on his forehead and could sense a warm sensation running down his cheek, he lifted his hand up to investigate, he was bleeding.

'Eaki-Trin, take care of our friend here.' ordered Jinx.

'I'll say this again Rhoadan, I'm deeply sorry. I take full responsibility for what has happened,' grovelled Jinx.

Yak stomped through to the kitchen, swinging the door wide as he went, Rhoadan spotted a few of the tribe glaring out at him. He was drawn to their bright eyes. Yak barged through, elbowing them as he went.

Yak came back into the room with a rag slung over his shoulder, he was trailing a small set of ladders behind him, he set up the ladders under the shelf and made his way to the top, once he was there he stretched his arm out until he was able to grab a small jar which contained a clear bubbling brew in it.

'Rhoadan, could you take a seat and let Eaki-Trin see to your wound,' Jinx asked as he pulled up a seat next to Rhoadan.

Yak jumped down from the ladders and climbed up onto the chair.

'It will sting a little' Jinx said. Yak tipped the bottle upside down onto the rag and without warning, he slapped it on Rhoadan. The concoction fizzed and hissed as it made contact with Rhoadan's skin.

Rhoadan grunted and inhaled deeply through his nose as the liquid got to work.

'Ouch, I thought you said it would only sting a little, well that stung a lot!' Rhoadan gasped, he inhaled heavily through his nose.

'Eaki-Trin, will you try to be gentle!' Jinx warned Yak, before placing his hands over his eyes in shame.

'As subtle as ever, our Eaki-Trin is,' laughed Ooseriz.

'Everyone of my tribe has embarrassed me today' groaned Jinx, cupping his hands and sinking his head fully into them.

'Right, can someone please tell me what just happened?' Rhoadan asked. Jinx sighed.

'When you were eating the bloodshrooms, I took the opportunity to play a little prank on you, all was going well until you got out of your seat, I was about to tell you that I was pretending and that's when it turned bad and I instantly regretted my decision,' explained Jinx.

'What happened next?' Rhoadan asked.

'Well, once you were out of your seat, you were clearly panicking and you just fell to the ground and you hit your head on that sideboard there,' Jinx explained.

'I got up to help you, but you were on the floor before I even got to you, I think you must have clipped the leg of your chair and that's when you went hurtling into the sideboard,' Ooseriz added.

Yak had finished applying the ointment to Rhoadan's head. He muttered something and sat down on the chair and watched Rhoadan, Ooseriz and Jinx interact.

'It honestly felt like I was paralysed, I couldn't move my legs nor my arms, nothing.' Rhoadan groaned.

Ooseriz couldn't take her eyes off of Rhoadan's forehead, expecting it to bleed again.

'What happened next was out of my control, you crashed into my sideboard, with your big frame—' Jinx was cut short.

'Are you saying I'm fat?' Rhoadan laughed.

'No I... uh... no, I'm not. I'm just stating that you are sturdy and when two sturdy items collide and smash into each other, well, I'm sure you can imagine what the consequences would be,' Jinx said awkwardly.

'I think you are calling me fat,' laughed Rhoadan.

'I'm genuinely not calling you fat. If you would care to have a look over at my sideboard, you will see exactly what I'm referring to,' explained Jinx.

Rhoadan looked over at Jinx's sideboard, or what was left of it. It stood there in a sorry state with a massive Rhoadan-sized crevice right in the middle.

'And when you collided with my sideboard, that's when my tribe's instinct kicked in and they came to protect their leader,' Jinx explained.

Rhoadan checked his head for any blood, flinching with pain as soon as he touched it.

'That's when they ran through from the kitchen. They were piled on top of you before we could stop them. I can appreciate that they are small, but they are also sturdy little things and that's why you couldn't see or feel anything,' said Ooseriz.

'So, they heard the commotion and ran through to save you?' Rhoadan asked Jinx, trying to picture it all in his head.

'Yes, exactly,' replied Jinx.

'Yak tried to defend you, but no matter how hard he tried he kept getting pushed to the side,' Ooseriz explained.

Rhoadan turned and smiled at Yak, then looked over at the sideboard again.

'I'm sorry for the state that I have left your sideboard in. I will pay you for the damage,' said Rhoadan.

'That won't be necessary, it wasn't intended. You are our guest and it's my fault it happened in the first place and my tribe assisted to the overall damage, so I don't want any payment,' Jinx replied.

'The bloodshrooms are tasty, but I don't think you should ever try to play a prank on anyone ever again Jinx, I say it with all due respect of course,' Ooseriz laughed.

'Believe me, my pranking days are over, on the very day they had begun,' Jinx replied awkwardly.

'As long as I'm not the butt of the prank I don't mind,' laughed Rhoadan.

Jinx cringed at the thought.

'So, before the unfortunate event happened, you were telling me where your tribe caught those delicious fish,' Ooseriz reminded Jinx.

'Chinqwacho, sho sho!' Yak yelled, slamming his little fist on the table.

Rhoadan, Jinx and Ooseriz all turned and looked at Yak simultaneously.

Yak remained silent.

'So, back to the fish' Jinx said, raising his eyebrows at Yak.

Ooseriz was shocked at the way Yak was being with Jinx. She had never seen this side to him before.

'You walk past where the bloodshrooms grow and you should come to an arched tunnel, walk through it and you will notice the beautiful lights within it change colour, it's almost like a rainbow tunnel if I remember correctly, anyway, keep going until you hear the sound of water trickling and that's when you will have reached Babblebrook Lagoon. There is several small piers there, and each one is sturdy enough to fish up these delicious fish from,' said Jinx.

'Wow, that was a mouth full,' laughed Rhoadan.

'I know, I didn't want to be disturbed again,' laughed Jinx.

'Well I shall be heading there tomorrow before I leave, could I borrow a fishing rod and a net?' Ooseriz asked.

'Yes, that would be fine. We can arrange it for you in the morning,' Jinx replied.

'Chinqwacho, sho sho' Yak stated again.

'Yak seems to think Chinqwacho is his friend,' said Rhoadan.

'Yes, he does indeed, I wonder why,' Ooseriz replied.

'Eaki-Trin, you must stay away from Chinqwacho, I won't repeat myself,' Jinx ordered.

Rhoadan knew then, that he would have to seek out Chinqwacho before he left the forest, even just to see why Yak had such a fascination.

'Speaking of friends, how did you and Ooseriz meet?' Rhoadan asked.

Jinx and Ooseriz slowly turned to look at each other. Neither of them spoke a word.

Chapter Ten

-A Rekindling

Entrapment-

Jinx and Ooseriz both looked at Rhoadan, with Jinx breaking the momentary silence.

'That my friend, is a tale for when your friends are in our company. I'll have the tribe clear up our table and I'll go and check on your friends,' explained Jinx.

Rhoadan sighed out loud unintentionally.

Jinx ordered his tribe to come through from the kitchen and clear the table, they sheepishly entered the room, each as timid as the one in front, they were still embarrassed because of what they did to Rhoadan. Rhoadan's presence inadvertently made the tribe nervous, they kept on bumping into each other as they cleared the table and they were more focussed on Rhoadan than the task they had been set.

'It's okay, I forgive you,' Rhoadan told the tribe, even with his explanation they still acted nervous around him.

Rhoadan, Jinx, Ooseriz and Yak observed the tribe as they cleared up the plates and anything else that lay about, they wiped down the table and cleared away any mess made by the smashing incident earlier.

'I'll just nip upstairs and speak to Aedin-Kaori and see how your friends are doing,' Jinx said as he left the room.

'I hope they are okay' sighed Rhoadan, he yawned.

'They are in good hands with Aedin-Kaori, they'll be fine. Try not to torment yourself too much,' Ooseriz replied.

'Sho sho' said Yak, this seemed to settle Rhoadan.

Rhoadan rubbed his itchy eyes, he felt lethargic, so he closed his eyes for a moment.

Jinx climbed up the stairs making sure not to touch the wall, he couldn't face the sound that came as a result of disturbing the camoglows. He stopped and sighed when he reached the main hall because the thought of climbing more stairs wasn't welcoming to him.

'Moss, bugs and stairs, that's all the place is, blooming moss, bugs and stairs.' he moaned. He reached the top, he turned left and continued along the hallway until he arrived at Aedin-Kaori's door, he Knocked twice and waited for an answer, even though he was the ruler of this abode, he still gave the occupants of the room the privacy and respect that was needed.

'Come in,' came the reply he was waiting for, so Jinx did just that.

'Hello Aedin-Kaori, how are our guests doing?' asked Jinx; peeking his head around the door.

'They're doing just fine, have a look for yourself and how many times do I have to remind you not to use my full name?' Aedin-Kaori asked.

'I'm sorry Aedin, you know I'm a stickler for formalities,' replied Jinx.

'I know you are, but we've known each other for many years and for the past few weeks it seems like I've told you a million times. Is everything okay?' she laughed.

'I'm sorry, I've had a lot on my mind recently' replied Jinx, running his eyes over to the three cloaked beds, the occupants were sound asleep. 'I'll let them sleep, I just wanted to check on them, I'll come back later' as he exited the room.

Jinx walked along the hall and followed the stairs right down to Rhoadan who was waiting eagerly for his return.

'Blooming moss, bugs and stairs,' shuddered Jinx as he walked through the door.

'Well, how are they?' Ooseriz asked.

'They're still asleep. Aedin said they're doing fine though,' Jinx replied.

'That's good. Rhoadan's fallen asleep,' Ooseriz said, nodding over to Rhoadan.

'Let him sleep. It's getting late and having an early night would benefit me, so I'm just going to head up to my bed,' said Jinx.

'I'll stay down here for a bit, if Rhoadan wakes up I can show him up to his room, he won't know where to go. Yak has already headed up to his bed, he was struggling to keep his eyes open.' Ooseriz replied.

'If he wakes up, just show him up to the main guest room. Good night Ooseriz.' said Jinx.

'I'll do that. Good night Jinx.' replied Ooseriz.

Jinx headed up the stairs.

Ooseriz rested her eyes and listened to the hustle n bustle of the tribe settling down for the night.

Rhoadan awoke in a strange room, he didn't know where he was and the dimly lit room wasn't helping him figure it out. He looked around trying to lay his eyes on something that would jog his memory, it was a few unsettling moments until he remembered he was in Mossguard.

He rubbed his face and stretched his arms and legs out. His eyes were drawn to a glass of water sitting on the bedside cabinet, he reached for it and gulped it down greedily until it was gone; he felt instantly hydrated. He got out of bed and walked across the room to the bathroom door; he opened it and went in. Once he had finished; he left the room and closed the door behind him harder than he had anticipated, it slammed against the door frame, making Rhoadan jump, the bedroom door and Yak burst into the room, giving Rhoadan another fright.

'Sho, sho' yelled Yak. He ran over to Rhoadan and gave him a hug.

Rhoadan smiled and hugged him back.

Yak tugged on the bottom of Rhoadan's top and then led him out the door, along the hall and down the big set of stairs he had stood in front of when he first entered Mossguard. Yak and Rhoadan made their way down the second set of stairs and into the dining room.

Yak burst into the room yelling* 'Sho, sho' over and over until Jinx reprimanded him for doing so.

'Morning' Rhoadan said.

'Good evening you mean,' laughed Ooseriz.

'Evening?' Rhoadan asked; he was puzzled.

'Yup' laughed Ooseriz.

'How long have I slept?' asked Rhoadan as he pulled out a seat and sat down.

'You fell asleep down here last night hunched over the table, and you've slept right through until now,' replied Ooseriz.

'Wow! I did need it I suppose, I didn't realise just how much so,' Rhoadan laughed nervously.

* Yak had an irritating habit of bursting into rooms and yelling.

Jinx, Ooseriz and Yak all laughed.

'How did I get upstairs?' Rhoadan asked mid-yawn.

'I stayed down here so I could show you to your room in case you woke up. I also fell asleep, but you stirred and I woke up. You were muttering something about gems, so I nudged you until you started waking up then I walked you up to your room and got you into your bed, I don't think you were fully awake at any point though.' Ooseriz answered.

'Thanks for making sure I got up there,' said Rhoadan.

'Yak has sat outside your room ever since he got up this morning. I've spotted him trying to get in a few times, but I warned him to let you sleep on,' Jinx said.

Rhoadan looked and Yak and laughed.

'How are my friends?' Rhoadan asked.

'I was just about to go up and see how they're doing before you came in, they were still sleeping when I checked in on them this afternoon,' replied Jinx.

He got up and made his way to the door, 'I'll check on them now' Jinx left the room and made his way up to Aedin's room, he knocked on the door and just entered the room this time without waiting on an answer.

'How are they now? Are they awake yet?' Jinx quietly asked.

'Have a look for yourself.' Aedin said and smiled.

Jinx walked over to the beds. He stopped when he reached the one on the far left. He ran his eyes up the white linen that was draped from the high velveteen ceiling, right down to the sturdy oak floorboards. He cracked his neck and peeled back the linen, revealing Kadence. She was shocked to see Jinx standing there, she gasped and held her hands up in front of her.

'It's okay you're safe. My name is Jinx-Amora, I'm a friend. I'm here to check on you for your friend Rhoadan,' he explained.

The other drapes were flung back simultaneously at the very mention of Rhoadan's name, startling both Kadence and Jinx alike.

'Did you just say Rhoadan?' Elk asked.

'Where is he?' Delph asked.

'He's downstairs, he's safe don't worry,' Jinx responded nervously.

'Can we see him?' Elk asked.

'Of course, I'll send him up soon. Let me explain where you are first,' replied Jinx.

'I've already explained everything Jinx, so you won't need to,' Aedin added.

'Thanks, that's saved me a bit of time,' replied Jinx, secretly glad he didn't have to.

'Thank you for taking care of us,' Kadence said graciously.

'It's been my pleasure, the only people I have had to take care of are the tribe you see, so a change of face is very welcoming,' replied Aedin.

'I'm so happy to see you all up and awake.' Jinx said.

'Thank you,' Elk said.

'Where are our clothes?' Delph asked.

'Let me get them for you,' Aedin replied, as she got up out of her seat and hobbled over to the walk-in cupboard and she disappeared inside.

'Right, I'll leave you all to get ready and I'll send Rhoadan up shortly. I bet you're hungry, I'll have some food brought up,' Jinx confirmed.

'Thank you ever so much for your care and hospitality. I don't know how we would have survived without it,' said Kadence.

'I dread to think, let me fetch Rhoadan for you,' Jinx replied, as he exited the room.

'How are they then?' Rhoadan asked Jinx excitedly the moment he stepped foot into the dining room.

'They're doing great, I spoke to them and they would like it if you went up to see them,' replied Jinx.

'That's smashing, absolutely wonderful,' yelled Rhoadan, raising both hands up into the air.

Ooseriz smiled.

Rhoadan couldn't remove the grin from his face if he tried.

'Let me fetch a few helpers, they can show you the way to the room, I need them to do an errand for me anyhow,' Jinx explained, he walked over to the kitchen door and opened it.

'You two, come here please,' Jinx asked two of his tribe to come over.

'How did they seem?' Ooseriz asked.

'They seemed fine, I didn't know what to expect if I'm honest. I certainly didn't expect as quick a recovery as that,' replied Jinx.

'Great news,' smiled Ooseriz.

'I need you both to take our friend Rhoadan up to see his friends, they are up in Aedin-Kaori's room, when you get up there I would like you to check for any clothes or dishes that need cleaning and then promptly leave the room and bring them down to the kitchen please,' Jinx asked his tribe.

The two tribe members nodded, they looked over at Rhoadan, they were unsure of him and wondered if he was planning any revenge.

Rhoadan smiled at them trying to ease the tension, the tribesmen returned the smile; they walked out of the room, followed by Rhoadan, who was closely followed by Yak.

Jinx and Ooseriz watched them walk out of the room.

'Oh Eaki-Trin, don't you dare touch that wall' yelled Jinx, before Yak disappeared out of view. He, lowered his hand as he was about to do just that. The smile quickly faded from his face. Rhoadan, Jinx and Ooseriz all laughed.

'Eaki-Trin follows Rhoadan where ever he goes doesn't he?' Ooseriz asked.

'I also noticed that. Hopefully, Rhoadan doesn't find it annoying,' replied Jinx.

Rhoadan, Yak and the tribe members reached the top of the stairs. They walked down the hall until they were outside Aedin's room.

Rhoadan was apprehensive although clearly relieved that he was about to be reunited with his good friends. Yak knocked on the door, they waited for Aedin to tell them to enter before they did so.

Rhoadan scanned the room for his friends. Yak walked straight over to Aedin and hugged her, whilst the tribesmen set about doing their errands.

Rhoadan, Delph, Kadence and Elk all looked at each other as Rhoadan walked over to the foot of the three beds, unsure of whom to hug first, he didn't need to wait for long, as Delph and Kadence approached him slowly and they hugged him tightly, Elk dived on the three of them from the bed.

'You lot had me worried,' Rhoadan said, although the hug muffled his words.

'Can you say that again?' Delph asked, as they broke up the hug.

'I'm saying, what a relief to see you as you had me worried,' replied Rhoadan, wiping away a tear.

There wasn't a dry eye in the room. They were so happy to see Rhoadan, who was equally happy to see them, the relief was astounding all around, not just from Rhoadan's point of view.

'We were told that we were captured by some sort of beast, who just about ate us. I'm definitely glad that didn't happen,' said Elk.

'You aren't alone with that thought,' sighed Delph.

'I can't believe we nearly died out there, one minute we were safe or so we thought and the next we were on the menu for some greedy monster looking to fill its stomach, oh Rhoadan, I'm so happy to see you,' Kadence cried, her eyes glazed over and became silent.

'Come here' Rhoadan said; as he leant down and gave her another hug.

'I'll leave you to it, I'm sure you have a lot of questions to ask, so I'll leave you alone and I'll head down and get some fresh air' said Aedin; she was also upset, even though she didn't really know them, there were a lot of emotions in the room, she had cared for them and brought them back from the brink after all.

Rhoadan turned around and thanked Aedin as she got up and walked over to the door. She was followed by the two tribesmen, who had both finished their task.

'I will be downstairs if you need anything just let me know,' said Aedin.

Aedin left the room and gently closed the door behind her. Her plan was to quickly nip in and speak to Jinx. Then she was going to go outside for some much-needed air, it was more of a chance to grab five minutes to herself. She walked down the stairs and she was met by Jinx and Ooseriz as she reached the main hall.

She stopped to speak to them, the tribesmen weren't watching where they were going and crashed right into the back of her legs, almost sending washing and dishes everywhere, they grunted and made clicking noises as they shuffled past her.

'Hello, I was just on my way down to see you,' said Aedin.

'Hello Aedin…' Jinx said, still finding it hard not to use her full name.

'We haven't been formally introduced, Jinx has told me about how amazing you are and how well the guys are doing, all thanks to your care,' said Ooseriz.

'Hello, I have also heard of you. Thank you for your kind words,' Aedin dipped her head and returned the greeting.

Jinx smiled and nodded his head, he agreed with Ooseriz.

'We are just heading outside into the courtyard for some air and I need to check on a few things if you would care to join us?' Jinx asked.

'Sure, I was thinking about heading out myself, I needed a break, if only for five minutes,' said Aedin.

'I completely understand.' said Jinx.

'I feel bad for saying that, but it's nothing against our friends upstairs, you have to understand that.' Aedin pleaded and clasped her hands together almost praying.

'Again... I completely understand, there is no need to explain yourself Aedin, we all need some time on our own, even if it's only for five minutes,' said Jinx.

Aedin nodded her head.

Mala was the first to greet them as they stood in front of the stable.

'Aedin, if you don't mind checking on Mika and I'll check on Mala, Ooseriz will tend to Brightbane and that way we can get this over with as quickly as possible,' Jinx explained.

They made sure there weren't any bramble-thorns stuck to Mika, Mala or Brightbane and that there was plenty of sleeping hay and water to see them through the night, the tribe had done a good job mucking out the stable earlier. Mala, Mika and Brightbane had been checked over and all was good, each of them received an extra long pet and clap.

'I think we're finished here for tonight,' said Jinx.

Ooseriz nodded.

'Let's head back in, it's getting chilly out here' Jinx said, as he turned to head back into his abode.

'Tonight's temperature is much to my liking, my fur gets me all stuffy you see,' said Ooseriz.

'I'm not a fan of the cold' replied Jinx as he reached the foot of the stairs.

'I'm going to sit out here for a little while, I need to clear my head' Aedin said, as she watched Ooseriz and Jinx ascend up the stairs, towards the main door.

Jinx stopped and turned around. Ooseriz carried on up the stairs.

'Take as long as you need, we will head in and I'll make sure supper is ready soon. Are you hungry Aedin?' Jinx asked.

'Yes, a little' replied Aedin.

'Okay, I'll get something made up for you as well then,' Jinx added. Aedin thanked him as he turned around and continued up the last few stairs.

Just before Jinx reached the door, he turned back around. 'Would you say our guests are healthy enough to come out of the room and meet us downstairs for something to eat?' Jinx asked.

'Yes, they seem better now, they have recovered and had plenty of sleep after all,' replied Aedin.

'Great, I would love to have a chat with them,' Jinx added.

Once again he turned around and faced the door and he stepped through it. Ooseriz was sitting back down in the seat she had previously sat in, she had just been in the kitchen to see if they had any crushed choco beans as she was thirsty and craved something sweet, she persuaded one of the tribe to make her a mug, although, there wasn't much persuasion required.

The tribe has had kind feelings towards Ooseriz for many years and the help she gave them in the forest earlier only reaffirmed that.

Jinx found himself outside Aedin's room. He knocked on the door and entered.

'Hello, sorry to interrupt, supper will be ready shortly, if you are all able to manage it?' Jinx asked.

'I'm starving. I will take whatever you have. I'm not fussy,' Elk piped in.

They all laughed.

'Well, I know that you've definitely recovered Elk,' laughed Rhoadan.

'You're always hungry' laughed Kadence, with a tear in her eye. Clearly still a little emotional after the past few days events.

'We will all take supper please,' Delph answered.

'Do you think you will be well enough to join us downstairs?' Jinx asked.

'I think we will be, I'm feeling okay. What about you two?' Delph turned his head to his right to ask Kadence and Elk.

'We have already established that Elk is doing fine,' laughed Rhoadan.

'Yeah, I feel fine, I will happily join you downstairs. How long will it be until you would like us to come down?' Kadence asked.

'Oh there is no rush, I will send someone up to tell you when it's ready,' Jinx replied.

'I'd appreciate that,' added Rhoadan.

Yak sat beside Kadence, he had taken a shine to her she was enjoying having him sitting beside her.

'Sho sho, sho sho,' said Yak, in an excitable tone.

'You're quite the talker aren't you,' Kadence laughed.

'What does it mean?' Kadence asked Rhoadan.

'It means friend, Yak is telling you that you are his friend,' Rhoadan explained.

'Where are our bags and weapons?' Elk asked.

Jinx seemed agitated and left the room without saying anything. He made his way back downstairs, Rhoadan remained in the room with his friends.

'Well Aedin got our clothes out of that cupboard over there earlier, so I'm assuming that they are probably in there.' replied Delph.

Elk jumped up and out of bed unexpectedly, startling the others and poor Yak nearly toppled right off the side of the bed, Yak was lucky he was pretty agile and has good reflexes, he clutched the blankets tight, saving himself from hurtling to the ground.

'Seriously Elk,' moaned Kadence as she helped Yak back up on the bed and gave him a loving cuddle.

Elk apologised as he walked over to the cupboard and Delph was correct, their bags were there, Rhoadan joined them, he wanted to check that his sack of gems was in there as well.

Rhoadan had a look inside.

'My sack of gems isn't here,' said Rhoadan.

'Our weapons aren't here either' gasped Elk, whilst rummaging through everything that was in the cupboard.

'You won't find any weapons stored in my room, I never allow it' explained Aedin, who had just come into the room, the sound of the door opening was muffled by the noise that Elk and Rhoadan made in her cupboard.

Rhoadan and Elk both stood up and turned around, somewhat surprised to see Aedin, their faces shone red with embarrassment, they had been caught raking through her cupboard.

'Do you know where our weapons are?' Rhoadan asked.

'I do' replied Aedin.

'Where are they?' Rhoadan asked.

'They are in storage downstairs, if you ask Jinx he will show you,' replied Aedin.

'Aedin, Jinx brought back a sack that is very important to me, do you know where he would have put it?' Rhoadan asked.

'I'm not sure, I would check with him, he will tell you where it is, he sent some of the tribe up here with some bags when you all arrived and I put them all in that cupboard, so if you are looking for something and it's not there, I would definitely speak to Jinx,' Aedin replied.

Rhoadan walked over to Aedin, 'Okay, I'll speak to him, thanks again for taking care of my friends,' he said, whilst clasping Aedin's tiny hands in his own.

'I'm a carer, I care for everything it's what I do, I would never turn away someone who needs my care, I would—'

The sheer amount of wrinkles on Aedin's face reminded him of a dried out riverbed, he glanced over the dark rings below her eyes and the small wisps of hair on her upper lip caught his attention more times than he wished.

He nodded his head and smiled, her voice drained away under his dreadful stare.

'Stop staring Rhoadan.' he told himself.

He noticed a faint smell of mushrooms coming from her, it caught his breath. It was the first time he had been this close to her, so he slowly backed away from her, but the more he backed away from her the closer she got, he felt uncomfortable.

'Stop staring Rhoadan,' he told himself again.

Rhoadan saw that she didn't carry herself well, she stooped over, he felt like he was being rude because he had zoned out and hadn't even bothered listening to what she was telling him.

He was momentarily fixated on her long, greying, hair, it reminded him of a thornberry bush except her hair was even thicker and was also matted, it just draped raggedly over her shoulders. He was just glad she didn't have any thorns in there or they would definitely jag into his skin if they were to hug.

'Rhoadan, are you even listening to me?' Aedin asked.

Rhoadan quickly snapped out of his fixation with Aedin's appearance.

'I'm sorry, I need some sleep. I'm sorry for being rude,' replied Rhoadan.

Aedin glared at him, her right eye and the brown ring below it twitched, she sighed out loud and hobbled away from him, she slumped down into her resting seat in the far corner of the room.

'I will be downstairs if you care to join us for some food' Rhoadan said; feeling rude and somewhat embarrassed, so he left the room to make himself scarce of the situation he just put himself into.

They had been travelling for so long now and had faced so many unfortunate events, none of which were enlightening or indeed fun.

Rhoadan had grown tired of them and rather tired of himself. He knew he needed sleep before he crashed and burned, his plan was to go downstairs, have something to eat and then make a sharp exit to his bed.

Rhoadan joined Jinx and Ooseriz downstairs.

The table was covered in bowls, some weird shaped crockery, utensils and night cups, Rhoadan had seen so many weird and wonderful things in his life, but never had he came across night cups before.

Jinx greeted him as he sat down at the table. He smiled and nodded his head. Rhoadan yawned, he was midway through it before he got his hand up to cover his mouth, his eyes nipped, he rolled his neck and rubbed his eyes and he clasped his head in his hands.

'Are you still tired even after that massive sleep?' asked Jinx; his right eye twitched.

'I'm still knackered, these last few days have been hectic,' Rhoadan replied.

'I'll be back in a moment. I'm just going to check on the progress of our supper,' Jinx said, as he disappeared through to the kitchen.

Ooseriz noticed Jinx's twitching eye. 'He's been acting awfully strange of late' she said to herself.

Rhoadan remained in the same position, he was too exhausted to move.

Ooseriz took the final gulp of her choco and put her cup down, she looked over at Rhoadan and just watched on in silence, Ooseriz was tired as well, she had also had a busy few days, she had been in a pretty relaxed state of mind right up until she saw Rhoadan, Kadence, Elk and Delph outside the cave.

Little did she know at that point she would be sitting here in silence just staring at Rhoadan snoring his head off as he caught up on some much-needed sleep, Ooseriz smiled.

'Supper will be ready shortly' Jinx peeked his head around the door. A little tribesman walked out of the room and headed up the stairs.

'Try not to be long.' Jinx shouted up to him.

A loud gnarly snore escaped from Rhoadan's mouth. Jinx cringed realising he yelled much louder than he meant to.

'Ooseriz, Rhoadan seemed particularly interested in finding out about The Guardian Four, do you think we should tell him anything?' Jinx took a seat across from Rhoadan and looked over to Ooseriz for an answer.

'I have to be careful about what I say, as you know if I reveal too much, it changes the events of the days in which we have yet to experience,' Ooseriz replied.

'You're right, we can't risk changing future events, I'm sure you can remember what happened the last time, we don't wish to repeat that,' replied Jinx.

'We can tell them a little bit about us though, I'm sure, Hopefully, we've put Rhoadan off from asking again,' replied Ooseriz.

Just then Elk, Kadence, Delph and Aedin all walked through the door, Jinx and Ooseriz both stood up and walked over and hugged each of them, Yak walked through the door after a few minutes.

'Come, let me get a seat for each of you,' said Jinx.

Jinx showed them to their seats. Aedin waited until they sat down before she took her own seat. Yak's seat was still in place from before, he ran around the table and in his initial haste to get back up on the seat, he almost became entangled within it.

He ended up having to swing his leg up and around the back of the chair, in the process he accidentally kicked Rhoadan smack bang on the side of his head and then continued as though nothing had happened.

Rhoadan awoke with a startle when Yak's foot clashed with Rhoadan's ear. He was brought back from his long overdue slumber.

'Sleeping on the job eh, Rhoadan,' laughed Elk.

Rhoadan squinted both eyes and looked over at Elk. He was delighted to see that his friends had joined them downstairs for some nourishment.

'Yeah, you could say that' said Rhoadan; still rubbing his ear.

Rhoadan turned to look at Yak, who was sitting patiently; as though butter wouldn't melt in his little mouth. Yak bashfully peered up at Rhoadan with an awkward smile and said, 'Sho sho' from the corner of his mouth.

Jinx waited for everyone to sit down before he stood up and peeked his head through the kitchen door.

'We are ready,' he told his tribe. 'They shouldn't be much longer now,' he told the group as he walked back to his seat and sat down.

'Before we go on any further, I would wholeheartedly like to thank you for the care you have given us here,' said Kadence.

'I agree,' replied Elk and Delph in unison.

'It's my pleasure,' replied Jinx. Aedin smiled and nodded her head.

The kitchen door swung open, and the tribe poured into the room.

'Let's say no more. For those of you who haven't already eaten at my table, we don't really have any formalities, so just dive right in,' said Jinx.

'That's the type of formality I like,' said Elk; rubbing his hands together.

Delph and Rhoadan laughed, Yak laughed at them laughing not really understanding what was said and Kadence just rolled her eyes at Elk.

They inhaled the wondrous smell as each plate passed them. Elk and Yak almost fell off their chairs trying to get a proper gander at what was being served.

Elk and Rhoadan made a quick start once the food was out on the table whereas Delph and Kadence took their time to choose which food they wanted, they were refined, unlike Elk.

Their meal was a choice of crispy tort bread with a choice of jellied syrups, some boiled oats and whey; topped up with gruffiot groats cream, or a mix of juice fruits and as much night tea and choco they could drink.

Delph and Kadence both opted for the tort bread and jellies, Jinx, Ooseriz and Aedin chose the broiled oats and whey and Elk, Rhoadan and Yak, messily grabbed a bit of everything.

Kadence inadvertently grimaced at the noise Yak, Rhoadan and Elk all made whilst they ate.*

* It would be unfair to the word eating to describe it as such, it was the type of noise that would attract a horde of male tri-tusks during mating season.

She felt queasy and embarrassed by their actions; more so Elk's actions, it was the first time they had sat downstairs and by tonight's standards, she rather much hoped it would be the last time.

'Ahem' Kadence cleared her throat.

It went unacknowledged because of the snorting noises that had invaded the tranquillity of the evening.

Delph and Kadence both looked along the table at Aedin, Jinx and then on to Ooseriz and back to Jinx again.

Jinx held up his hand and shook his head to show that it didn't matter. Kadence skulked and leant down into her seat and extended her leg to kick Elk's leg.

'What did you do that for?' he yelled; spraying his supper everywhere.

The moment he realised that he was spraying chewed food everywhere, he tried catching as much of it in his hands as quickly as possible. He was now experiencing the same embarrassment that Kadence was suffering.

He looked around at the faces observing him, Yak, however, didn't bat an eye and continued as he was.

Elk quickly finished what was in his mouth and apologised. He looked down at his food and decided that he was no longer hungry after his eyes followed the chaotic trail of spat out food.

'You must be hungry Elk' Ooseriz said; stating the obvious.

'He's always hungry,' Kadence laughed. Elk glared at Kadence and screwed up his face.

'It's all right, I'll get someone to clean it up,' said Jinx. He got up out of his seat and peeked his head into the kitchen to ask one of his tribe to clean it up.

'Jinx, can you remember when we were back in the forest, I handed you that important bag. Where did you put it? And where are our weapons?' Rhoadan asked.

'Yes, I remember, I had them taken into our storage room through in the kitchen, you can have them whenever you like, although like I said before, we don't condone weapons on show within Mossguard, unless it's required, of course, we can leave them locked up, if you're okay with that,' Jinx answered.

'Can I have a quick check on them before I head to bed?' Rhoadan asked. He would rather settle tonight knowing his gems and hatchets were where he was told they were.

'Of course you can. I'll show you where they are and you can see what you need to see once we are all finished here.' Jinx replied.

They had all finished eating, and they had chosen their desired drink. Elk, Rhoadan, Delph and Kadence all opted for night tea, they all made sure it was as sweet as possible. Aedin, Jinx, Yak and Ooseriz, opted for a big cup of choco. It was nowhere near as sweet as the night tea though.

Yak disturbed the silence by loudly slurping the dregs of the choco from his cup.

'So, what are your plans for tomorrow then?' Jinx asked.

'Well, I'm tired. I have a busy day tomorrow, so I'm going to turn in for the night, I won't be hanging around in the morning though as I have other matters in which I have to attend, so I will bid you a good night and I will catch up with you all very soon and once again, I'm grateful for your hospitality Jinx,' Ooseriz said.

They all said goodnight to her.

Ooseriz slid her chair back and stood up and hastily left the room.

'Wait, you still haven't told me how you and Jinx met,' yelled Rhoadan.

'Jinx can fill you in' Ooseriz yelled from the top of the stairs.

Rhoadan glanced over at Jinx and unknowingly raised his eyebrows.

'I will tell you in the morning, it's late' Jinx told Rhoadan, but he also made a sidewards glance at Aedin, their eyes met across the table.

Rhoadan began to think that Jinx wouldn't tell him. Jinx had avoided Rhoadan's question every time he was asked about it.

'How about I take you to your bags before I head off to my own chambers,' suggested Jinx, he stood up from his own chair, enticing Rhoadan to do the same.

'If you'll follow me please' Jinx said, he pushed the kitchen door open, and they both walked through. The blare of chatter from the tribe ceased as soon as Rhoadan placed his foot over the threshold. Rhoadan could still smell supper lingering in the air, he was impressed with how clean and organised it was in the kitchen, everything seemed to have its own place on the countertops. The ceiling light reflected against the metallic walls, it reminded him of his own kitchen back at his inn at Bramwich, except this kitchen was much cleaner.

'Jinx' yelled Aedin.

'Rhoadan, stay here for a moment' ordered Jinx as he peeked his head back through to the dining room.

'We're all heading up to bed it's been a long day, our guests can sleep in my care room for tonight, I'll send Eaki-Trin up to his bed as well,' said Aedin.

'That's great thanks, I'll show Rhoadan up to the room once he's finished here,' said Jinx. The others left for bed.

'Now, if you will follow me' ordered Jinx as he joined Rhoadan.

Rhoadan did as he was asked and he followed Jinx to a large metallic silver door. Jinx turned the long handle upwards and asked Rhoadan to help him open the door.

There were shelves full to the brim with food and tasty treats and had Rhoadan not just eaten, he would have surely overindulged on them.

'If you notice that door over there Rhoadan,' said Jinx; pointing to the golden door that lay at the far end of the cupboard.

'I see it, yes,' replied Rhoadan.

'Just head over to that, it's quite stiff, so you'll need to push in the handle and then lift it up to get in.' Jinx said, as he slowly backed out of the cupboard.

'I'll be there in a moment, I just need to have a word with my tribe, I need to relieve them of their duties for the night, just you carry on, I won't be long,' Jinx said.

Rhoadan walked into the golden room, it was full of satchels and backpacks and right at the back of the room he saw two small shafts sticking up.

He recognised them as Brother and Sister so he walked over to them and knelt down.

He couldn't help standing on top of the bags, there was far too many to dodge.

'Hopefully, there isn't any fragile objects in those bags' thought Rhoadan.

Rhoadan picked up Brother and Sister and kissed them both, he felt somewhat naked without them, he stood back up and lost his footing as his ankle became entangled in the strap of one of the bags.

He crashed to the floor, instantly feeling pain when his hand hit the ground.

Rhoadan tried to get up, however, soon realising that he was struggling to move his left arm as easily as he should have been able to. He tried to stand up again, yet in the midst of doing so, he felt a clamping sensation gripping around his index and middle fingers.

He tried moving his fingers frantically, but it was no use, they were truly stuck.

The sheer amount of bags prevented him from seeing what was stopping him from pulling his hand to safety, so he desperately moved them out of the way with his free hand, but it was taking too long, he wasn't enjoying his predicament one bit and wanted to be free.

The fear of his hand being restrained by an unseen horror was beginning to take its toll on him, he could feel the outset of helplessness lingering in his stomach, so with that, he leant over to his left to gain more support this time round, he pulled with every morsel of strength he possessed.

He felt some resistance however, it only fuelled his desire to be free, he yanked his arm upwards and groaned as his shoulder burned under the strain, Rhoadan clenched his teeth to try and take away the pain of his shoulder burning, he fought through it and just when he was starting to give up he heard an almighty cracking sound and his arm was free.

He immediately checked his hand, he wanted to make sure there was no damage, he was horrified when it came into view.

He couldn't quite make out what he was seeing at first, so he inspected it closer, his stomach churned once he realised that his fingers were stuck in the eye sockets of a skull, shocked, he turned it around and found that half of the spine was still attached, just hanging there like a discarded rope.

He tried to yell, yet he felt too nauseated to speak. He jammed the skull under his arm and he pulled his fingers free, instinctively, he threw it away from him, striking it against the wall.

Darkness raced into the room which only added to Rhoadan's apprehension, his fingers ached from clenching his hands up into fists, he felt his heart beating irregularly which left him struggling to breathe; resulting in a tight chest, his eyes widened as he tried to find a way out of this forsaken room, immediately feeling discouraged as he set his eyes on the door.

All he could focus on was two gleaming yellow eyes which were fixated on him as the door slowly closed in front of him, sealing him in from the outside.

To be continued...

Dear Reader,

If you enjoyed *Elk of Eshia*, please recommend it to your friends and family.

You can find me mooching around on social media:

Facebook: - https://www.facebook.com/elkofeshia
Twitter: - https://twitter.com/leenicollee

If you enjoyed *Elk of Eshia*, I would love an honest review.

Please send any feedback or comments to me on my social media profiles mentioned above, if you bought *Elk of Eshia* from Amazon, please remember to leave a review.

Thank you for your support.

Lee Nicol

-Reviews from Amazon-

Thank you to the people below for leaving a review.

★★★★★ **Great read.**
By Sara Brown on 23 April 2018
Format: Kindle Edition | Verified Purchase

I loved the book, I was intrigued and couldn't put it down, it kept me interested and left me wanting more.
Can't wait for book number 2. (P.s hurry up and release it)

★★★★★ **Great story**
By Rosemary Nicol on 29 June 2017
Format: Kindle Edition | Verified Purchase

I loved this book, a very enjoyable read with great characters and storyline. Left me wanting more and can't wait for the sequel to come out.
I highly recommend this book to anyone looking to escape for a few hours into a world of fantasy.

★★★★★ **Excellent work**
By Janet Dyet on 22 June 2017
Format: Kindle Edition | Verified Purchase

Excellent story and loved the characters. Looking forward to the sequel. Story had me engrossed from start to finish.
I gave the 5 star rating because I truly loved this amazing story.

★★★★★ **Escape to another world, well worth a good read**
By AMontie on 31 July 2017
Format: Kindle Edition | Verified Purchase

So enjoyable to read, takes your imagination away to intriguing & mystical places & people. I enjoyed the journey, the characters & the storyline.
Looking forward to the next instalment. Thank you Lee xx

★★★★★ **Enjoyable read**
By Tracy Cook on 16 July 2017
Format: Kindle Edition | Verified Purchase

Not normally my type of read but I thoroughly enjoyed this book. Took me onto another world for a few hours.
Can't wait for the next instalment

★★★★★ **Five Stars**
By Callan mackay on 2 July 2017
Format: Kindle Edition | Verified Purchase

Highly recommend this book. The story is amazing

★★★★★ **Fascinating read**
By caroline on 23 April 2018
Format: Kindle Edition

This is a great read for all lovers of the fantasy genre. I was completely lost is the world of Elk and his kin and found that I couldn't put this book down. Praise to Lee Nicol for producing a brilliant first novel.
I'm very much looking forward to the next adventure...

★★★★★ **Great storyline**
By SHARON MILLER on 1 May 2018
Format: Kindle Edition

Great book , couldn't put it down . Lee takes you to another fantasy world , brillant characters .
Can't wait until the second book to continue on their adventure

-Reviews from Amazon-

Thank you to the people below for leaving a review.

★★★★★ Hopefully the first of many.
By jean on 6 November 2017
Format: Kindle Edition | Verified Purchase

Hard to believe this is the writers first book. I thoroughly enjoyed it from cover to cover and I'm hard to please. Will be looking out for more titles from this author in the future.

★★★★★ Such A Good Read
By Shelley Doran on 15 May 2018
Format: Kindle Edition | Verified Purchase

I absolutely loved reading Elk of Eshia. Cannot wait till book 2 comes out. No doubt I won't be able to put that one down either once I start reading it.

★★★★★ Humorous
By Daniel Jackson on 9 May 2018
Format: Kindle Edition | Verified Purchase

Great read. Great first novel and looking forward to the next one. I found this book funny. Intriguing world and creatures.

★★★★★ Great read
By Amazon Customer on 7 May 2018
Format: Kindle Edition | Verified Purchase

Captivating read from start to finish. Thourghly enjoyable from a first time writer can't wait for second book.

★★★★★ I loved this book
By CharlotteW-BTON on 11 May 2018
Format: Kindle Edition

I loved this book. I wouldn't usually go for this genre, but I felt like a change, and it really opened up a whole new world of reading for me! Thank you Lee!

★★★★★ Everybody Must Read This!
By A. Munro on 27 January 2018
Format: Kindle Edition

Elk of Eshia is a rip-roaring fantasy adventure, brimming with thrills, humour and immense imagination. An absolute pleasure to read!

★★★★☆ Captivating storyline
By Mr Scott Campbell on 11 July 2017
Format: Kindle Edition | Verified Purchase

Lee has created a world that draws you in and makes you want to know more of what is going to happen. With myriads of creatures and adventures to follow. Cannot wait for the next instalment.

★★★★☆ Well worth reading
By Elizabeth Murdoch on 27 June 2017
Format: Kindle Edition | Verified Purchase

Not the kind of book I usually read, however, I really enjoyed it. Read it within 1 day, looking forward to the sequel